Remedy

NEW YORK TIMES BESTSELLING AUTHOR

KAYLEE RYAN

Cover Design: Sommer Stein, Perfect Pear Creative Covers
Cover Photography: Sara Eirew
Editing: Hot Tree Editing
Formatting: Integrity Formatting
Proofreading: Deaton Author Services

Chapter 1

GRADY

It's been three long years since I've been home. Three years of blaming it on my job at the hospital, the eleven-hour drive, and a host of other "reasons" I couldn't come home. Three years of acting as if the dick swinging between my legs is actually a vagina, when really there is only one reason.

Collins Ward.

My best friend's little sister.

Three years ago, I came home for a week right after my first year of medical school ended. I was supposed to be home for a full seven days before heading back to my apartment and part-time job in patient transport at Duke Medical Center. Instead, three days in, I went home early, claiming work needed me. I talked up how important the job was with me being a med student and all. I talked a good game because my parents let it go.

What I didn't tell them was that I crossed the line. I didn't tell them that the night before, the reason I didn't come home was because I was with her. Because I couldn't pull myself away from her; I couldn't resist her. Instead, I gave into temptation. We both did. I knew growing up

Collins had a crush on me. It's like a rite of passage for the younger sister to crush on the older brother's best friend. Collins was always just Caleb's little sister, four years younger than me. Tall and skinny, she was cute, but there was nothing there.

That night, things changed. It had been a few years since I'd seen her. Between hanging out with Caleb, our buddies, Alec and Bryce, and my parents during my trips home, we missed each other. The thought never crossed my mind when I was home. I never thought, damn I need to go see Collins. Caleb would bring her up in conversations, a guy she was seeing he didn't like or how he was glad she was staying close to home for college. I listened—she is his sister after all—but I felt nothing.

Not until that day three years ago. That day, when I laid eyes on her for the first time in two years, I felt everything. My heart had palpitated in my chest, my palms were sweaty, and my eyes were riveted on her. Let's not forget to mention how my cock saluted her. That day was when I realized that Collins was no longer just Caleb's little sister. She was a beautiful, sexy-as-sin woman who I couldn't take my eyes off, no matter how hard I tried. The end result was my mouth on every inch of her skin, and a whole hell of a lot of guilt.

When it was time to pick a residency, I knew coming home was the only option. Now here I am, three long years later, and it's as if history is repeating itself, and I can't seem to pull my eyes away from her. Luckily for me, Caleb is too preoccupied with his new fiancée, Emily, to notice. The rest of our friends are already feeling the effects of the alcohol and aren't paying me any attention. So here I sit, just like all those years ago in the corner of the room. This time it just so happens to be a crowded bar, drinking alone and watching Collins's every move.

I'm perfectly content, nursing my beer and taking in the view before me. It's not until she turns and catches me watching her that the contentment washes away and dread fills its place. I watch as she tells Tabby, her best friend, something and then heads my way. Quickly, I drain the warm beer I've been nursing, needing all the liquid courage I can get.

"Grady." Her sweet voice washes over me.

"Good to see you, Collins," I reply, trying like hell to keep my shit in check on the outside. Inside, my gut is churning. I hate how we left things. It's something that no matter what has been going on in my life over the last three years, she was never far from my mind.

"Is it?"

She's pissed, rightfully so. "Yeah, you look gorgeous." I let the words tumble free, knowing that it will only piss her off even more.

"Right." She laughs humorlessly. "I remember you telling me that exact thing. Funny how I believed you then. I'm no longer that naive."

She doesn't believe me. I penetrate her with my stare, letting her know I'm being honest. "I meant it then and I mean it now."

"That's why you left?" she asks, never taking her eyes from mine.

"No."

"Look, this is the first time we've seen each other since that night. I know you're back, so I just wanted to clear the air. It never happened, that night." With a disgusted shake of her head, she turns to walk away, but I'm up and out of my seat, reaching for her. I grab her elbow, and she spins to face me. "Let me go." She tries to remove her arm from my grip, but I hold tighter.

"No," I say, my voice low.

"Grady," she says with a sigh. "I'm not doing this with you." I give her a pleading look. "What? You don't want me to hate you? Fine, I don't hate you. I won't tell Caleb. Hell, I've kept it to myself this long. I won't ruin your bromance. Now let me go."

She tugs again, but I hold steady with my grip on her arm. Not tight enough to hurt her, but tight enough to keep her here. "It happened," I say through gritted teeth.

"Trust me, I remember," she replies, anger lacing her voice. "I also remember waking up alone. I want nothing more than to erase that night from my memory and pretend it never happened. That's what I plan to do. This is closure, Grady. You should do the same."

Not giving a fuck who's around, I back her up against the wall, bracing my arms on either side of her head, palms flat, boxing her in. The sweet smell of lavender and something uniquely Collins washes over me. I can't help but close my eyes and breathe her in. It's been too damn long. Three long years without her, helps put things into perspective. Sure, it would suck to lose my best friend, but losing her, it's not an option. I'll fight for her, for both of us.

"Grady," she breathes.

Although it's not meant to be, my name is a plea on her lips. She wants this as much as I do, but she's fighting it. I can feel it coming off her in waves. My eyes pop open to see her watching me. "I can't do that, Collins. I won't do that," I say adamantly.

"Please," she whispers.

Bending, I place my lips next to her ear. "No way could I forget you or that night." She sucks in a deep breath when I place my lips just below her ear. Lifting my head, I see her breathing is labored, and that tells me all I need to know. She doesn't want me to stay away any more than I want to.

"Someone will see us, and then we both have a lot of explaining to do." Her voice is breathy, and her eyes are closed. She's not as unaffected as she would like me to believe.

"Fuck that. We're both adults. We don't have to explain shit to anyone."

Her eyes flutter open. "So you're going to tell Caleb what happened between us? Are you going to tell him how you snuck out while I was sleeping? You willing to lose your best friend since birth over that one night?"

"If that's what it takes," I tell her honestly. It's been three fucking years, and I can't get that night out of my head. Can't get her out of my head. At first, I thought it was the guilt, but then anytime I would even think about attempting to date, it was always Collins who was front and center in my mind. Then there was today and my reaction to seeing her for the first time since the night I left her in bed alone. Ignoring this, whatever this connection is and forgetting the night happened is not an option.

"Don't," she says, panic in her voice. "That solves nothing. It was a mistake, one that won't be repeated, so why ruin a lifelong friendship over one night?"

"Is that all I was to you? One night?"

Something flashes in her eyes, but it's gone before I can work out what it is. "It was years ago, Grady. Let's just agree to be cordial and forget it happened."

"Did you not hear what I just told you? I can't forget."

"You're going to have to," she says, leaning up on her tiptoes and kissing my cheek. I'm so shocked by the act, by the feel of her lips against my skin, she's able to duck under my arm and scurry away. I could have stopped her, but she needs time.

Turning, I rest my back against the wall and watch her go. I'll let her have tonight. She can run and pretend that what happened between us is a figment of her imagination. Seeing her again has everything all rushing back, and no way am I going to let this go without a fight.

Chapter 2

Collins

MY LEGS FEEL AS IF they could fall out from under me, sending me crashing straight to the floor. I focus all my attention on each step that carries me further and further away from him. When I finally reach the table, I drop into my seat and exhale the breath I've been holding.

"What's up with you?" Tabby asks.

"Nothing. I need another drink."

"I thought you went to get another drink?"

Shit. "I went to the bathroom instead," I lie, and I know I'll regret it because now I've mentioned the bathroom, my bladder is screaming at me to be relieved.

My best friend gives me a look that tells me she knows I'm full of shit. "Really? I could have sworn that I saw you talking to Grady." She sits back in her chair and crosses her arms over her chest, raising an eyebrow. We both know I'm busted.

"I might have run into him," I confess.

"Uh-huh, and what happened?"

"Nothing. I said hello. He said hello, and now I'm back." Tabby doesn't know what happened that night. She knows that my crush turned into something more, something all-together different than just a crush, but that's it. I never told a soul. When I woke up, and he was gone, I knew that was it for us. The fantasy of him feeling about me the way I've always felt for him was shattered. I didn't see the point of telling anyone what a fool I'd been. I was so blinded by his words, the attraction, and the longing I've had for him for years, that I let all of it cloud my judgment. I'll not make the same mistake twice.

"I'll let that go, but don't think I don't know something happened. Your face is flushed, and you looked like a newborn deer on those legs on your way back to the table. I know it's been a while since you've seen him. Did the near sight of him knock you on your ass?" She laughs.

If she only knew. "Ha ha. It's been three years, and no, the alcohol is getting to me. I haven't eaten much today."

Her eyes soften. "I don't know how you do it, working in the ER."

"I like helping people. Sure, there are times the job gets to me, but at the end of the day, the rewards outweigh the downfalls."

"I'm gonna give you a pass." She grins. "I'll order us some wings while you go to the restroom."

"How did you know?"

"Your knees are bouncing up and down so fast you're shaking the table. Go." She waves me off, and I don't have to be told twice. I'm up and out of my seat and headed toward the restrooms. I don't look around, instead keeping my eyes focused straight ahead. I can't get pulled under his spell.

Not again.

After I take care of business, I head back to the table with the same avoidance as before. Head down, no eye contact. To my surprise, when I reach our table, we have guests. My brother and his fiancée, Emily, have joined us, and just my luck, Grady and Alec are with them as well.

"Hey." I lean in and give Emily a hug.

"Did you get the email I sent about dresses?" Emily asks. They've been engaged less than a month, and she's already in full wedding planning mode.

"I did, and I love them. Is that your pick?"

"Yeah, I think so. Everyone seems to agree."

"I'm so excited for you," I say, giving her another hug.

"Thank you. Did you put in for the time off?"

"I did. I still can't believe that you're planning a wedding in three months."

She waves off my concern. "It's nothing. It's all coming together, and Caleb wants to make it happen before he starts his new job."

My brother is an attorney. He was able to land a job at a big law firm here in Indianapolis. He signed on to start after taking his boards which will be at the end of August. The wedding is the end of July, just two short months away. I was happy for him when he told us, but concerned about his job if he doesn't pass his boards. Ever cocky, he assured me that after all his years at law school, he could pass in his sleep.

"It makes sense," Tabby chimes in. "This way you can take your honeymoon. I'm sure being the low man on the totem pole, he's not going to get much time off that first year."

"Jesus, it's not prison." Caleb laughs. "I get vacation time and floating holidays, but I want some time with my wife, just the two of us before I start working long hours again. She's put up with me all through law school. I want to give her that time, but I want it to be as my wife."

I can feel Grady's eyes boring into me, but I continue to pretend he's not standing mere feet away. "Anything I can help with?" I ask my future sister-in-law.

"Not at the moment, but don't worry. I'll call you if I need you."

"Me, too," Tabby agrees. "I'm happy to help." Tabby and I are roommates, so chances are she'd end up helping me anyway.

"So, Grady, how long are you in town for?" Tabby asks.

"I have a month before my residency program starts."

"Who would have thought that you two would end up being a doctor and a lawyer," Bryce says.

"Not me," Alec says.

"Fuck off." Caleb grins, taking a sip of his beer. That reminds me, I definitely need another drink.

"You ladies not drinking tonight?" Bryce asks, throwing his arm over my shoulder.

"We are. We're just pacing ourselves."

"How are you getting home?" Caleb asks immediately, realizing we're both drinking.

"Ever heard of these things… they're usually bright yellow, with the letters C-A-B written down the side? They actually pick you up and take you anywhere you need to go. You just have to pay a small fee," I quip at my older brother.

"Ha ha. Have you ever heard of two beautiful young girls drunk off their ass in a cab alone at night? Not a good outcome."

"You've read too many case files, lawyer boy," I tease.

"Just be careful, yeah?"

"Fine," I mutter. "You've killed my buzz anyway." I look over at Tabby. "You ready to head out?"

She studies me, knowing there's more to it than just arguing with Caleb. He and I go round and round all the time; he's just being my protective, big brother. It's never had me wanting to head home early. My best friend knows this, and I know she's going to want answers as soon as we are in the cab and headed back to our apartment. I have the cab ride home to decide what or how much to tell her. I don't make it a habit to keep things from my best friend, but this… it was over before it began, no point in dishing details when he acted as though it never happened.

Chapter 3

GRADY

"I CAN DRIVE YOU," I rush to offer. Anytime with her is a bonus. Maybe I can get her to talk to me. "I've had one beer all night. No point in wasting money on a cab when I can take you."

"I'm sure you have better things to do," Collins replies. Her tone of voice tells me she's not impressed with my generosity.

"No, actually, I don't. First day back in town, I'm beat from my day of travel."

"You staying at your parents' place?" Caleb asks.

"Yeah."

"Perfect. These two live just about two miles from there at the Sunny Glen Apartment Complex."

I watch her as she gives her brother a death glare. Yeah, she's not impressed. "Even better." I step toward her and place my hand on the small of her back. "Ready to go?" I'm trying on my best "I'm just being a nice guy" face though the truth is, my body hums with the feel of her warmth against my palm. It's been too damn long since I've been this close to her. Only in my dreams.

Stepping to the side and away from me, I'm now the one receiving the death glare. "Fine," she mutters, grabbing her phone from the table and stomping off toward the front door.

"What crawled up her ass?" Caleb asks Tabby.

"Caleb." Emily swats at his arm, scolding him.

"What? She's being a bitch for no reason. Grady, let her get a cab so you don't have to deal with her shit," he tells me.

"I got it," I say, then look over at Tabby. She's studying me. "You ready?"

"Yeah." Picking up her drink—something pink—she downs it and turns for the door.

With a quick wave to my friends, I follow after her. I find both of them standing beside my old Toyota 4Runner. I click the lock and watch as Collins rushes to climb into the back seat, leaving the front open for Tabby. As soon as I'm in the car with the door shut, her scent washes over me. Lavender. It's been too long since I've seen her, but every time I smell that scent, I think of her, of the night we shared together.

"So how long have you lived at Sunny Glen?" I ask no one in particular. Glancing in the rearview mirror, I see Collins with her arms crossed over her chest and is staring out the window.

Tabby looks over her shoulder at Collins before turning to look at me. "About three years. We both graduate from nursing school next week. BSN," she says excitedly.

"Good for you. Both of you," I say, looking in the mirror again. Collins is still just staring out the window, watching as the night passes us by. "I didn't realize you were both in nursing," I admit. That's my fault. I should have paid more attention anytime my parents or Caleb talked about her. I just couldn't though. I didn't want to hear about who she was dating or worse, engaged to. Instead, I blocked them out and skipped over the conversation completely. If they caught on, they never said.

Tabby looks over her shoulder again, then turns back around. "Yeah, we both went to IU, roomed together all through college. We moved into our current place right after our freshman year. Neither one of us were feeling dorm life."

"Yeah, I did the same. It helped that my two roommates were both med students as well. We didn't have to worry about raging parties when we needed to have our noses stuck in a book."

"What? No raging college parties for the infamous Grady Carmichael?" She places her hand against her chest as if the shock is just too much for her to take.

"I went to Duke for both undergrad and med school. Undergrad there were a few, and by few, I mean, literally maybe three or four. I had to stay focused. Duke Med School is no joke, and I had to keep my grades up. Then med school was a bitch, no time for parties. Any spare time I had was spent sleeping."

"So, what's next for you? Are you a doctor now?" she asks.

"Yeah, Grady Carmichael, MD at your service." I laugh. "However, I still have to complete my residency before I can practice on my own."

"Damn, that's a lot. How long is residency?"

"Three to seven years, depending on my specialty and if I go for a fellowship."

"Are you?" she asks.

"Nah, that's not the plan. At least, not for now. Three years of residency and I'm good to go." I can tell she wants to ask more, but I pull into their complex. "Which unit is yours?"

"That one on the end." Tabby points through the front window at the end of the lot. After pulling my SUV into a space, I turn off the engine and hop out.

"What are you doing?" Collins asks. It's the first time she's spoken since she stormed out of the bar.

"Walking you to your door."

"We can handle it," she says, slamming the door and heading toward the building. Tabby shrugs in confusion and follows her.

Not letting her attitude stop me, I follow along behind them. Collins stops at the door and turns to face me. "Really, Grady?" she seethes, hands on her hips.

"Um, I'm just going to go on inside. Thanks for the ride, Dr. Carmichael." Tabby grins and waves before disappearing behind the door.

Collins's long dark hair is covering those big, blue eyes, the same ones that I see every damn time I close mine. When I lift my hand and gently tuck the loose strand behind her ear, she sucks in a breath. "I'm just looking out for you, making sure you make it inside safely," I say softly.

"Oh, yeah?" She swallows hard. "Where were you three years ago, Grady? Huh? Where were you after I gave myself to you, when you disappeared into the night? Where were you?" she asks, her voice breaking.

"Col—"

"No." She takes a step back until her back hits the apartment door. "I don't need your excuses. If you were worried, if you cared, you would have been there." Tears well in her eyes.

"There is nothing in life I regret more than leaving you that night."

"You sure have a funny way of showing it." She turns, opens the door, and closes it quickly.

I don't try to stop her. The pain in her eyes, the tears threatening to fall have my stomach in knots. I fucked up, I know it, she knows it. However, what she doesn't know is that there is no one for me but her. I just need to figure out a game plan to prove it to her. To show her how sorry I am. That I know I made a mistake, but if she were to give me another shot, I can prove to her that she's my girl. She has been since that night three years ago.

Chapter 4

Collins

S AFELY INSIDE MY APARTMENT, I close my eyes and fall back into the door. Grady Carmichael is back in town after all these years, and I thought I was ready for it. I thought I was ready to see him. I had convinced myself that I could act as if nothing happened between us. One look and that theory was blown right out of the water.

He's still sexy as hell. Tall with a trim build, and I know the peaks and valleys of the muscles that lie just underneath his tight-fitting shirt. By the looks of it, he is even more defined now. His shaggy brown hair, those green eyes, and his five o'clock shadow wrap up the sexy package that is solely him. Grady fucking Carmichael is back, and I'm a mess.

"It was him, wasn't it?" Tabby asks.

Slowly, I open my eyes and see her sitting on the couch watching me. I never admitted to anyone what happened that night with Grady and me. I did tell Tabby there was a guy, but I told her he wasn't worth naming since he snuck out on me while I was sleeping. She didn't pressure me for details, something I love about my best friend. She knows when to push, and I'm sure she could tell that the details of that night were not on my "hot topic for discussion" list. I can't seem to form the words, so I nod.

She pats the couch cushion beside her. "Come sit."

One foot in front of the other, I make my way to the couch and plop down beside her. "I'm sorry I never told you who it was."

"You don't have to apologize. That's your secret to share. I know what happened. You knew that if you needed to talk, I was ready to listen, at least I hope you did."

I nod. "Yeah, I just didn't want to admit that it was him. I crushed on him for years and that night… he made me feel special, like all along he had felt it, too. I was humiliated to know that I was just a night of fun for him."

"You have nothing to be humiliated about."

"Yeah, easier said than done. You try giving your virginity to your older brother's best friend and have him sneak out of bed like a thief in the night. I texted him you know. I asked him what I did wrong, but never once did he reply. I blamed myself. I was inexperienced, and a whole list of other reasons and emotions I'd rather not talk about."

"You probably don't want to hear this, but he doesn't look at you like a man who was disappointed." She nudges me with her elbow, trying to lighten the mood.

"It was just easier to keep it to myself. I never want Caleb to find out. Why have him pissed at me and Grady for a one-time thing."

She cringes. "Yeah, Caleb would be pissed for sure."

"I was willing to risk it, you know? To be with him. I thought he felt that way, too. I was wrong. It hurt, and now I'm over it. Well, as over it as I can be. I can't be friends with him or whatever it is he has in mind. At least, not yet."

"Maybe one day, when you're ready," she says gently. Tabby knows how big my crush was on him. Freshman year, I might not have told her all the details, but I did tell her about my older brother's best friend that I've always had a crush on. Hell, if I'm honest, it's still there, but the anger overshadows it. I can still feel the hurt of waking up alone, reaching for him, only to find him and his clothes gone. I called and texted him with no reply. Later that day, I found out that he went back to college, claiming work called and needed him. I never bought that excuse. In my messages, I begged him to come home for Christmas so we could talk. My messages went unanswered, and he never showed up for Christmas. That was answer enough for me. I was a fling. My first time, meant to be special, was forever tainted by the feeling of being tossed to the side. Even if he didn't want me, I would have thought that with our families being close, with him being my brother's best friend, he would have at least let me down easy. Nope. Instead, he disappeared, and tonight was the first night in three years since I laid eyes on him.

"Maybe," I say, not committing. I don't know that I can ever be friends with him. I would like to think I can forgive and forget, but my heart just isn't onboard with that idea just yet. "I'm calling it a night. Thanks for listening, and I know you won't, but please don't say anything."

"Never," she says adamantly. "Get some rest."

I hug her tightly, grateful to have her in my life. I might have kept his identity from her, but not because I didn't trust her. I just... wanted to keep him to myself. I had a small part of him, even though he discarded me. I wanted that small piece. Not to mention, I was able to avoid embarrassment.

In my room, I shut the door and fall face first onto my bed. I want to forget this day ever happened. Forget what he looks like—older, more defined. I want to forget what he smells like—musky and uniquely Grady. I want my heart to forget that it craves him. One day, I'll get over him. One day.

My phone pings with a message, rolling over, I dig my phone out of my back pocket and tap the screen. My chest heaves at the sight of his name. I contemplate not opening it, but I'm a gluten for punishment, so I do it anyway.

Grady: Goodnight, Collins.

That's it. Two little words that are three years too late. Why is it so damn easy for him to text me now? Where was this message, this confidence of his three years ago? Why in the hell does my heart beat just a little faster knowing he was thinking about me? I'm supposed to be getting over him.

I want to text him back and ask these questions, but then I think about my messages and calls that went unanswered. He doesn't deserve a reply. I should have deleted his number years ago, but for some reason, I just couldn't bring myself to do it. At least I won't be up all night wondering who the message is from. I would have more than likely replied asking who it was, opening up a line of conversation I'm not willing to start. Turns out not deleting him was a good thing. Tossing my phone on the nightstand then grabbing some clothes, I head to the bathroom and take a steaming hot shower to wash away the day and get ready for bed.

⟞⟞⟞⟞♡⟞⟞⟞⟞

The sound of my phone alerting me to a text message pulls me from my slumber. Glancing at the clock, I see that it's a little after eight. Who in the hell is texting me this early in the morning, on Sunday no less? This is my sleep in, "lounge around and do nothing if I want" day. Reaching for my phone, I swipe the screen and open my messages. I have to blink twice to make sure I'm not imagining things. It's another message from Grady.

Grady: Morning, beautiful.

What. The. Fuck? I wish I knew what his end game was. Why all of a sudden is he Mr. Nice Guy and trying to butter me up? The time for that has passed. And last night, I lay awake longer than I care to admit breaking apart piece by piece his actions. His words, *"There is nothing in life I regret more than leaving you that night,"* a constant loop in my mind. No matter how I manage to spin it, it still doesn't justify his actions. None of it makes any sense to me. He's wasting his time. There will never be anything between us. Not anymore.

Chapter 5

GRADY

IF I'VE LOOKED AT MY phone once today, I've looked at it a thousand times. It's foolish to think she'll reply after all these years, especially after what happened and how things ended. That's on me, and I know that. I'm trying to fix it, but she's not having it. Granted, I understand that I need to do more than just send her a couple of text messages to prove to her that I'm sorry. That I was wrong, and I want her. All of her.

That night, there were hundreds of scenarios running through my mind. First and foremost, nothing had ever made me feel the way being with Collins had. It was her first time. The knowledge had rocked me. I should have stopped right then, but I was too far gone. I needed her. I still do. Then there was the fact that she's my best friend's little sister. I knew Caleb would be pissed, but I couldn't resist her. Another huge factor, I was in medical school, over twelve hours away. I knew getting to see her would be sporadic at best and that my time was not my own. It belonged to Duke University Medical School. She deserved better than a long distance relationship, so I let my fear win, and I bailed while she was sleeping.

I remember watching her sleep as I held her close, knowing I was leaving her and wishing there was another way. At the time, it seemed the best and only option. Looking back, I know that I was wrong. I'm man enough to admit it. Now, I just need her to accept my apology so we can move forward.

I know she thinks that I left her lying there sleeping and forgot all about our night together. She's wrong. She's all I thought about. Fuck, she's all I think about. Medical school was brutal, but on the off chance that me and my roommates went out, every girl who crossed my path I compared to Collins. None of them stacked up to her. It only took me until about five miles out of town to realize how badly I'd fucked up. That there would never be anyone else for me but her. I should have called her then, begged for her forgiveness, but I couldn't do that to her. I read every message, listened to every voice mail, but still I remained silent on my end. I didn't know what to say, and I knew if I reached out to her, I would go home. I'd worked too hard to just leave it all behind. I was going to become a doctor. Not to mention, there was still the fact she was Caleb's little sister, and I had three more years of medical school. So, instead, I put all my energy into school. I never went out, I kept my nose in the books, and my heart in Indiana, with her.

My phone rings and I fumble it in my hands, rushing to answer. I don't even look at the screen, hopeful that it's her after staring at the silent device all day. "Hello."

"Hey, man. What are you into?" Caleb asks.

I sigh. "Not much. What's going on?"

"Don't sound so thrilled to talk to me." He laughs. "Nothing. Emily and Collins are working on wedding plans. Thought I'd see if you wanted to come over. I ordered some subs from that shop down the street. I need some testosterone to level out my apartment. Ouch," he says, laughing. I can hear Emily telling him he's cut off, and he immediately tells her that he's sorry.

Collins is there. I know she would rather not see me, but that doesn't exactly work for me. Not to mention, it does nothing for my master plan to win her over. "Yeah, need me to bring anything?"

"Beer. Bring lots of beer."

"What about the subs? I can swing by and pick those up on my way."

"Sure. I'll get you some cash when you get here."

"No need. I'll be there soon." Hanging up the phone, I realize I have yet to shower today. I've sat around in my old bedroom at my parents' place, moping, waiting for a glimmer of hope from Collins. Rushing, I grab some clean clothes and take a shower. Downstairs, I find my parents sitting in the living room.

"He's alive," Dad jokes.

"Where you headed?" Mom asks.

"Caleb called. Emily and Collins are working on wedding stuff, and he feels outnumbered. We're going to have dinner. Catch up."

"Be safe. Let us know if you won't be coming home," Mom instructs.

"Will do." With a wave, I'm out the door and firing up my 4Runner. Caleb and Emily live in a condo on the edge of town. It's about a fifteen-minute drive. I'm so focused on seeing her that I almost forgot to stop and pick up the subs. Checking the time, it's just after six, which means I made the cut off for Sunday beer sales. After stopping for the subs, I rush into the market, grab a twelve-pack, and then I'm on my way. Not three minutes later, I'm pulling up outside of their condo.

Caleb meets me at the door, taking the beer from me before I can even climb out of the SUV. Reaching into the passenger seat, I grab the bag of subs and follow him. "Were you watching for me?" I ask, amusement in my voice.

"Yes. I'm starving, and it's fucking wedding central in there. Man, I don't give a shit about flowers or napkins. I just want her to be my wife. She can have anything she wants, but she insists on asking me, and I have no fucking clue."

"Did you tell her that?"

"Yeah, in so many words. I don't want to hurt her feelings. I care about our wedding, I do. I care that she's my bride and is going to be my wife. That's it. Everything else is just fluff. She could tell me I had to wear a hot pink suit and I would be there with bells on."

"You could rock pink," I say, barely able to keep a straight face.

"Hey, Grady. Thanks for picking this up." Emily greets me as we enter the small kitchen.

"No problem." I look at the table that looks as though wedding central is taking place. "Heard you had your hands full."

She beams. "Just a little."

Finally, I allow myself to look at Collins. Her long dark hair is pulled up into a messy bun. She's in short, tight, little athletic shorts, at least that's what it looks like to me, and a tank top. Her face is free of makeup, and I can't take my eyes off her. "Hey, Collins," I greet her.

"Grady," she says. Her face, and even her voice, is void of emotion. She looks down to the color samples in her hands, effectively dismissing me. I want to pull the chair out next to her, rub my thigh against hers, anything to gain her attention. I can't take the silence, even though I know it's what I deserve.

I thought that I had made up this fantasy of her in my mind. Over the years as she had gotten older, I noticed her. I also knew she had a crush on me. I should have fought harder to resist her. Then again, I should have had the balls to not walk away. No matter how hard long distance was, or what Caleb thought. I should have stayed. I told myself that my stolen time with her was just that and nothing more, that the electricity that pulsed through my veins anytime I looked at her was just the chemistry, the endorphins of the night. Even the alcohol. Even though that's what I told myself, I still remember the way my heart galloped in my chest the night I drove away. I still feel the anger at myself at life on the drive back to school. It's why I kept to myself. I didn't see the point in forcing what wasn't there with other women.

Last night, it all came rushing back like a tsunami of emotions. The regret, the heartbreak, the fear, and most of all the need. I have a need for her that burns deep in my soul. It's like nothing I've ever felt before. I pushed it away, the distance allowed me that luxury. I'm back and she's here, and the need is consuming me.

I want to pull her into my arms and tell her how sorry I am. I want to tell her that even though I never responded I read every single message, and listened to every voice mail, time and time again. I was weak, and I knew it. I knew if I reached out that I would leave school. Being a doctor was my dream, then again, so was she.

"Let's eat," Caleb announces, already digging into the bag of subs. I take his lead and grab one for myself and a bottle of water. My hope is that she drinks, and I have to drive her home. A guy can dream.

Chapter 6

Collins

*D*AMN! WHY DID CALEB HAVE to call him? I know I'm going to have to get used to seeing him around, but I thought I would get a day or two, this week at least, before I ran into him again. I take my time studying each color sample, blocking out the conversations around me. It's not until I feel his hot breath against the side of my face, I realize my mistake. Pretending is not a good option if I don't want to get ambushed.

"You going to eat?" he asks softly.

Looking up from the samples that are not nearly as interesting as I'm pretending, I find him in the chair next to mine. He motions to the island where the bag of food and the beer he picked up is sitting. "Not hungry. Thanks," I add as an afterthought. If I'm too big of a bitch, Caleb and Emily are sure to catch on that something is off.

"Here," Emily says, handing me a sub and taking the seat on the opposite side of me at their tiny four-person table. "You said you were starving."

I know she didn't hear me tell him that I wasn't hungry, and I'm sure if she knew she just made things even more awkward she would have kept quiet. Chancing a glance at Grady, he's holding his sub to his mouth ready to take a bite, a smirk on his lips. Well, damn. Standing from the table, I grab my sub and act as though I need a drink. Twisting the cap of a bottle of beer, I take a long pull. I'm going to need liquid courage for this for sure.

My stomach growls as I unwrap my sandwich and take my first bite. I really was starving, but I was willing to sacrifice to not eat his food. Instead of going back to the table, I stand at the island and eat.

"You too good to eat with us?" Caleb asks as he reaches back and grabs another beer.

"No, just got up to get a drink and decided to stand. We've been sitting there for a while." I take another bite to avoid having to say more. Hoping he buys my excuse.

"We're making great headway." Emily looks over at me. "Thank you for all of your help."

"That's what sisters are for, right?" I ask. She smiles wide, and I can't help but think that my brother hit the jackpot when he met Emily. I'm just glad he was smart enough to put a ring on it. She's perfect for him, and him for her. One day I want what they have.

"So, where are we?" Caleb asks his fiancée.

"Well, we have the dresses picked out for the bridesmaids, the suits for you and the groomsmen. Flowers are picked, and we selected colors for the napkins and decorations. You sure you don't want a say?" she asks him.

"Nope. This is your day. I'm already getting everything I want." He kisses her on the corner of her mouth, and I know I should turn away, but I can't.

I love how easy this comes for them. They make love look effortless, and I envy that. I've had exactly one experience, from a man who used me. Chancing a glance at Grady, I see he's watching me. His eyes are soft as he takes me in. I want to lash out. I want to tell him how he hurt me, but I know that none of it matters. Three years is a long time to harbor this pain. I need to move forward, and I thought I had until he showed up back in town.

"What colors?" Caleb asks.

"Well, the bridesmaids are going to be wearing black dresses, and the groomsmen are going to wear dark gray pants, with black button-down shirts, dark gray ties."

"Really? I love that, babe."

The smile that his compliment causes is blinding. "Thanks, it's going to be a great day."

"Of course, it is. It ends with you being my wife."

"Grady," Emily addresses him, "will you still be here for the wedding, if not, you are able to come home for it, right?"

"Yeah, I'll make sure when I start my residency, to tell them. It's usually easy to find coverage. I might end up working two weekends back to back, but that's a small price to pay to be at my best friend's wedding." He takes the last bite of his sub and wads up the wrapper. "Speaking of, are we doing a bachelor party? Just so I can plan ahead."

"Nope. We're not doing best man or maid of honor either. Neither of us could choose, so we decided it's our wedding, we don't have to. You, Alec, and Bryce will stand up with me. Collins, Samantha, and Cindy, who are Em's sisters, are going to stand up with her."

"Yeah, and since we couldn't decide which order, we're just going to have the guys draw names out of a hat. The name you draw is the person you'll be paired with for the wedding festivities."

His eyes find mine, and they sparkle. "Sounds easy enough. When do we get to draw?"

Emily looks over at Caleb. "How about we get everyone over here next weekend and do it then?"

"I'll call the guys," Caleb assures her.

"Grady, can you be here? Will you still be in town?" Emily asks.

"Yeah, I'll be here," he says, glancing over at me.

"Where are you applying?" Caleb asks.

I don't know much about Grady and his career endeavors. I do know he's always wanted to be a doctor. It has something to do with his little brother who died when he was three or so. I know that they were close. I don't know all the details of what and why, but I know that was his driving force. I don't even know what kind of doctor he's going to be. I try to tune out conversations about him. It helped that he stayed away the last three years. Now here I am faced with spending time with him and being in my brother's wedding with him. I send up a silent prayer that he doesn't draw my name out of the hat. How will I handle that? How will he? Maybe he'll talk one of the other guys into trading with him. Yeah, no… that's not going to happen. That's not the vibe I've been getting from him. He'll take every opportunity he can to get me to talk to him. I don't know what the reasoning behind it is. If I end up paired with him, I guess I'll find out eventually.

"Right, so what's left to do?" I ask Emily.

"I think we've got it. Thank you for all your help. I couldn't have done this without you."

"Yeah, thanks, sis," Caleb adds. "I'm not much of a wedding planner. I picked the ring and the girl, that should be enough, right?" He laughs.

"Your ass is lucky she said yes," I goad.

"Trust me, little sister, I know this." He whispers something in Emily's ear, making her smile and blush at the same time.

My eyes stray to Grady and find him watching me. Again. "Well, I guess I need to get going. I have to work early tomorrow."

"It's six." Caleb states the obvious.

"Yeah, but I have to do laundry, and get ready for the week." It's a lie. I have more scrubs than most. I just can't pass up the cute patterns, and the patients seem to love them. I could go a couple of weeks or more without doing laundry. Wearing scrubs everyday is like wearing your pajamas to work. Of course, I'm going to stock up.

"Thanks again." Emily stands and offers me a hug.

"Call me if you need help with anything else. Are we still on for Saturday to work on centerpieces?"

"Yes, if you're still available. Sam and Cindy want us to FaceTime with them so they can be here." She laughs. "That's the bad part about your family living so far away."

"Florida, right?"

"Yeah, my plan was to always move back home, until I met this guy." She places her hand on Caleb's shoulder. "Funny how plans change."

"This is selfish of me, but I'm glad you're here." I motion toward

Caleb, who is in deep conversation with Grady. "You're good for him."

"He's good for me." She grins.

The happiness that is gleaming from my brother and his fiancée is insane. Emily has changed him. He's still a fun-loving prankster, but there is a maturity about him. Then again, he's getting older, getting ready to start his big boy job as a lawyer. It's hard to believe. Life seems to be moving forward at a rapid pace for everyone around me. I'm still stuck on my past, pining for a man who left me and never looked back. I want to have what Caleb and Emily have, but letting go is harder than I expected.

Chapter 7

GRADY

I HAVE TO MAKE MYSELF keep my attention on my best friend as he talks about… I'm not really sure, to be honest. I'm looking at him and nodding, trying to look interested when really all I want to do is leave with his sister. I want to be going home with her, hell, at least walking Collins to her car and kissing her goodbye, but I can't. I lost that opportunity three years ago, and although that night changed things for me, she doesn't know that.

She doesn't know that I stopped dating and instead chose to drown myself in medical school. If I wasn't studying or working my shift at the hospital, I was thinking about her. About that night, about my life changing in more ways than one.

"Reds game Sunday," Caleb says. "You interested?"

I shake out of my Collins thoughts and focus on our conversation. "What time?"

"It's an early game. Noon I think. Plenty of time to make the three-hour drive there and back on the same day."

"Sure, man, sounds good. Been ages since I've been to a game."

"Yeah, you know, saving lives and shit." He laughs.

"What about you, fancy lawyer?"

"I deal with DUIs and divorces all day. Nothing fancy or heroic about that."

"What time we heading out?"

"I was thinking eight thirty. Give us time in case we hit traffic."

"Sounds good, man." We bullshit some more, and I try like hell to pay attention. He's my best friend, has been since we were in diapers, and our families have always been close. Our times together have been few and far between over the years, but that's on me. I could have made time to come home, but I was a coward. I couldn't face her, not yet. Truth be told, I wasn't sure I was ready last night. I'd stayed gone long enough, and when Caleb called to tell me that Emily said yes, and the wedding was at the end of the July, I knew I couldn't avoid home, avoid her any longer. It was time to come home and face the music, the disaster I'd created on my own. Not to mention, that my residency is here in Indy. I missed my family, my friends, and I missed Collins.

When it was time to pick a program, she was all I thought about. Being closer to her. A chance for me to right the wrongs of my past. I know I'm going to have my work cut out for me, and then there's Caleb. I need to tell him, but I need to talk to Collins first. Really talk to her. I need to earn her trust, get her before we tell him. I'm sure he's going to be pissed, and rightfully so, but this is Collins and, in the end, no matter how many years of friendship, I choose her. Makes me sound like an asshole, but my heart can't live without her. I tried, honest to God tried, for three long years. Besides, I'm hopeful once Caleb realizes that she's all I see, he'll come around. I hope.

I spend the next couple of hours catching up with Caleb and getting to know Emily. Just from our brief interactions, I knew my best friend was a lucky man, but today confirms it. She's sweet and keeps him on his toes. Exactly what he needs. I can't help but let my mind wander to Collins. Can we ever get to that point? Have I fucked up so badly that the one girl who owns my heart will never truly be mine?

Standing from the couch, I walk to the kitchen and toss my empty water bottle. I had one beer, and that was hours ago. "I'm going to head out."

"Thanks for stopping by, man. It was good to see you in the flesh. It's been too damn long since you've been home."

"Yeah," I agree. It has been too long for a lot of things.

"Next weekend," Emily reminds me. "We're going to have you guys draw. We'll order some pizza or something."

"Sure. Just text me when and where."

"Be safe, Grady." She smiles and waves while Caleb kisses her cheek.

In my SUV, I pull my phone out of my pocket and text Collins.

Me: It was good to see you tonight.

I place my phone in the cupholder and head back to my parents' place. I don't wait for a reply; I know I'm not going to get one. Hell, I'm not even sure that's still her number. The silence from the other end tells me it is. I hope so. At least she knows I'm thinking about her. In her eyes, it's three years too late, but that's not the case. One day soon, I'm going to get her alone so we can talk. So I can tell her I don't regret her or that night we spent together. The opposite in fact; it's consumed me.

The house is dark when I pull into the drive. My parents have always gone to bed early and get up just as early. Some things never change. As quietly as I can, I make my way inside the house and down the hall to my room. Stripping out of my clothes, in the dark, I slide under the covers in nothing but my boxer briefs. Tapping my phone screen, the light blinds me in the dark room. Dimming the screen, I scroll through my pictures until I find the one I'm looking for. Collins lying on the bed in my parents' camper. Her dark hair tousled in her sleep. It's longer now. Back then it had just been past her shoulders. Now it's long and hangs down her back. Her bare shoulders are peeking out from under the sheet. The very same sheet that I was under just moments before I took the picture.

I stood there for I don't know how long, watching her sleep. She took my breath away, yet I knew what I was about to do would destroy us, but there was too much going on inside of me. I knew it was best if I left, even though I wanted nothing more than to snuggle back under that sheet with her in my arms and wake up the same way. Never did I dream that three years later, it would still be her. It's only her.

Me: Goodnight, beautiful.

Rolling over, I stare at her picture until I can no longer keep my eyes open, dreaming she was here with me.

Chapter 8

Collins

I SLEPT LIKE SHIT. I turned my phone off after I received my second message from Grady. Then I spent the rest of the night tossing and turning, wondering if he sent more. It's a vicious cycle that's done nothing but lead me to be dragging my ass into work this morning. Not something, as an emergency room nurse, I should let happen.

"Good morning, Collins," Angie, my coworker, greets me. She's the always smiling, always super happy, bubbly kind of girl. Don't get me wrong, there is absolutely nothing wrong with that, but today, today her sunshine and rainbows just make me feel worse.

"Morning, Ang," I say, trudging past her at the reception desk to the break room to put my things in my locker.

"Rough weekend?" she asks from behind me, causing me to jump.

"Just didn't sleep well last night. How's the day looking so far?"

"Not too bad. Brenda said last night was slow."

In most cases, a slow night drags by, but in this case, working at the emergency room for a pediatric hospital, it's a good thing. I'd much rather have my night drag on than have all our triage rooms full of little boys and girls who are sick. "That's a good thing," I say, grabbing my stethoscope out of my bag and placing it around my neck. Taking inventory, I realize my phone is still in my purse. Reaching into my locker, I dig for it. I don't use my phone during work hours, a text here or there if we are slow, but I still like to have it on me. Not to mention you never know when an emergency might happen, and you need to be able to call for help. We've been through more disaster preparedness drills than I can count. All suggest we keep our phones on our person, on vibrate, or silent to not disturb patients. Ah ha! Feeling my phone, I pull it from the depths of my purse and see I have a new text message.

Grady: Morning, beautiful.

My heart beats a little faster seeing his name. I don't know what the hell his game is, but I'm not falling for it. Not again. He played me once; it won't happen twice. Just as I'm slipping my phone into my pocket, I feel it vibrate. Looking at the screen, I see another message from Grady. A follow-up to the one he sent just minutes before.

Grady: Have a great day.

I don't bother to text him back. Eventually, he will get the message. Maybe one day we can be friends, but right now, I'm too confused from seeing him again and from this… attention he's suddenly giving me. I'm sure he's just worried that now he's back in town, I'll tell Caleb and our families. He should realize that if I didn't say anything then, when I was dealing with a newly broken heart from the way he rode away like a thief in the night, I'm not going to tell them now. Besides, what good would it do? My brother would lose his best friend, and right before his wedding. Our families have lived next door to each other for years. It would cause a rift between us, and I don't want that to happen. I'm over it. I'm over him.

Sliding my phone into the pocket of my scrubs, I go check the board to see where we are. I need to keep my head in the game. This is not a job that I can be distracted from. Little lives are in my hands. Most of the time, it's an ear infection or other minor illness, but there have been times when the diagnosis is not that simple. Like cancer or diabetes. My heart squeezes when I think about my childhood friend Jared. Jared was Grady's younger brother who was my age. He and I were close and played together a lot when Grady and Caleb would lock us out of their rooms. He was sick for so long. The doctors would not listen to Debbie, their mom, that was not until it was too late. Jared was misdiagnosed. What they were calling reflux and irritable bowel was really cancer. By the time they discovered the real issue, he was stage four, and we lost him a few short months later.

I remember Jared telling me how nice the nurses were to him. How they would hold his hand when he was having a test or a shot. He said things were not so scary when the nice nurse was there. I remember thinking that I wanted to be that for someone. I wanted to make them comfortable when not feeling well, or give them a sense of peace, make sure they knew they were not alone when they were fighting for their life like Jared was.

I remember the day Grady told us he was going to be a doctor. It was after Jared's funeral. Caleb and I were sitting with him on the back porch while friends and family were in every room of the house. I can still hear the conviction in his voice when he declared "I'm going to be a doctor." At the time, I didn't think much about it, but when he started college and declared premed, I knew he would do it. I'm so damn proud of him, despite how hurt and angry I am. I wish I could tell him. He was such a huge part of my life growing up, and then he was more for a brief moment in time before he was nothing. The pain is still there, and I can only hope that one day I'll be able to let it go and maybe, just maybe he will be a part of my life again.

One day.

Shaking out of my thoughts, I dive into my next patient, a three-year-old little boy who is in town visiting his grandmother. He's crying and pulling at his ear, which is a pretty good sign he has an ear infection. I talk to him, asking him if he knows the characters on my scrub top. When he sniffs and says in a super sad voice, "Sponge Bob," I smile at him and make a huge deal about how smart he is and how I can't believe he knew.

"I loves Sponge Bob." He sniffs again.

"Well, then I'm glad you're my patient. You can tell me all about it." With his hand on his ear, he tells me about Sponge Bob and how he's really a sponge that lives in the sea. I'm able to take all of his vitals and get a good intake of what's going on from his mom. "You are my new best friend," I tell him, and he smiles up at me.

"My ear hurts."

"I know, sweetie. Dr. Larson will be in soon to take a look. We're going to get you fixed up so you can enjoy the rest of your time with your grandma," I tell him.

"She's old," he says unapologetically.

His parents scold him while the three of us try to hide our smiles. From the mouths of babes. The rest of my day goes at a steady pace. Nothing out of the ordinary, but my feet are killing me by the time I get home. Twelve-hour shifts are brutal. I work Monday, Tuesday, Wednesdays, and pick up others when my coworkers need time off. It works for me, and I'm damn lucky to be on first shift right out of nursing school. So the long days are worth it.

"How was work?" Tabby asks when I walk through the door of our apartment.

"Just another day. Yours?" I kick off my shoes and plop down on the couch next to her.

"Good. Gramps was in rare form today, among other things." She laughs.

"What did he do this time?"

"He pinched my ass!" She snorts. "He thought I was Lucy." She shakes her head.

"Are you sure working at the same assisted living your grandparents are in is a good thing?"

"Yeah, I need to hook them up." She throws me a grin.

Tabby's mom's mom and her dad's dad are in the same assisted living home where she works. That was her motivation to work there. We all have our reasons. "You think?" I ask, amused.

"Yeah, I mean, if Gramps can hit on Grams, then he'll leave the nurse alone."

"And what about your poor grams?"

"Pfft, you do realize that STDs are a big thing in nursing homes and assisted living homes, right?"

"What? No!"

"Yep. I was shocked, too, but we had training on what to look for and everything."

"So, wait a minute. You're telling me that they…. Can they still do that?" I stare at her wide-eyed.

She shudders. "Yep. I was skeptical too until today."

"Uh-oh, this must be the 'among other things' part of the conversation. Do I want to hear this?"

"Doesn't matter. I had to see it so, as my best friend, you have to hear it." She turns to face me on the couch. "So, I'm doing rounds after lunch, and I see that Miss Ida is not in her room. She fell last week, so I was worried about her. I went looking room to room, and I found her all right. She was in bed with Mr. Gordon!"

"By in bed, you mean they were just sleeping, right?"

"Nope. Both of them were naked as the day they were born. That's all I saw before running out of the room." She shudders again. "Then Theresa informed me that most of them are swingers. They don't care who they are, as long as they are getting it." She bursts into laughter.

"No!" I study her as her shoulders shake. "You're joking, right?"

"I wish I was. Now I will knock and listen before entering. Hearing it is a hell of a lot better than walking in on it."

"Oh my." I cover my mouth as laughter bubbles up.

"Right? I bet you can't top that."

"Nope. Not even going to try." I stand from the couch. "I need a quick shower. What do you want to do for dinner?"

"Going to Mom and Dad's. You want to come?" she offers.

"Nah, I should probably go see my parents as well. I told Mom I would stop by one night this week and show her the bridesmaid dresses."

"She still hasn't seen them?"

"No, we changed them since she saw the first version. I was going to text it to her, but she said I could show her when I stopped by. You know Mom, always thinking of reasons to get us to visit."

"Right? It's a mom thing I guess. How are the wedding plans? Does Emily have it all squared away?"

"Yeah, we wrapped up most of it last night. Now it's kind of a waiting game. She should get invitations in the mail in the next few days. Save the dates already went out."

"I can't believe Caleb is going to settle down."

"You and me both. If you're gone by the time I get out," I say, heading to my room to grab some clothes and take a shower, "have a good time. Tell the parentals I said hello." She yells down the hall with her agreement, and I close myself inside the bathroom. A long, hot shower is exactly what I need. I want to spend the rest of the night curled up with a good book, escaping my world for one of fantasies and happily ever afters.

Chapter 9

GRADY

I'M SITTING OUT ON THE back deck at my parents' place, just relaxing. It's not something I've done much of the last three years, and the next three are going to be the same. Although there is more time off in residency, it's not much. The hours are long and brutal, but I'm on the home stretch. I'm also back in my hometown. The more I'm here, the happier I am with my decision to come home for residency. I got the email earlier letting me know that I start on Monday, it's earlier than I thought I would be starting, but I'm ready for it. I'm anxious to get started, but I wish that things were better with Collins before I did. I know from the way she's been ignoring my text messages that's not going to happen. I did sneak a look in Mom's phone last night and confirmed it's still her number. That gave me hope, unless she blocked me.

"It's a great surprise." I hear Monica Ward, Collins and Caleb's mom, say.

Our houses are right next door. Although the lots are big, voices still carry.

"Mom, you're acting like it's been weeks since you've seen me."

"It was last week," Monica counters.

"You're impossible." Collins laughs.

"Well, sweetheart, we miss our only daughter," her dad, Roger, chimes in.

"I feel the love," Collins says. "Oh, Mom, before I forget, let me show you the bridesmaid dresses."

"Didn't Emily already show you those?" her dad asks.

"Mom!" Collins mock scolds her. "You didn't tell me you saw them already."

I smile at their banter. Our families are so similar I guess that's why our parents have been so close all these years. Wanting to give them privacy, I head inside and move to the front porch. I stare at her old beat-up Mazda. It's the same car she drove all those years ago. Not that there is anything wrong with that. I'm still driving my first car as well. I guess there are some things that don't change.

I have the house to myself. Mom and Dad are at bowling league. Apparently, it's a new thing for them. I should go inside and grab some food, maybe head to bed. I feel like I could sleep for a year and never wake up. Of course, it doesn't help me sleep knowing I'm in the same city as her. Just a few miles away in fact. I wish I could convince her to talk to me. I have things I need to say.

I must have been deep in thought because the sound of her voice pulls me back to the present. "Thanks, Mom. I'm sure Tabby will love them." I watch as Collins holds up a small container of what I'm sure is some type of baked concoction from her mother. Man, that woman can bake.

When I hear the front door close, I stand from the steps and walk across the yard. I make it to her car at the same time as she does. "Hey." I shove my hands in my pockets to keep from reaching for her.

"What are you doing here?"

"I live next door, remember?"

"You're just visiting."

"Not this time. I'm here to stay."

"Good for you. I really need to go," she says, pointing at her car door that I'm now standing in front of.

"Can we talk?" I want to pull her into my arms and just... hold her.

It's been too damn long. I know it's my fault, but I'm trying to fix that.

"We have nothing to talk about. I told you, it's over. I'm over it. Just forget it happened." She steps forward, and I move to stand in front of her.

"We do have things to talk about. At least I do."

"Funny, I stopped caring what you had to say a long damn time ago."

"Collins."

"Move, Grady. I had a long day and have to get ready for work tomorrow."

"Can we meet for lunch? Dinner? You name the time and place."

"Nope. Now, if you would please move." She reaches around me to open the door, and I can no longer take it. I place my hand on her arm to stop her.

"I'm sorry, I know you deserve more than that."

"You're damn right I do. I did three years ago when I gave myself to you, and you walked away as if it never happened. Where were you when I was calling you every day? Where were the replies to my text messages?"

Tears brim in her eyes and pain laces her voice. "I know. I ran scared, and I'm an asshole, I am. I own what I did, but never, not once, did I forget you or that night." She's still not looking at me, so I keep going, hoping that she's at least listening. "I know the gift that you gave me. I know that I didn't deserve it, not with how I acted after. I need you to know, no, I need you to tell me that you understand that night altered my life. Every day since then, it's been with you in mind. To coming back to you and winning your heart."

"Right." She laughs humorlessly. "Just let it go, Grady." Her eyes move to the house.

"I can't." I know this is not the place to be having this conversation, but damn, she's here in front of me. I can't let the opportunity to talk to her slip through my fingers.

"You don't have a choice."

"You see, that's where you're wrong." My free hand, that's not holding onto her, lifts her chin so that she's looking right at me. "I do have a choice. I realize that three years ago I made the wrong one, but I won't make it twice."

"Well, I hope whoever she is, you keep that promise."

"There's no one but you." I cup her face in my hands. "Please."

"I have to go." She pulls out of my hold, dips under my arm, and opens her door. I step out of the way, letting her leave. I did this to her, but now I need to find a way to fix it. Pushing her won't do it. Slow and steady wins the race.

I stand here in her parents' drive and watch her leave. My gaze follows her car until I can no longer see her taillights, and then I make my way across our yards and back to the front porch. I hate that she's driving when she's upset, I hate it even more that I upset her, but I have to make her understand. I watch the time of my phone, and as soon as fifteen minutes have passed, I send her another text.

Grady: I hope you made it home safe.

Nothing. No reply, not that I expected there to be. With a heavy sigh, I head into the house to heat up some of last night's leftovers. I barely taste the food as my mind replays our conversation. I wanted to kiss her, pull her into me, and slant my mouth over hers, maybe then she would have listened. I'm trying to be the guy she deserves, giving her space to come to terms with me being back in town, but I don't know how much longer I can do that. I don't know how much longer I can be this close to her and not touch her. Sure, I had my hand on her arm, and I cupped her face in my hands. Her silky-smooth skin reminded me of exactly what I've been missing these past three years, but it's not enough. I want my arms around her, and her body aligned with mine. I want to taste her. I want it all, and it's fucking driving me crazy that I can't have it. Maybe the nice guy routine is not what it's going to take.

Heading up to my old room, I strip down and climb into bed. Just like I have every night for the last three years, I pull up the picture of her from that night. I fucked up. This is on me. My eyes grow heavy, and I know it won't be long before sleep claims me.

Grady: Goodnight, beautiful.

I don't wait for a reply this time. I know it's not coming. Instead, I go back to her picture and fall fast asleep.

Chapter 10

Collins

THIS PAST WEEK HAS BEEN… off. If I'm honest, I've been off since the night I realized Grady was back in town. The night my world, the one I pretended was not filled with pain and abandonment, came crashing down. Every day since that night, he's sent me a message. Good morning, goodnight, how was your day… simple messages. I hate that three years ago, I would have clung to them, taking any morsel of attention or affection from him that he was willing to offer. What I hate even more is that the temptation is there. Three years later and he still makes my heart pump a little faster. He still sets off a swarm of butterflies deep in my gut. The only difference is this time, I know the hurt. I know what it feels like when he walks away, slipping into the night as if our time together never existed. This time, I know better than to let him break down my walls.

Each time a new message pops up, I have to read it. It's become so frequent in the last week, that it's almost as if his messages are now a normal part of my day. Rolling over in bed, I look at the clock. It's just after eight in the morning, and I'm already eager for this day to be over. This afternoon, we're all meeting at Caleb and Emily's for the guys to draw names for who they are walking with in the wedding. I don't have to be there. Emily's sisters are not going to be there, but I live close, and they know my work schedule, and I couldn't think of a reason to get out of it. Not one that would have gone over as a good alibi. So in six hours, I'll be face-to-face with him. My only saving grace is that there will be other people there. His friends that he's not seen much of since he's been away at medical school. I hope they keep him occupied. My phone pings with a message, and I know it's him. I count to one hundred slowly in my head, instead of rushing to read it like I want to. I need to learn to pace myself. I want to know what he has to say, even when I know I shouldn't. Another ping has me reaching for my phone before I reach my goal of one hundred.

Grady: Good morning, beautiful.

Grady: I can't wait to see you tonight. Maybe we can talk after.

"Not happening," I mutter. After throwing the covers off, I head across the hall to the bathroom. Tabby's door is still shut, so I'm assuming she's taking advantage of sleeping in today, something my mind didn't seem to want me to do.

I pop a bagel in the toaster, then slather it with cream cheese and grab a bottle of water from the fridge. I'm not a coffee girl, never have been. Some of it smells heavenly, but the aftertaste is a hard no for me. I'm just about to take my first bite when my phone rings. Glancing at the screen, I see Emily's smiling face. "Good morning," I answer.

"Hey, you're still coming this afternoon, right?"

No. "Yep. Need me to bring anything?"

"No, I'm just going to order some pizzas. I called to tell you that you should pack a bag and stay if you're going to drink."

"Um, I thought the guys were just drawing names for the wedding?"

"Oh, they are, but Caleb decided to involve alcohol since they'll all be together."

"Were they not just together last Saturday night at the bar?"

She laughs. "Yeah, but he misses his friends," she says in a whiny voice.

"Please tell me that's how he said it," I sputter with laughter.

"No, but he might as well have. Like he needed to convince me. He was laying it on thick. Since my sisters are not coming in from out of town, you're my only ally. I need you."

And here I thought I could skip out early. "We'll just engross them in all-things-wedding. That will scare them away."

"Why didn't I think of that?" she asks, humor lacing her voice. "So, pack a bag." She gets back to the purpose of her call.

"Yeah," I say, unable to tell her no. "What are we drinking?"

"Vodka cranberry is what I have. You want anything else? Caleb is running out to pick up some beer and snacks."

"That's my poison of choice."

"I know. You've got me hooked. Thanks, Collins, you're saving me from a night of pure testosterone."

"Anytime. I'll see you later." We end the call, and I mentally chastise myself for not being able to say no. If Grady were not back in town, I would have been jumping at the chance to hang with them, with no hesitation for staying over. Now though, now life is all messy and confusing again. His presence does not mean a damn thing. I just need to keep reminding my heart that.

His presence does not matter, which is why I took extra care when getting ready. I made sure I shaved everywhere and smoothed my favorite lavender lotion all over my skin. It took me longer than I care to admit to pick out an outfit. I want him to see what he's missing, what he willingly gave up. I put curls in my hair, letting them hang down my back and go with subtle for my makeup. I didn't want to look like I'm trying too hard or trying at all for that matter. I settled on a pair of cut-off denim shorts, and a burgundy flowing tank top. Completed with black flip-flops and I'm good to go.

I made sure to pack some short shorts and a matching tank to sleep in, as well as another outfit for tomorrow. That one, I chose at random. I added some toiletries and zipped the bag. How is it possible that I'm both excited and dreading this night all at the same time? I want him to see me, to see what he can never have, not again. I also don't want to deal with it. I want to forget the pain and the loneliness and just live. Clearly, my head and my heart are in battle. Why I'm not sure; they both remember the pain. I wish I could say that I was over it, over him, but that nervousness when he's around—even mixed with anger—tells me that's not the case. He was my first love. He also took what he wanted and then disappeared from my life. Why can my heart not understand that?

"Where you headed off to?" Tabby asks when I come out of my room carrying my overnight bag.

"Caleb's. They're drawing names for the wedding party today."

"That's right. Are you staying?"

"Maybe, not sure yet. Thought I would take some clothes just in case. I guess Caleb and the guys are going to be shooting the shit and Emily didn't want to be the only woman there. You want to come?"

"Nope. I have a date." She grins.

"Do tell." I take a seat on the arm of the couch waiting for more details.

"Just this guy I met at work. His mom is there, and she's in my hall. He asked me to dinner."

"Good for you. Call me if you need me to come and get you or bail you out. Text me where you will be."

"I'm sure it will be fine." She waves me off.

"Still, text me so I don't worry."

"Got it, Mom," she says with a laugh.

"Ha ha. I'll see you either late tonight or in the morning."

"Have fun," she calls over her shoulder as I head out the door.

Chapter 11

GRADY

I'M EARLY. NOT BECAUSE I want to see the guys, and not because Caleb and Emily need help setting up. I'm early because I know she's going to be here. I don't know how long she plans on staying, but I don't want to miss the opportunity to see her. Caleb called last night to remind me and mentioned she was coming, too, but Emily's sisters couldn't make it. They live out of town, and this is not really a wedding festivity.

Reaching in the back seat, I grab the bottle of Crown that I picked up earlier today. This is the apple flavor, and when you mix it with Sprite, it's lethal. I didn't go out much in medical school, but my roommates and I would indulge at home. This is something we learned in undergrad. College education at its finest.

"Hey, Grady," Emily answers the door. "What you got there?" She points to my hand, smiling.

"Crown Apple." I hold up one hand and the twelve-pack of Sprite in the other. "Have you had it?" I ask, following her into the kitchen and setting the items on the counter.

"No, is it any good? I don't drink much, but Collins has me hooked on Cape Cod's vodka and cranberry juice."

"I've had a Royal Flush, but never just vodka and cranberry."

"Then you'll have to try one tonight. That's pretty much the only drink Collins and I will drink. Well, she loves those Wild Grape Smirnoff, but I'm not much of a grape fan."

I take in every morsel of information that she's giving me about Collins. I can use every advantage I can get to convince her to listen to me. "Where's Caleb?" I finally ask when I realize we're just standing here in their kitchen.

"He's in the shower. Bryce and Alec called not long ago and are on their way as well. You must be glad to be home?"

"Yeah. It's been a while. School and my job at the hospital kept me busy." It's not a complete lie. I was busy, but I could have made time. It's not like I can tell her I slept with your soon-to-be sister-in-law, my best friend's little sister, then couldn't face her or the fact that I knew it would cause me to lose my best friend. I can't tell her that Collins made me feel more in one night than anyone before her and any who attempted to come after. It's the half-truth that she gets, that they all get until I can talk to Collins, and ideally for longer than a couple of minutes. I'm hoping tonight I'll get my chance.

"Well, I know Caleb is glad to have you home. I'm pleased your residency is going to be close. Where did you say you're doing it again?"

"I didn't." I grin. "Riley," I say, and her smile widens.

"That's awesome! Did you know that Collins works there? She's an ER nurse. She just started a couple of weeks ago."

Hell yes! "No, I wasn't aware. I knew she was a nurse, her roommate, too, right?" I'm going for casual when all I can think about is us being in the same place for the next three years. Fuck, I hope it doesn't take me that long to win her over. *You were gone three years, asshole. That's what you deserve.*

"Yes, they went to nursing school together. You know, I don't think she knows that Riley is where you will be doing your residency either," she studies me.

"Yeah, let's just keep that between us for now." I know she's trying to process why I would say that. "This is about your wedding. She'll find out soon enough." The smile comes back to her face.

"I have pictures of my sisters and Collins. I put them in envelopes. The three of you are going to draw straws at who gets to go first. Once you have all drawn, you get to open your envelope and see who you're walking with." She claps her hands as she radiates with excitement.

"Are you cheering?" Caleb asks, stepping up behind her and wrapping his arms around her waist.

"Maybe a little." She turns to look at him. "I was just telling Grady about the plan to draw names."

He smiles at her. "You're cute." He kisses her nose and then looks up at me. "Hey, man. Thanks for coming."

"Oh, he brought this." Emily lifts the bottle of Crown from the island.

"Nice." He grins. "Been too long since it was the four of us hanging out."

"Hey, don't forget that your sister and I will be here as well."

"I could never forget you, babe."

"Come on now, if this is how it's going to be all night, I'm going to go back to my place," Collins says from behind me.

I fight to not turn to look at her. I can hear her footsteps as she gets closer, her lavender scent surrounding me. Then she's there, right beside me. I glance at her out of the corner of my eye, and her attention is on her brother and Emily.

"Thank you!" Emily rolls her eyes playfully. "I was about to be outnumbered. As it is, we still are, but I needed you," she says dramatically, causing Collins to laugh.

I turn my head to look at her, her laugh captivating me. "Hey," I greet her. I'm going for casual, but fuck it. I feel like it's anything but.

"Hi," she says with a smile that doesn't reach her eyes. "Where is everyone?" she asks Emily. We all know she's running this show.

"On their way. Alec was stopping to pick Bryce up." Just as the words leave her mouth, there's a loud knock at the door. With their fingers laced together, they both go to greet our friends, leaving me alone with Collins.

"You look beautiful," I tell her.

"Cut the shit, Grady."

"I'm being honest. Listen, do you think that maybe after this you and I could go grab a drink so we can talk?"

"Nope."

"There he is," Bryce's deep voice booms as he enters the room. He wraps an arm around my neck and pulls me in, rubbing the top of my head.

"Fucker." I laugh and push him away, only to receive the same exact treatment from Alec. I push him away, too.

"My future wife." Bryce wraps his big muscled arms around Collins and pulls her into his chest, kissing the top of her head.

Here's the thing. The four of us have been thick as thieves since kindergarten. Caleb and I have been neighbors even longer. In this moment, it's taking everything I have in me to not punch one of my oldest friends in the face. Collins laughs and places her arms around his waist, giving him a hug. My fists clench at my sides.

"Oh, yeah?" she asks, amused, looking up at him. Those blue eyes giving him all of her attention. "I need a rock." She holds up her left hand and wiggles her fingers.

I want to drop to my knees and tell her I'll buy her any damn ring she wants. I don't care what it costs if she'll just talk to me and remove her hands from him.

"My turn," Alec says, pulling her from Bryce and hugging her to his side.

I watch as Bryce goes to Emily and pulls her into a hug as well. He doesn't seem to mind or notice that Caleb is staring daggers at him. Alec releases Collins and does the same. I want my turn to hug her, to hold her to my chest and let her lavender scent wash over me. I fucked that up, but I'm back, and I'm not giving up until that exact scenario is our reality.

"Right," Alec says, laughing when he sees the look that Caleb is giving him. The one that says you have mere seconds to get your hands off my future wife. I know the look well. I've been giving it to both of them since they walked through the door; they just don't seem to notice. "Are we doing this?" he asks.

Emily claps her hands. "Yes. Okay, so each of you are going to draw a straw. Longest goes first and so on. You'll each pick an envelope. Inside is the picture of either one of my sisters or Collins."

"I've seen your sisters, Emily, and this one." Bryce points to Collins. "We win regardless." He smirks.

"Fuck yes, we do," Alec agrees.

I stay silent. I watch Caleb waiting to see if he mouths off to them the way they are talking about his little sister. He says nothing. Was I that wrong? Would he have accepted her and me? Would he have been okay with the two of us being together? Did I run for nothing? Mess up the best thing to happen to me, for nothing?

Bryce smacks his hands together and rubs them. "Let's do this."

Emily reaches into the drawer and pulls out three straws that are already in her hand. I stand back. It doesn't matter what order we go in; there is still a one in three chance that I get paired with Collins. Instead of worrying about when I get to pick my straw, I send up a silent prayer that it's her picture in my envelope.

"Hold them up," Emily says after I draw mine. "Alec, Grady, then Bryce," she announces. Reaching behind her, she grabs three black sealed envelopes from the cabinet and lays them in a line.

"Come on, at least you could have made the envelopes white so we could attempt to cheat," Bryce jokes.

"Nope. We want this to be fair. Too much pressure the other way." She laughs. Caleb leans in and kisses her cheek.

Alec moves the envelopes all around until finally picking one. He starts to open it when Caleb tells him to wait.

"She wants you all to open them at the same time, right, Em?" he asks his fiancée.

"Yep." She looks at me. "Your turn, Grady."

I look across the island at Collins and she's biting her bottom lip, her eyes focused on the two remaining envelopes. I know her silent plea is the exact opposite of mine. With a deep breath, I close my eyes and blindly reach for one of the envelopes.

"All right," Bryce says. "Can we open them now?" He reaches for the last remaining envelope.

"You're enjoying this way too much," Caleb jokes.

"Hey, can you blame me? They're all three hot as hell." He winks at Collins and again, I fight the urge to punch him. "Either way, we all win. I just need to know which beauty I'll be cuddled up with that night."

Emily laughs. "They're all three single, too." She hip-checks Collins.

"Hey, now." Caleb laughs. "I don't need to hear that shit about my little sister."

That's it? No warning to keep our hands off? No warning that if we touch her, he's going to kick our asses? Growing up, I heard that speech so many damn times I can recite it. It has to be the thrill of the wedding.

"On three," Emily counts us down. At the sound of three, I slowly peel open the envelope and slide the picture from its depths. I look at it, blink, and then look again. She's still there. Collins with her long, dark hair and her bright blue eyes are staring back at me. I got her. I hate to think that I don't get her to myself until the wedding, but I'll take it. I'll take anything and everything I can get of her.

"The sexy Samantha." Bryce shows us his picture.

"I like older women." Alec holds up a picture of Emily's other sister, Cindy, I think she said her name was.

"She's two years older than us." Emily shakes her head.

"Sam's what, two years younger?" Bryce asks.

"Nope. Four, she and Collins are the same age." She looks at me. "You get our girl here." Once again, she hip-checks Collins.

"Yeah," I say, looking at Collins. "I get our girl." My voice is soft and my eyes are fixed on her, but no one seems to think a thing of it as they start passing out drinks.

Chapter 12

Collins

"COLLINS, GRADY HAS A NEW drink for us to try," Emily tells me.

"Oh, yeah?" My palms are sweating and my heart is beating faster than it should be for a leisurely Saturday afternoon. He drew me. I knew it was possible, but I figured the fates would take pity on me. How am I going to do this? Let him walk me down the aisle? Dance with him at the reception, sit next to him at the reception, photographs? The list goes on and on, but the fact remains it's the two of us paired up for the entire event. I have weeks, mere weeks to come to terms with the fact. I'm an adult, I remind myself. It's two nights—the rehearsal and then the wedding. If I can get through him walking away, I can handle being nice and smiling for the cameras. It's *just* two days. This is for my big brother and soon-to-be sister. I can be the bigger person. Maybe if I keep repeating that, I'll actually believe it.

"It's Crown Apple and Sprite," he says.

I look up to find him watching me. "I don't drink much." I don't know why I tell him that, but I feel like I need him to know I'm not out drinking myself into a stupor over him.

"Me either, really. My two roommates during med school turned me onto this. None of us went out much, but we would indulge here and there after a study session at our place. It's good," he says, adding Sprite to a cup of Crown and pushing it across the island toward me.

"Try it," Emily says.

I'm tempted to let it sit and walk away, but that would be obvious that something is wrong. I need to learn to act as if he's just some guy. He's no longer *the* guy, at least that's what I keep telling myself. I take a sip and surprisingly, it's not bad. "It's good."

"Here." Grady slides a cup toward Emily, and she takes it, immediately taking a sip of her own. "Wow, this is really good. I need to add this to my short list of likes." She smiles and takes another sip.

"Yeah," I agree with her, taking another sip. I look over at Grady, and he's smiling proudly, observing me.

"You want one, man?" he asks Caleb.

"Why not," he says. Grady goes about making him a drink while I pretend to not be watching him over the rim of my glass. I know he knows, but I'm still pretending that's not the case.

"Serve it up, G," Bryce says, placing his arm over my shoulder and grabbing my glass. I study him as he places it to his lips and tilts his head back, draining my cup. "Make my girl another," he says, setting my now empty glass on the counter and sliding it toward Grady.

"I was making you one, asshole," Grady grumbles.

"Might as well pour me one, too, if you're serving," Alec tells him.

Grady nods as he adds Sprite to the solo cup that was meant for Bryce. Instead, he picks it up and holds it out for me. "Collins," he says softly.

I take the offered cup, telling my heart that he served me first because Bryce drank mine. It makes good sense, but I know Grady. It's been years, but I know the kind of guy he is. Ladies first. I've spent three years trying to forget that's his motto in everything he does. It's a plan that I once upon a time greatly benefited from. Now, I hate it. I hate the memories that it brings up. I hate to remember them, but I hate to let them go. It's a no-win situation.

Grady makes Bryce and Alec their drinks and puts the lid back on the bottle, without making one for himself. "What's up with that?" Caleb asks him.

"Just not feeling it right now," he says as an explanation.

Cup tilted to my lips, I watch him over the rim, and he's watching me. He gives me a small smile, and I close my eyes, taking a big gulp. When he looks at me like that, like he wants me, it unnerves me. The time for that has passed. If he thinks he can roll back into town after fading away for three years and things are just fine, that we can be friends or whatever in the hell it is that he wants to say or ask, he's wrong. He's so damn wrong. I know I need to remain strong, to resist his charms and his eagerness to talk. There is however, a small part of me that wants to hear what he has to say. Will he grovel? Even more so when he apologizes again, because from our interactions this far, that's a given. Will I ever be able to forgive him?

"So, Emily," Alec speaks up, "are your sisters coming in any time before the wedding?"

"I don't think so. Collins has been great at helping with the wedding plans and of course my future mother-in-law has been helpful as well." She beams just from talking about Mom being her mother-in-law.

"So, what are the plans before the wedding? Anything we need to do?" Grady asks.

"Nope. It's all taken care of. We do need the three of you to go get measured for your pants and shirts."

"No monkey suits." Bryce throws his hand in the air in silent celebration.

"Nope. I want everyone to be comfortable. That's why I chose the dresses that I did. They could technically wear them again if they wanted to."

Grady glances at me and smiles. I turn to Emily and pretend to be listening to her tell Bryce and Alec what they will be wearing. However, I don't hear a damn word she says. All I can see is his smile and the way it affects me. I hate it. I hate that after all this time his smile still causes butterflies to take off in my stomach. I hate the way I long for that smile to be directed at me every day.

"Collins." His deep voice brings me out of my thoughts.

Blinking, I look at him and realize it's just the two of us left in the kitchen. "They went in the other room, you okay?"

"Fine." I raise my drink to my lips and drain it.

"You want another?"

I nod. He takes my empty cup from my hand, his fingers brushing against mine. There's a jolt of electricity. I quickly pull my hand away; luckily, he already had the cup. Thankfully, preventing a spill, and the need for me to fumble through an explanation for the cause. How is it possible that three years later, my body still reacts to his touch?

"Your hair's longer," he says, placing the lid back on the bottle of Crown, and opening a new can of Sprite. I don't bother to respond. Instead, I watch his every move. When he slides the now full cup across the counter to me, I grab it and take a small sip, knowing I need to pace myself.

"Collins—" He stops and swallows hard. "I'm sorry. There is so much that I need to say."

I laugh humorlessly. "The time for that has passed, Grady. Where were your words when I was texting and calling you? When I was begging you to talk to me?" I close my eyes and take a deep breath. When I open them, he's watching me, sadness and what looks like regret written all over his face. "We're done here," I say, turning on my heel and making my way toward the living room. I find the others sitting around the living room, just shooting the shit. Caleb and Emily are huddled together in the chair, while Bryce and Alec are on the couch. There is one open chair and an open spot on the couch. Neither appeal to me, so I wave and point to the patio doors. I need some fresh air.

When I reach the door, I can't see outside because of the inside light, but I know what I will find behind the door. A small patio with a table and chairs. After sliding open the door, I pull it closed behind me. I forgo the table and chairs and head toward the banister. Solo cup in hand, I lean my elbows against the banister and close my eyes. The warm night air surrounds me, as do the sounds of the town, cars driving by, voices in the distance. I take a deep breath and slowly exhale.

"You okay?" a deep voice asks, a voice that haunts my dreams. When I don't respond, he places his hand on the small of my back. "Collins," he says again.

Too lost in my thoughts, I didn't even hear him come out here. That's what he does to me. "What are you doing out here, Grady?"

"Checking on you."

"No," I say forcefully. "What are you doing here? Back in town?"

"I live here."

"No, you don't. It's been three years since you stepped foot into this town."

"It was time."

"It was time," I mock. "Go back inside, Grady." Tilting my head back, I drain the rest of my drink.

Instead of walking away, he steps closer. "Collins," he says softly. "I'm sorry for leaving. It's my biggest regret. Please, can we talk about this?"

"Nope," I say, popping the *P*.

He steps closer, and I can feel his heat on my back. He braces his arms on the railing beside mine, caging me in. A step closer and his front is aligned with my back. Closing my eyes, I fight the shiver his touch causes.

"I was wrong, Collins. I was scared for so many reasons, and I acted like a coward." His hot breath brushes my ear and this time, the shiver is evident. When I feel him bury his head in my neck, I begin to panic.

"What are you d-doing? They could see us," I say, trying to step out of his hold, but he's too close, too strong.

"I don't care about that, any of it. All I care about is you. Please, talk to me."

Eyes closed, I let his deep timbre wash over me. I want to turn in his arms and wrap mine around his waist. I want to feel his warmth surround all of me, but that's my heart talking, the one who still longs for him. My head knows better. "No, we can't do this. Not here."

"Meet me. You tell me when and where, and I'll make it happen."

"Right." I laugh. "You're so trustworthy." His lips press against my neck, and I fight the urge to melt into him. "We need to go back inside."

"I don't care if they see us," he insists.

"You might not, but I do. Why do they need to know about our one night of bad judgment? It's not like it will ever happen again. No need to ruin friendships."

"It wasn't a night of bad judgment," he says through what I'm sure are gritted teeth. I look down at his hands that are gripping the railing. "Please, can we go somewhere and talk?"

"No." I manage to turn in his arms. When I look up at him, his green eyes are focused solely on me. "It was a night of lapsed judgment. You regretted it as soon as it happened, and me, well I learned to deal with the rejection. We aren't going back there. It was years ago." I don't know what makes me do it, but I stand on my tiptoes and press my lips to his. His grip on the railing releases, and he rests his hands on the small of my back, pulling me into him. Breaking the kiss, I step out of his hold. His arms drop to his sides, and he's breathing heavily. "This, whatever it was back then, no longer exists." I step around him and walk back inside.

I find myself in the kitchen so I make myself another drink. This time, more Crown than Sprite. I don't want to think about Grady, or that night, or the way his lips felt against mine. I don't want to give my heart the chance to latch onto him, or the thought of him. That was long ago. We can never go back.

"There you are," Emily says. "You okay?"

"Yeah, just wanted some fresh air and needed another drink."

"Pour me another." She grins.

I do just that. I make hers just as strong, and we head back into the living room. Grady is sitting on the couch with Bryce and Alec, leaving the chair for me. I avoid looking at him, pretending he's not even there. I need to learn how to deal with him being back in town.

"Never have I ever." Alec claps his hands together, moving to sit on the edge of the couch.

"Are we back in college?" Caleb laughs.

"I'll go first," Bryce says, ignoring him.

My eyes wander to Grady on their own accord, and he's watching me. This is going to be a long-ass night.

Chapter 13

GRADY

SHE KISSED ME. THAT'S ALL I can think about, the feel of her soft lips pressed against mine. I want to grab her and haul her into my lap, bury my face back in her neck, and just hold her. I want to show them all that she's mine. I hurt her, I get that. I know that I'm going to have to work hard to prove to her how sorry I am. I was young and dumb, and if I'm honest, scared out of my mind at the feelings she evoked in me.

"Never have I ever went to law school." Bryce grins.

"What the hell?" Caleb laughs. "You trying to get me drunk?"

"Drink up, brother," Bryce taunts him.

"Wait," Emily says. "Grady, you need a drink."

"I'm not drinking tonight," I tell her.

"Of course, you are," she says, standing.

"No, really. I have some residency stuff to deal with tomorrow, and I need a clear head." It's a lie, but I get a free pass anyway.

"Fine," she grumbles. She disappears into the kitchen and comes back with a can of Sprite and hands it to me.

"Thanks."

"Okay, now me. Never have I ever had sex in a public place," Alec says, smirking. Bryce curses under his breath and takes a drink.

"You're holding out on us," Caleb taunts him.

"Nowhere in the rules does it say we have to give details." He smirks.

Caleb laughs. "I see how you are. Right, my turn." He looks up at Emily, who is still sitting in his lap. "Never have I ever had a one-night stand."

She smiles down at him, and that's when I remember their story. They were a one-time thing, until he ran into her again and convinced her to go out with him. One date led to two, and here we are, fast approaching their wedding day. Bryce, Alec, and Collins all drink, but I don't.

"Right," Collins scoffs.

I raise my eyebrow at her, daring her to say more. I've had three years to think about this, and if I lose my best friend to have her, it's worth it. She's worth it. If I could go back in time and have a do-over, I never would have left. I would have slept with my arms locked tightly around her, soaking up every fucking minute I could before I had to go back to school.

"Moving on," Caleb chimes in. "I'm going to pretend that my baby sister did not just drink to that one."

"Never have I ever seen the ocean," Emily says quickly.

Alec and I are the only two to drink. I make a mental note to one day take Collins to the beach.

"Col," Caleb says.

"Okay." She sits up a little straighter in her chair. "Never have I ever turned my back on someone I care about." Her eyes bore into mine.

I did, but I didn't. She smirks, waiting for me to bring the can of Sprite to my lips, so I do. I don't like it because I'm here now, but it's the truth all the same.

"Grady." Bryce nudges me with his elbow.

"Never have I ever had a speeding ticket." It's lame, but it gets everyone to drink except for Emily and Collins.

"Never have I ever been in love," Bryce says.

I watch as Caleb and Emily quickly take their drinks. Turning my attention to Collins, she frowns as she places her cup to her lips and takes a drink at the same time as I do. I don't take my eyes off her, hoping she understands.

"You?" Alec asks, looking around Bryce at me.

"I thought we didn't have to defend our answers?" Bryce saves me without even knowing it.

"There is a big difference between one-night stands and love," Alec says.

"Yeah, me," I say, still looking at Collins. It's risky, but I can't seem to look away from her, not when I say. "She's amazing, smart, beautiful." I swallow. "I messed up, but I'm working on getting her back." Wide-eyed, she looks away.

"Who is she?" Bryce asks.

"He doesn't have to tell us, remember? Now, Alec, it's your turn." Emily rescues me.

Funny thing is I didn't really want to be rescued. I was ready to tell them all that it was her—Collins. I was prepared for my best friend to punch me. I'm not the same guy I was three years ago. Time and distance have made me realize what I walked away from.

"I need another drink." Collins stands and is wobbly on her feet.

"Hey there, little sister. Maybe you've had enough?" Caleb watches her.

"I'm staying, remember?"

"That doesn't mean you need to drink yourself into a stupor where you don't remember the night."

Her eyes find mine. "Maybe I want to forget." Her words are a soft confession that cut right through my chest. "Actually, you know, I am pretty tired. I think I'll head to bed. I'll see you all in the morning." She waves over her shoulder and stumbles down the hall.

I have to force myself to sit in the chair and not rush after her. To take her in my arms and hold her while she sleeps off the alcohol.

"So, you find a place yet?" Alec asks.

"Not yet. I need to figure it out this week. I love my parents, but living with them is not something I want to do after being gone for so long."

"I think Collins said that there was a vacancy at her complex. In fact, it's the unit right next to hers. The girl got married a couple of weeks ago," Emily says.

"Really? I'll have to ask her about it."

"You better go now before she crashes." Bryce chuckles.

"Good idea." I stand and head toward the hallway, as if just inquiring about an apartment is all that's on my mind. I'm taking risks, which I'm sure she hates, but her being a secret is something I hate more. I would be okay with getting caught.

When I reach the spare bedroom, the door is open, and the bedside lamp is casting a soft glow over the room. Collins is on the bed, curled up in a ball. I think she's sleeping until I hear a soft sob break free from her chest. Pushing into the room, I drop to my knees beside the bed. Slowly her eyes open, big, beautiful blue eyes that are wet with tears.

"I don't understand," she confesses. Her voice is soft and filled with pain. "Why now? After all these years, why now?"

Reaching out, I cup her face in my hands and wipe her tears with my thumb. "I knew the minute I drove away that night that I was making a mistake. I knew leaving you there in that bed would be my biggest regret in life, but I let fear control my actions, and I kept the car pointed back toward school."

"I called you," she whispers.

"How drunk are you, Collins? Will you remember this conversation in the morning?"

"I'm buzzed, but not so much so that I won't remember."

"I want to tell you, Collins. I want to tell you everything, but, baby, I want you to remember it."

"I'll remember," she assures me. "Just like I remember the way it felt to have you hover over me, the way your eyes never left mine." She stops and swallows hard. Footsteps carry down the hall and disappear behind the noise of the bathroom door shutting. "Now is probably not the best time."

"I don't care if they know," I remind her.

"So, you said."

"You tell me when and where, and I'll be there. That's all I ask... for the chance to tell you my side. It doesn't make what I did right, but I hope it might help you understand."

"Why now?" she asks again.

"Because, my beautiful, Collins, I want you in my life."

"Grady—" I place my fingers over her lips.

"Just give me the chance to explain, please?" I ask softly. Her answer is to nod. "I need to find a place to live, not with my parents. Emily says there is a unit beside you that's vacant?"

Again, she nods.

"Can I call you tomorrow, get the information?"

Another nod.

Leaning in, I kiss her soft lips. Just a peck, but a kiss all the same. "Get some rest, baby. I'll call you tomorrow." She closes her eyes. I stand and make myself turn to leave.

"Grady," she whispers.

I turn to look at her over my shoulder. Her eyes are still closed. "You hurt me."

Turning, I walk back to the bed and drop back to my knees. I rest my hand on her hip and give it a gentle squeeze. "I know I did. I can't tell you how sorry I am. I want to make it up to you. Prove to you that I'm a man deserving of you."

"You left me."

I know the alcohol is taking her under, and her whispered confessions not only cut me like a knife, but they also confirm that having the conversation that we need to have tonight, would not have been a good idea. "I know, baby, but I promise you I'll never leave you again. I'll never hurt you again." I wait for a reply but get nothing. This time, I kiss her forehead and again have to force myself to walk away.

With every step I take down the hall away from her, my heart is screaming that I need to go back. That I need to be here when she wakes up tomorrow. I need to show her that I'm not going anywhere.

"Well?" Caleb asks.

"She's a little out of it. I'm going to call her tomorrow and get the information."

He nods. "It's good to have you back, man."

If he only knew my driving force for coming home. Caleb and I couldn't be any closer if we were brothers, and I hope that once he gets used to the idea of Collins and me together, that will still be the case. I won't live without her. I can't. I tried that for the last three years. I tried to tell myself that what I felt that night was a fluke. That my heart was not fused with hers, but it was a lie. All of it.

Chapter 14

Collins

WHEN I WOKE UP THIS morning, my head was pounding and my heart ached. I declined breakfast with Emily and Caleb and headed home. I barely remembered the drive, too lost in the memories of last night. As quietly as I could, I went straight to my room and climbed back in bed. I wanted to sleep the day away.

"Wake up, sleepy head," Tabby says from her perch on the edge of my bed.

"What time is it?" I ask her.

"One."

I groan, knowing that I have things to do today to get ready for work this week. "I guess I need to get my lazy ass motivated."

"Rough night?"

"You could say that."

"I heard you come in early this morning."

"Yeah, Caleb and Emily were too damn chipper. I needed more sleep." It's not a complete lie.

"Well, your phone's been going off like crazy. You should check it. I'm heading out to Mom and Dad's, I'll see you later."

"Later," I say, reaching to the nightstand and grabbing my phone. I have four missed text messages from Grady from various times throughout the morning.

> **Grady:** Morning, beautiful. How are you feeling?

> **Grady:** I guess you're still sleeping. Call or text me when you wake up.

> **Grady:** Caleb said you left his place hours ago. Are you okay?

And the last one.

> **Grady:** If I don't hear from you in thirty minutes, I'm coming over.

Looking at the time on my phone, I see it was sent twenty minutes ago, I'm quick to type out a reply. The first I've given him since he waltzed back into my life.

> **Me:** I'm fine. Fell back asleep.

> **Grady:** I was worried.

> **Me:** Don't be.

> **Grady:** I'll always be.

Gah! Why does he have to be so damn charming? I toss my phone and throw the covers off. Grabbing some clothes, I head to the bathroom to take a shower. I let the hot spray wash over me, massaging my sore muscles. I must have slept wrong. When the water starts to run cold, I shut it off and climb out, and that's when I hear the knock at the door. Shit. Rushing, I tie my hair up in a towel, slip into my robe, and open the bathroom door. My wet feet drip on the carpet as I rush to the door. Pulling it open, my mouth hangs open when I see who it is.

"Hey," his deep voice greets me.

"Grady, what are you doing here?"

He holds up a bag. "I brought lunch. I thought we could eat while you fill me in about the apartment next door."

I groan, remembering that I told him we could talk today. Stepping back, I motion for him to come in. "I'll be right back." I rush back to the bathroom, closing and locking the door behind me. I brace my hands on the counter and take a deep breath. I don't know how long I'm standing here, but it must have been a while because Grady knocks on the door.

"Collins, you okay?"

"Yeah, be out in a minute," I call through the door. Rushing, I get dressed, sliding into a pair of athletic shorts and a tank top. I remove the towel from my head and brush out my long hair. Instead of putting any effort into my appearance, I tie the still wet strands in a knot on the top of my head. It's not my best look, but what do I care? It's not like I'm trying to seduce him or catch his eye. With one more deep breath, I open the door and slowly make my way back to the living room.

"Hungry?" he asks as soon as he sees me. He points to the white bag on the table. "Burger and fries, perfect hangover cure."

"Thanks, you didn't have to do that." I take a seat on the couch on the opposite end.

"I wanted to." He grabs the bag and passes out our food. He then hands me a bottle of water. "Found it in the fridge," he explains. I nod.

We eat in silence. When I've finally taken my last bite, I have to admit I feel better. "So, you're in the market for an apartment?"

"Yeah, living at home with Mom and Dad is not what it's cracked up to be after living on my own all these years."

"And you want to live here?" It's a stupid question, but I ask it anyway.

"Sure, I mean, it's a nice place, right?"

Grabbing my phone from the coffee table, I pull up the landlord's information. I take a screenshot and then text it to him. His phone beeps, but he makes no move to check it. "I just sent you the landlord's information."

"Thank you." He still makes no move to check it. "Is now good?" he asks.

"Good for what?" I'm playing dumb, but I don't know if I'm ready to have this conversation. I'm still reeling from last night.

"Collins, I'm not sure how much of last night you remember, so I'll say it again." He takes a deep breath, looks down at his hands that are clasped together, then back up at me. What I see has me sucking in a breath. Remorse is clearly written in his eyes. "My biggest regret in life is walking away from you that night." He pauses but never takes his eyes off me. "I don't know when it started, but before I left for college, I noticed you. Noticed you as not just the girl next door or my best friend's little sister. I knew you were off limits, so I let it go and went away to college. Not to mention, you were underage."

He takes a drink from his water bottle, screws the lid back on, and sets it on the floor, next to his feet. "Then I came home, and you were even more beautiful than I remembered. It was as if my being away and not seeing you, then seeing you again, made me want you even more," he confesses. "That first night, we had dinner with our families. It took everything I had not to just stare at you. I could feel you watching me. I knew that those gorgeous blue eyes were taking me in. I told myself to ignore it, to ignore you. But that next night, nothing could have kept me away from you."

I want to tell him to stop, that I don't want to hear it. Tell him that my fragile heart can't take it, but I don't. Because my fragile heart wants to hear it. Every single word.

"I never thought it would go that far. When you dragged me by the hand and out to the backyard, I told myself that I just wanted a taste. I wanted to know if your lips were as soft as they looked. I needed to know if they were as sweet as I imagined."

I can see the night so vividly in my mind. He'd been watching me, I'd been watching him. Caleb was distracted by his new girlfriend, our parents were playing cards, and I wanted some time with him. Just to talk to him. I'd always crushed on him, but the attention he was giving me that night set my blood on fire. I remember grabbing his hand and leading him out onto the deck.

"It's such a nice night." I wrap my arms around myself to ward off the chill. It wasn't freezing, but it was far from warm.

"You're shivering." He leans in and wraps his arms around my shoulders. "Better?"

Grady Carmichael has his arm around me! "Yeah, thanks." I take advantage and burrow a little closer.

"I have an idea. Come with me." He laces his fingers through mine and leads me across my backyard into his. Behind their garage is his parents' camper. Grady opens the door and holds the door open for me. Cautiously, I step into the camper. "The heat isn't on, but it will keep us out of the night air."

I turn to thank him, and he's there, standing so close I can smell him, a musky scent that's completely Grady. And his eyes, even in the dark of night, I can tell they're focused on me. I have all of his attention. "Thanks," I whisper.

He places one hand on my hip, the other reaches up and tucks a stray strand of hair behind my ear. "I needed to keep you warm."

Having his eyes on me all night, combined with lusting after him for years makes me bold. "You think maybe if you kissed me that might help?" I ask shyly, yet it's bolder than I've ever been. I know he knows I like him. How could he not? This though, this is altogether different.

"You want me to kiss you?" His voice is soft. His large hand cups my cheek, and he traces my lips with the pad of his thumb.

"Do you want to kiss me?" My voice is shaky but not from the cold; it's from the adrenaline racing through my veins. I can't believe I'm here with him, like this.

"More than anything," he confesses.

The next thing I know, he's leaning in and pressing his lips to mine. I gasp, surprised that it's happening, and he slides his tongue past my lips. Slowly, his tongue duels with mine. I grip his shirt and hold on for the ride.

"Collins," he murmurs, pulling away from the kiss.

"Please, don't stop," I beg. I'm aware that I'm begging, but that's what he does to me. I've never been kissed like this before. Like he needs to mold his lips with mine, as if kissing me is the only way he can gain oxygen. It's a heady feeling, and I want more.

"They'll know we're missing."

My shoulders fall, knowing what that means. My time with him is over. "Yeah," I reluctantly agree. I know he's right, but that does not mean that I like It.

"Can you meet me out here later?"

My head pops up to look at him. "Later?"

"Yeah, after my folks come home, and yours are in bed. We could meet out here.

If you want."

"I want."

"Come here." He pulls me into him and kisses me again. Just as deeply and just as caring as the one before it. "Text me when you're ready. I'll meet you."

"Okay."

"Okay." With one more quick kiss to my lips, he takes my hand and leads me out of the camper and back over to my yard. We take a seat on the back deck, just as Caleb comes out of the house.

"Hey, man. I've been looking for you."

"Just getting some air," Grady says.

"You want to ride with me to take Sara home?"

"Nah, go ahead. I'm going to head home soon. I'm tired."

"All right, man, I'll see you tomorrow then. Later, sis," Caleb says with a wave, and then he's gone.

Once the door shuts, Grady stands. "Text me, Collins. Even if you change your mind, text me to let me know."

"Okay."

"I clutched my phone in my hand that night, waiting for your text. I told myself that I was just going to kiss you some more. I knew it was wrong, sneaking around with you, but I couldn't seem to help it. I wanted you, Collins."

Chapter 15

GRADY

MY FUCKING HANDS ARE SWEATING, but I keep pushing on. I have her full attention, and I have no idea how much longer she'll give me. I need to get this all out.

"I wanted you," I say again. "I never meant for it to lead to making love to you." Her beautiful blue eyes mist with tears, but I keep going. "That's what I did that night, Collins. I made love to you. It wasn't something I'd ever done before."

"Yeah, right," she scoffs. "I know it wasn't your first time."

"I'd had sex before you, yes. But I'd never made love. That's what it was for me. When I finally got your message, I was nervous because we were sneaking around, but I didn't care." She'd been all I could think about, the taste of her sweet lips. I was already addicted.

"Hey," I whisper into the night.

"Hi," she says shyly.

I quickly open the camper door and usher her inside out of the cold. "I brought some extra blankets out. I didn't want you to get too cold."

"I just assumed you would keep me warm." Her voice is soft and unsure.

I growl and pull her into me. My lips crash down on hers, and she doesn't hesitate to open for me. Her taste explodes on my tongue, and I know already that she's different. I know that this night is different from any other night, from any other girl. She pulls at my shirt, and it's a tight space standing in the little walkway of the camper. Breaking the kiss, I guide her to the bedroom in the back. That's where I left the extra blankets. I climb onto the bed and pat the empty space beside me. No hesitation, she takes her place right next to me.

"You want me to keep you warm?" I ask, placing a hand on her hip and pulling her as close as I can get her.

"I've wanted that for a long time," she confesses.

"Your brother is my best friend."

"Should we call him and get his permission?"

"No." My voice is firm, and so is my decision. I don't want anyone to break this bubble that we seem to be in tonight.

"I don't either."

I cup her face in my hand. "Can I kiss you?"

"I'd be disappointed if you didn't."

Tilting my head, my lips meet hers. My mind is scrambled, and all I see, all I can think about is her and her soft sweet lips. I kiss her like she's the air I breathe. When she pulls away and sits up, I want to beg her to come back to me. Instead, I watch as she pulls her shirt over her head and tosses it on the camper floor.

"Collins." I breathe her name as I take in the creamy, flawless skin. Her breasts are spilling out of a light pink lace bra. I can see her hard nipples through the thin fabric. She lies back down beside me, snuggling close. Slowly, so I can gauge her reaction, I trace the swells of her breasts with my index finger. "Beautiful," I murmur.

Her hand slides under my shirt, and she lifts it. I know what she wants. Sitting up, just as she did a few minutes ago, I reach behind my head, grab the back of my shirt, and lift it over my head. I don't know where it falls when I release it. All I can think about is getting her skin on mine. When I lie back down, she's sliding her bra straps over her shoulders.

"Collins, I just wanted to kiss you," I say lamely. Hell, I need to just keep my mouth shut. I'd be a damn fool to pass up anything that she's willing to offer.

"Kiss me here," she says, taking my hand and resting it on her bare breast.

My hands shake as I run the pad of my thumb over her tight nipple. I don't understand it. Why is she affecting me like this? She releases what sounds like a sigh and a moan mixed together, causing my dick to throb in my pants. Sliding down the bed so I can get a better angle on her, I close my mouth around her nipple. She buries her hands in my hair as I suck, nip, and lick at her as if she's my last meal. My heart gallops in my chest, so much so that she has to be able to hear it. My fingers tingle from the feel of her soft skin. My senses are on overload, and I can't seem to control it. This is new, she's new, but she's more. I never want to stop this high that I'm on right this minute. Collins is consuming me, tilting my world on its axis. I want more.

Shaking out of my vivid memories, I keep going. "Every experience before you, before that night paled in comparison. It rocked me to my core, scared the living hell out of me, the way my body reacted to yours. The way my heart was hammering in my chest. I was holding you while you slept, thinking about when I could make love to you again. When I got a text message from Caleb asking if I wanted to go to the batting cages the next day." She wipes at her tears, and I want to pull her into my arms, but I know she's not ready for that, no matter if I am or not. "I was holding you so close I wasn't sure where I ended and you began, thinking about doing it again, and then it hit me that Caleb was not just my best friend but your brother. I panicked, Collins. I panicked and ran." A sob breaks, and I stand to go sit next to her on the couch. Reaching out, I lace her fingers through mine, surprised that she lets me. "I laid there for hours trying to come up with a solution. The only one I could think of was running. I didn't want to lose my best friend. I didn't want you fighting with your brother. Our families were close, and it was all crashing in. I couldn't explain this pull I felt toward you, and that scared me even more. So, I ran. I slid out of that tiny bed and quietly got dressed. I took a picture of you because I knew that leaving was going to destroy anything we might have been able to have. That picture got me through the last three years."

She's quiet, her tears silent as they coat her cheeks. I wait, my hand in hers, giving her all the time she needs. Finally, she looks up at me, her blue eyes wet and filled with sadness and pain. "What do you mean, about the picture?"

With my free hand, I reach into my pocket and unlock my phone. I scroll to the picture I took that night three years ago. The night I broke both of our hearts. I take a long look, even though I no longer have to actually look at it to see her. I've studied it so much it's a permanent memory. "This one." I hold my phone so she can see it. "Every day for the last three years, I've looked at this very picture. I've fallen asleep looking at this picture. Anytime something good or hell, even bad, happened I would tell this picture, as if I was telling you. It made no sense because, before that night, we were never close, not really. But that night changed me. It changed us."

"Grady, I—" She stops, closes her eyes, and sucks in a deep breath. When her eyes open again, they're still sad. "I don't know what to think, or what to say. I just… need some time I guess."

"I know, baby. I'll give you all the time you need, but I need you to know something. I want you, Collins. I don't care who knows it. I don't care how much time you need. I'll wait for you."

"How can you say that? It's been three years. It was one night, and you ignored me after. *Three years,* Grady," she says again.

"I know exactly how long it was. I also know that my heart has been yours since that night. Like I said, I can't explain it, but, Collins, I don't want to. I just want to prove to you that I can be the man you deserve. We can call Caleb and our parents and tell them what I did. I don't care. I know I could lose my best friend, but, baby—" I cup her face in my hands. "—you're worth it. You're worth that and so much more. All through medical school, I kept my nose in the books. I never went out. I told myself I was doing it not only for Jared, but for you, too. I needed to be a man you would be proud of."

"You were!" she yells. "Don't you get that? You were everything." Her voice breaks on a quiet sob. "I need you to go."

"Collins, please," I beg. I'm not above that when it comes to her.

"I need time, Grady. I have to process this."

"Okay," I concede. I knew it would take time, that I was going to have to work for it, work for her. "I have one more thing before I go. My residency starts next Monday. I had to accept a program back in April. Collins, my residency is at Riley."

She laughs through her tears. "Of course, it is. Just go, Grady."

"I hate leaving you when you're upset like this."

"Right," she scoffs. "This is nothing compared to three years ago. You should have stuck around for that."

I feel her words like a dagger to my heart. "Call me… when you're ready to talk again, call me."

"Just go," she says, and I can see that she is battling another round of tears.

"Collins—" I reach for her, but she stands.

"Please, ju-just g-go."

Standing, I lean in close and place a kiss to her forehead. "I'm so sorry for how I ended that night, but I'm not sorry it happened. Up until the time I walked away, that was the greatest night of my life." With that, I turn on my heel and force myself to leave her, the girl I love in tears, her heart shattered to pieces because of me and my stupid decisions. I'll never stop trying to gain her trust. I don't care how long it takes or what other relationships it costs me. I know I should have said that three years ago, but I can't change the past. I can only change the future, one I hope to share with her.

Chapter 16

Collins

I FLINCH AT THE SOUND of the door closing, and a sob breaks from my chest. I want to hate him. I do. I want to tell him to go to hell, but my heart has other plans. My heart yearns to reach out and hold onto him, have him hold me close like he did that night. One night, a few hours of time, and yet he's branded me. How is that even possible? Locking the door, I grab my phone, a bottle of water, and disappear into my room. I just need a minute to regroup. I don't want Tabby to come home and see me. I would have to explain the tears, explain the pain, and I'm not ready for that. I don't know that I ever will be. So, instead, I burrow under the covers and let the tears fall. I replay that night in my head, just like I have thousands of times before.

I bury my hands in his hair as he plays with my breasts. When he sucks a nipple into his mouth, gently nipping it with his teeth, I tug hard. "You okay?" he whispers into the night.

"Yes." One-word answers are about all I can muster.

"All you have to do is say stop and I will."

"Please don't stop," I beg. I don't know where this new brazen Collins is coming

from, but he doesn't stop, so I'm thankful she decided to make herself known. He takes his time moving his mouth from one breast to the other, his thumb and forefinger play with the other, and it's sensation overload. Heat pools between my legs, and I would be embarrassed if I couldn't feel his hard length against my belly. He wants this, wants me as much as I want him. I've thought of this moment a hundred times, maybe more. Dreamed is more like it, and I never thought in a million years that dream would come true.

He kisses his way up my neck and nips at my ear. His large hands press on my bare back, bringing me even closer than before. When his lips find mine, I open for him. I want to taste him again and again. I never want this night to end. My hands roam his chest, taking in every line, every curve of his chiseled body. When I reach the waistband of his jeans, I pass over the button to cup him in my hands.

"Jesus," he mutters. "Collins, baby, you can't do that. I'll lose it," he whispers against my lips.

"What? This?" I ask, taking him in my hand once more.

"That." He kisses me.

I feel wanton and powerful at his admission. Going for brave, I pop the button on his jeans and lower the zipper. Grady sucks in a deep breath, burying his face in my neck, but he doesn't stop me. With shaking hands, I reach under the band of his briefs and stroke his hard length.

"Fuck," he murmurs against my neck. He lifts his head and even in the dark, I know he's looking at me. "Collins, what do you want?"

"You."

"I need you to be sure."

"Never been more certain in my life."

"Have you ever?" he asks, working the button on my jeans.

"N-no," I say, equal amounts of nervous and excited.

He stops. "Collins," he whispers.

"No, don't stop. Please, this is what I want. I want it to be you."

He takes my mouth in a slow kiss as he slides the zipper down on my jeans. I suck in a breath when his hand slides under the band of my lace panties.

My phone vibrating in my hand wakes me from my dream, my

memories of that night. My eyes are swollen, and I'm sure I look like hell from the tears I've shed. Cracking them open, I look at the screen and see his name—a new text message. I don't want to know what he has to say, I don't, but that doesn't stop me from swiping the screen to read the message.

Grady: Just checking on you. You okay?

Grady: Need me to come over?

I hesitate before replying. It's not something I've done since he's been back in town, but I fear that he'll show up at my door. Tabby should be home soon, if she's not already, and I don't need that.

Me: No need for you to come over.

I don't tell him I'm okay, because honestly, I'm not sure I am. My heart aches, my head hurts from the tears, and I honestly just don't know. I don't know if I'm okay or if I ever will be. What I felt for him runs deep, and the scars are there, still red, swollen, and fresh from the pain. I can only hope one day it will get better.

My phone vibrates with another message.

Grady: I'm sorry for everything, Collins.

This time I don't reply. I can't say it's okay because it's not. I can't say that I accept his apology because, well, I'm not sure that I do. I feel like everything is hanging in the balance, and I'm just waiting for the other shoe to drop.

Climbing out of bed, I gather my laundry and carry it to the laundry closet just off the kitchen. That was the best perk to this place when Tabby and I were looking, no laundromat. I stuff the washer, add soap and fabric softener, and shut the lid. Glancing at the clock, it's just after six and my stomach growls, reminding me it's time to eat. I settle for a slice of left-over cold pizza and make my way to the couch. That's how Tabby finds me not ten minutes later.

"Hey," she says, plopping down on the opposite end of the couch. "How was your day?"

"Meh, I slept off and on. My allergies are acting up," I lie. I feel like shit for doing it, but I can't tell her he's been relentless with his efforts. Not yet. "I decided to drag my lazy ass out of bed and get started on laundry."

"Yeah, I need to do that, too. But I'm not doing it tonight. I'm exhausted. Aunt Tabby was a jungle gym all afternoon. I swear I don't know how Roger and Beth do it. Those boys are balls of energy."

"Yeah, but twins, they can keep each other occupied."

"I guess, but not when I'm around. Those little buggers were all over me." She laughs.

"You love it."

"I do." She nods. "Anyway, I'm taking a shower and calling it a night."

"I'm not far behind you. I need to put my clothes in the dryer and then I'm turning in, too. It's been an… off day."

"We all have those." She smiles, stands, and heads to her room.

When the washer beeps, telling me that my load is done, I swap it out, turn out the lights, and head to my room. How pathetic am I? In bed, a little after seven on a Sunday night. I'm just about asleep when my phone pings with a message. I have a pretty good idea who it is before I even look at the screen.

> **Grady:** Good news. Your landlord called me back. I'm your new neighbor.

> **Grady:** I can move in right away, so I'm going to get that taken care of before I start residency next week. Thanks for the number. I'm exhausted, so I'm heading to bed early.

> **Grady:** Goodnight, beautiful.

Immediately I think about something that he said earlier, *That picture got me through the last three years,* and I fight the urge to ask him if he's looking at it now. Instead, I place my phone back on the nightstand and close my eyes. It's hours before sleep finally claims me.

Chapter 17

GRADY

TURNS OUT THAT "RIGHT AWAY" was Wednesday. I spent all day Monday and Tuesday getting things I would need. My first purchase was a bed, a king-size bed. The landlord gave me a tour on Monday, and I was glad to see that the bedroom was big enough. Living in a tiny, cramped apartment the last three years, I'm ready to stretch out. All through college, I slept on a twin. I'm a tall guy and need more space. So, I took a big chunk of the money I was gifted for graduating medical school and bought me a big-ass king-size bed. My mom insisted on buying me sheets and bedding as a housewarming. I'm a guy living alone. I don't need anything fancy. Not to mention, there will be no one to impress with my fancy new bedroom digs. The only girl I want refuses to speak to me.

Still.

I've walked by her apartment door more times than I can count, making extra trips, with smaller loads just for the chance I might get a glimpse of her. My efforts were fruitless as I've not laid eyes on her since Sunday, the day hers were filled with tears when she told me to leave.

I've texted her multiple times, and even called a few, but still no reply.

I know I laid a lot on her and that she needs time, and I'll give her as much time as she needs. In the meantime, I just wish she would talk to me. After three years of wishing she was close, she's now literally right next door, and I still feel as though we are states away.

"Thanks again," I say, shutting the door behind the delivery guys. They just delivered and set up my new bed. It looks massive being the only piece of furniture in the room. I'm taking a spare dresser my parents have at their place. Mom tried to get me to bring all of my furniture from my old room, the one that remains the same as the day I left for college right after high school. I declined; you never know when you might need to move home again. Besides, I know Mom, and she likes that it's still the same, makes her feel like I'm still living at home, which is all the more reason I needed to get out on my own. I'm twenty-six years old and starting my residency. I'm a damn doctor. I need my own place. I'll have weird, crazy hours and shifts over the next three years, so having my own place is just another perk for my parents really. I won't have to disturb them at all hours of the night.

Grabbing my keys, I head out to get some groceries. Now that my bed is here, I can officially move in, but a man needs food. As soon as I step out of my door, hers opens. My eyes stay glued to the door, hope blossoming until I see it's her roommate, Tabby.

"Grady?" she asks confused.

"Hey, Tabby." I wave at her.

"What are you? Wait, are you our new neighbor?"

Glad to see Collins has been talking about me. I'd like to think I'm wearing her down. "Yeah, they just delivered my bed, so technically this is my first day living here," I explain for no reason at all, except that maybe Collins will hear her talking and come out to see what's going on.

A man can dream.

"Does Collins know?"

Shit. I don't want to throw her under the bus, but... "Yeah," I confess.

She grins. "Interesting. Well, welcome to the hood." She laughs. "Have a good day, Grady. I'm on my lunch break and need to get back to work."

"You, too." I watch her until she disappears down the hall. My feet carry me to their door, and before I can think about it, I'm knocking. I shove my hands in my pockets and wait. When the door opens, Collins's eyes go wide. "Hey," I murmur. She's gorgeous; it's been too long since I've laid eyes on her in the flesh.

"Grady," her sweet voice greets me. "What are you doing here?"

"We're neighbors," I remind her.

"I get that. But what are you doing here, knocking on my door?"

Oh, that? "Well, I'm headed to the store. I thought I would see if you needed anything." It's not a complete lie. I know that telling her I just needed to set my eyes on her even for a brief minute would be too much.

Her shoulders relax. "I'm good. Thank you."

"You're welcome to come with," I offer before I can think better of it.

"N-no, that's okay. I've got some things to do around here. Congrats on the new place," she says and starts to close the door. "Bye, Grady," she says softly.

Before she can get it closed, I place my hand on the door, keeping it open. In one step, I'm standing right in front of her, right on the threshold. "Can we have dinner tonight?"

"I don't think that's a good idea."

"Collins." After reaching up, I press my palm against her cheek. "I need you to know I'm not going to back off. You can push as much as you want, and I'm going to push right back." Knowing it's a risk, I do it anyway. Leaning in, I place a light kiss on the corner of her mouth. "I'm going to fight for you." I whisper the words, but the meaning is there, screaming loud and clear.

Pulling back, I drop my hand. "Please, have dinner with me?"

"I cook dinner on Thursday nights," she tells me. "It's Tabby's late night, and I cook."

"Tabby can come, too. I'll make dinner." It's not ideal, but I'll take what I can get.

"Grady," she sighs.

"Collins," I mimic her.

"I'll make dinner," she concedes. "Tabby will be home at seven."

"What can I bring?"

"I'm making chicken enchiladas."

I nod. "I'll figure it out." Reaching out, I grab her hand and give it a gentle squeeze. "I'll see you soon, babe." With that, I turn and walk away. As soon as I'm facing away from her, I let the grin break free. I'm wearing her down.

When I make it to the grocery store, I'm still smiling, and I've gotten more than a few strange looks, but I don't give a fuck. I'm having dinner with Collins. Sure, Tabby will be there, but I'll be in her space. Just... time with her. It's a step in the right direction. Making my way to the bakery, I grab some vanilla cupcakes with white whipped icing, my girl's favorite. I can use all the help I can get.

Chapter 18

Collins

O NCE THE DOOR IS CLOSED, I come to my senses. What in the hell was I thinking inviting him to dinner? I'm losing my damn mind. I blame the smile. I know better. My mind is still jumbled from our talk on Sunday. He's texted me every day, texts that still go unanswered. It's not that I don't want to reply, as much as I don't know how. How do I forgive and forget? How do I let him back into my life and not ache to be more? Who am I kidding? I'm already aching for more. All week I've thought about the fact that he's now my neighbor. Why did I not tell him the place was rented or that the landlord is a dick? Anything but willingly give him the number to call.

Looking at my watch, I see it's just after one in the afternoon. I have six hours until I see him again.

For dinner.

Here.

In my apartment.

Shit!

Grabbing my phone, I text Tabby.

Me: So we're having company tonight.

Tabby: Oh, yeah? Is he hot?

Me: ?

Tabby: When were you going to tell me we have a new neighbor?

Me: We have a new neighbor.

Tabby: I know. I met him on my way back to work.

Tabby works just about ten minutes from here versus my twenty-minute drive to the local children's hospital. She often comes home on her lunch hour. I can rush home if I need to and then have to rush back and hope to not meet any traffic. It's not worth the effort in my opinion.

Me: Well... he's coming to dinner.

Tabby: About that. Lucy called in sick. I'm working until ten until her replacement shows.

Tabby: I was getting ready to text you.

Me: Tabby!

Me: One—that's a long ass day.

Me: Two—you can't abandon me!

Tabby: Sorry.

Me: I'll just cancel.

Tabby: You CANNOT cancel on him.

Me: Of course, I can.

Tabby: Chicken.

Me: You don't understand.

As soon as I type the words and hit Send, I feel guilt wash over me. She doesn't understand because I've kept to myself since he's been back in town. She's the only one who knows about our history, yet I shut her out, too. I just need some time to process this. I need to figure out where we go from here.

Tabby:	I have an idea.

Shit!

Me:	It's complicated.
Tabby:	It always is. Don't cancel and I want details when I get home.
Me:	Fine.
Tabby:	Yay!

She knew exactly what she was doing. Being called a chicken goes deep. I would beg to hang out with Caleb and his friends. They would call me a chicken, daring me to do the things they did. Ride wheelies on my bike, jump off the swinging rope into Grandpa's pond. Come to think of it, Grady's the only one who I don't remember ever goading me. At least, not that I remember.

I now have just under five hours until he's knocking on my door for chicken enchiladas. Jumping off the couch, I rush to my room, strip down, slide into my robe, and head to the shower. Yeah, I've already showered today, but I skipped shaving my legs. Not that I think anything is going to happen tonight, but I need the confidence boost that freshly shaved legs give. That's my story, and I'm sticking to it.

I want to show him what he's missing. What he walked away from.

The enchiladas are in the oven. I started to make some Spanish rice as well but decided that would look like I was making too much of an effort. I have two huge pans of enchiladas. That's enough. It's double what I normally make for just Tabby and me, but with Grady coming over, I wanted to have enough. I guess I get that from my mom. She always has too much food, but her saying is, "I'd rather them leave full and satisfied than hungry." She's a smart woman, my mother.

He's going to be here any minute, and it's going to be a whole lot of awkward. I should have canceled. I'm not ready to spend a night in with him, just the two of us. It's ironic that three years ago, I would have given anything for this to be my life, now... not so much.

A loud knock bounces against the door, and even though I was expecting him, I flinch. After standing, I make my way to the front door. A big deep breath, slowly exhaled, I open the door.

"Hey, beautiful," he says softly. Pulling his hand from behind his back, he hands me a bouquet of flowers. "Lilies. Are they still your favorite?"

"How did you…?" I take the flowers when he hands them to me again.

"I pay attention, Collins. Even before that night, I paid attention."

What do I say to that? Not that I can form words if I tried. Instead, I step back and allow him to walk in.

"I brought dessert. White cupcakes with white fluffy icing." He holds up a container of cupcakes. "I wasn't sure if Tabby liked them, but really, you're all that matters." He leans in and kisses my cheek. "In the kitchen?" he asks, already walking in that direction.

Closing the door, I stare at the bouquet of lilies in my hands. They're beautiful and fragrant, and I'm still in shock that he knows they're my favorite. Is it possible that all those years ago, I wasn't the only one paying attention like he said? How could I have missed that?

Shaking out of my thoughts, I head toward the kitchen to put my flowers in water. Grady takes them from me as soon as I walk into the room.

"You have a vase or something? I should have thought of that. I can run out and get one," he says quickly.

"I have one." I open the cabinet door under the kitchen sink and pull out a vase. Oddly enough, it's not because I have been sent flowers that I have it. When Tabby and I moved in here, Mom cleaned out her cabinets bringing up a few things. She insisted we needed upgrading from poor college students. This vase was one of those items. My dad sends her flowers out of the blue, and she has a shelf full of vases. I think she keeps them all.

"You have one," he says, eyeing the vase. "That's good," he says, but his tone of voice tells me he doesn't really believe his words.

Is he jealous? No, can't be. "Yeah, Mom gave this to Tabby and me when we moved in here." I don't take my eyes off him. I can visibly see his shoulders relax and his jaw that was clenched tight eases.

Interesting.

Chapter 19

GRADY

I HAVE TO KEEP REMINDING myself I'm not allowed to be pissed off that another guy has sent her flowers. I walked away, that's on me, but damn it, I can't seem to control it. To say that I was relieved when she said her mom gave her the vase is an understatement.

"It smells amazing." My stomach growls loudly, reminding me that it is indeed time to eat.

"Thanks. It's Mom's recipe."

I groan. "Your mom is a damn good cook. I've missed her cooking." Her face scrunches up, and I know what she's thinking. Reaching out, I touch her elbow, getting her attention. "Not as much as I missed you."

She steps away from me, breaking our connection. My arm falls away, and although it was brief, I miss the feel of her skin beneath my fingers. "So," I say, trying to get her talking, "Tabby on her way home?"

"About that." She turns to face me, biting her bottom lip. "She had to stay late. She's working until ten, so it's just us. Just you and me," she rambles.

I have to work hard to not let my smile shine through. I get her all to myself. The stars are starting to align in my favor. "Well," I say, trying to sound as though this is not the best news I've heard all day. "That just means more for us. However, we should probably save her a cupcake. That's a long day."

"Yeah. How did you know?"

"Know what? That white cake with fluffy white icing is your favorite? I told you, I paid attention. That night, it was more for me. I know you don't trust that right now, and my actions speak otherwise, but it was more, Collins."

"There's water or beer in the fridge," she says, ignoring everything I just told her.

"Water or beer?"

"Water for me, please."

I pull open the fridge door and grab two bottles of water. "Can I help with anything?"

"Nope, just need to pull these out of the oven." She opens the oven door, and I peek inside. Two large pans that smell damn good are sitting side by side on the rack.

"Here." I take the pot holder out of her hands. "Let me."

She steps aside as she says, "I can do it, Grady."

I set both hot pans on the stove before I turn to look at her. "I know you can, baby. But if I'm around, you can let me do some of the heavy lifting."

"I've managed the last three years just fine," she mumbles under her breath.

Placing the pot holders on the counter, I don't take my eyes off her. Her long dark hair is in loose curls hanging down her back. I push them off her shoulder, revealing her slender neck. "I know that," I say gently. "I left. I regret it. I'm willing to do whatever I have to do to prove to you that I want this. Me and you, Collins. I want to see if everything I felt that night still holds true." I step a little closer. "I want to see if your breath hitches when I kiss you here." With my index finger, I trace the line of her neck down to her collarbone. "I want to know if these still respond to just the simplest of touch—my lips, my fingers, my tongue," I say, dragging my index finger over the mounds of her breasts.

Her chest is rising and falling as her breaths come faster and shorter. Her eyes flutter closed, but she doesn't pull away. Instead, she bites down on her bottom lip. "I want to know if these," I run my thumb over her lips, pulling it from the torture of her teeth, "feel as soft pressed against mine. I want to know if they are still as sweet as I remember." Her eyes slowly open and her blue irises are dark with desire. She's still not stopping me, so I keep going.

Stepping closer, so close I can feel her body heat even through our clothes, I place one hand on her hip, pulling her close, while the other slides under her hair and around the back of her neck. "I want to know if it feels like my world is falling when I slide inside of you. That's the only way I can explain it. It's a feeling like nothing I've ever felt before. I want to know if the replay in my mind the last three years is just a figment of my imagination."

Her hand grips my arm and pulls it from behind her neck, and she steps out of my hold. "I'm sure in the last three years you've found it with someone else. I'm not playing this game with you, Grady."

I can't help it, I laugh. Not just a chuckle, but a throw-my-head-back and deep belly laugh. "Collins, I can assure you, I have not. There's no one but you."

She freezes, then turns to face me. "What did you say?"

"There is no one but you."

"Now," she scoffs.

"Since that night," I fire back.

Her entire body is still, as if she was made of stone. "Explain that," she whispers.

I step closer to her, needing to be near her. This time I place both hands on her cheeks and stare into those gorgeous baby blues. "You heard me. There's been no one since that night. Not a kiss, not a one-night stand, not a relationship. Nothing. Not one single date."

"That's not possible."

"Baby, I was in medical school, working at the hospital, and missing you like crazy. I craved more of you, but I was too damn stupid to see the fucking forest for the trees. I threw myself into school and work. My two roommates, Jeff and Andy, they did the same. We would throw a party of three after studying. We kept each other on the straight and narrow, and our grades stayed up. Jeff, he's one of those people who really has to work for it, so Andy and I helped him out." I pause, letting it all sink in. "There was no one I wanted but you. I knew before I even made it back to North Carolina that I had made a mistake. I also knew it was better for you. I was states away in medical school. We would have seen each other a couple of times a year, if that, and I didn't want you to wait around. Not to mention, I didn't know how to break the news to your brother. So I pretended that my heart was not here in Indiana and focused on becoming a man you can be proud of."

"Grady, I—" She stops, appearing to not know what to say.

"I'm that man, Collins. I'm that man today standing here before you, begging you to give me another chance. I'll prove to you that you can trust me, that I'll never walk away from you again."

Her eyes shimmer with tears. "This is... too much. I don't... Grady, I don't know what to say."

"Say you'll think about it. Say that you'll let me see you, more than just bumping into you in the hallway of our apartment building. Let me show you what you mean to me."

"You broke my heart," she whispers.

"I know, baby." I pull her into me, her head resting against my chest. I lock my arms around her, cherishing the fact that she's in my arms. "I broke my own foolish heart. Just let me show you. I know I don't deserve a second chance, but I'm asking for one anyway."

"I don't know if I can." Her words are muffled against my shirt, but I hear them all the same. The pain they bring slices through my chest.

"Please. We'll start slow. You set the pace. I don't care how long it takes. I'm not walking away. Not now, not ever. Never again."

She pulls away from me and walks to the couch. She sits down, rests her elbows on her knees, and places her head in her hands. I don't say a word. I know I've laid a lot on her and I know she needs to process it all. I take a seat next to her on the couch and gently run my hand up and down her spine, soothing her and something inside of me as well. I just need to touch her and calm washes over me.

That's how it was that night. It was unlike anything I've ever felt. The moment I pushed inside of her, it felt... right. Like I was exactly where I was meant to be. It scared the fuck out of the younger me. Now, I'm begging and pleading to be there again. I can guarantee being inside of her is a gift I will always cherish.

She lifts her head, pulling me out of my thoughts. Surprising me, she turns sideways on the couch and crosses her legs. She takes a deep breath. "Grady, I'm scared," she admits. "I grew up crushing on you, but that night I gave you a piece of me that no one else will ever have. I thought I loved you. When your lips pressed to mine, I was certain I did. Then everything that happened after, I thought maybe I imagined it. That I didn't really know what love was." She pauses to collect her thoughts.

Reaching out, I lace my fingers through hers, needing to feel connected to her.

"I know it was my first time, and I've played this over and over in my head. Did I imagine the moment? Did I make it out to be this earth-moving experience because of my crush on you? Honestly, I'm not sure, Grady. I know that night I fell madly in love with you. Hell, I was close to it for years, but I fell off the cliff, hands raised, enjoying the fall."

Reaching out with my free hand, I catch a tear with my thumb that has just fallen from her eye. "It wasn't a fantasy, Collins. I was there and felt it, too. It scared me."

"How do I know you won't run again? Grady, I can't go through that again. I was crushed. It was just me, you know. I couldn't tell my family, our families. No matter how upset I was with you, I couldn't do it. I didn't tell anyone, not even Tabby. These past three years I've been fighting the pain all on my own, and I can't… I can't do it again."

Her tears, her words rip my heart to shreds. "You won't." I say the words with as much conviction as I can. "I will never walk away from you."

"You don't know me. It's been three years, Grady. People change."

"I know you love lilies. I know your favorite cupcake. I know you have a passion for helping others. I know where you got this." I run my thumb over a scar on her right knee. "I know you, Collins. I know what if feels like to be on the receiving end of your kisses and your hugs. I know that you are home to me. Not this town, not my parents' place. You. I've never felt more connected to someone. Three years ago on a cold winter night, you captured my heart." I pause to wipe another tear. "I want you to keep it, Collins. I never want it back."

"I've missed you so much, and I'm so scared," she says again. "I'm scared of how badly I want to bury my face in your chest and let you hold me. I'm scared of how strong the urge is to pretend that you never left. You're all I've ever wanted, but a part of me is still angry. My head..." She gives me a weak watery smile. "My head is angry with you, and my heart is pleading to fall into you."

I place my hand that's not holding hers over her chest, right over her heart. "Follow your heart," I whisper.

"I want to," again a watery smile. "I just need some time, Grady."

"I'm not going anywhere," I assure her.

She nods. Turning, she uncrosses her legs and rests her head on my shoulder. Raising my arm, I wrap her up and hold her close. Closing my eyes, I feel the tension fall away. It's like three years of stress have just vanished. This right here is where I belong—with her in my arms. I'm going to prove it to her. Her breathing evens out, and I whisper her name. When she doesn't reply, I know she's fallen asleep. I should get up and go to my place, but I don't. No way am I missing out on the chance to hold her like this. I hope there will be more opportunities in the future, but from our talk tonight, that won't be immediate. I know she needs time. I hurt her, hurt us both. Those wounds are still fresh, but I think we're on our way to healing. She surprised me by opening up to me, and we need that. We need to be open and honest if we're going to get through this.

I lose track of time, holding her. When she adjusts her position, she startles when she feels my grip on her. "It's just me," I say softly.

"I'm sorry." She sits up, pulling away from me.

"I'm not." My words earn me a sweet smile.

"Let me get you some of this food to take home with you, since we never got to eat."

Just like that, she's dismissing me, but it's getting late, and I haven't earned my spot back in her life just yet. I'll get there. "You sure?"

"Yes, I made way too much." She heads toward the kitchen, and I follow her like the lovesick fool I am. "Thank you for dinner, and for the talk."

"It was nice." She slaps the lid on the container and hands it to me.

"I'll walk you to the door," she says again, clearly dismissing me.

I walk slowly, so much so I'm sure it's painfully obvious to her. When I reach the door, I turn to face her. With one hand holding my leftover container of enchiladas, the other cups her cheek. "This isn't me walking away." I know we both know that, but I feel like I needed to say it.

"I know. Goodnight, Grady."

Bending, my lips kiss the corner of her mouth. "Goodnight, Collins." With that, I turn, open the door, and walk the mere feet to mine. I hate leaving her, but there is something comforting knowing she's just next door.

Chapter 20

Collins

TABBY GOT HOME NOT LONG after I sent Grady back to his place. She kicked off her shoes, went straight to the kitchen, made herself a plate, and then settled on the couch. "Talk," she said before she began shoveling food into her mouth. I'd been holding onto the details of this secret for years, so talk is what I did. I spilled it all from that night, up until right before she walked through the door.

"Wow," she says, setting her now empty plate on the coffee table. Then she surprises me when she smacks my arm. Not hard enough to hurt, but still shocking all the same.

"What was that for?" I rub my arm. Again, no pain, but it's the shock.

"You should have told me. I'm your best friend." She pouts.

"I know, but it was complicated. Honestly, Tab, I was embarrassed. I crushed on him for years, and I fell for him. He didn't have to work to get me into that camper that night," I tell her. "I went willingly. In fact, I initiated it."

"So," she says, confused.

"So, I was a naive girl who thought he wanted me, not just a warm place to stick his dick on a cold winter's night."

"Collins, you know better than that. If anyone has a good head on their shoulders, it's you. What is it your mom always says, you're wise beyond your years? She's right, and you know it." She takes a drink of her water, letting her words sink in. "So, what are you going to do?"

"What do you mean?"

"What I mean is that hot piece of man candy is fighting for you. What are you going to do? Fight him back or let him win?"

"I don't know."

"Nah," she says, grinning. "You know."

"I know what I want to do, but wanting and doing are two different things. I can't do that again, Tabby. I can't."

"You're stronger than you realize. Besides, *if,* and that is a big-ass if, it happens again, I'll be there for you. No shutting me out."

"I'm sorry."

She waves me off. "There is no best friend law that says you have to tell me everything, but it's important to know that you can."

"I do know. I *did* know, but I was—"

"Embarrassed, I get it. No more of that. Now, we need to invite him over for dinner again, ooh… or maybe out for drinks. I need to see how he acts around you to give you sound advice." She nods as if she agrees with her own assessment. "I mean, from what you've told me alone, my guess is he's sincere, and he's not going to let go easily. However, I would like to see it for myself."

"What? No, we're not doing that. Either of them." She's lost her damn mind.

"Oh, my bestie, we are." She grins. "You need to spend time with him and see where your head is at. Take it slow, hell, move at a snail's pace, or don't. Either way, you can't string him along."

"I'm not," I say defensively.

"Not yet, but you have to decide if you can forgive him. Not just forgive him, Collins, but be willing to let the past remain in the past. You can't move forward and hold this over his head."

"That's not what I'm doing."

"I know that. But I felt as though it needed to be said. I'll always be honest with you." She pauses then asks, "What do you want, Collins?"

"Grady."

She nods. "All right then. You decide the pace, maybe make him work for it a little longer, but not too long. Don't play games."

I give her the "did you really just say that to me" look. "You know me better than that."

"I do," she agrees. "I also know there is a lot of time, hurt, and distance between the two of you. We don't always think rationally in those types of situations."

"Who are you, and what have you done with my best friend?" I chuckle.

"It's all those years of dating wisdom you've bestowed upon me. I've never been able to use it on you until now. I'm pulling out the big guns." She makes a gun with her hand and pretends to blow smoke off the barrel, which is her index finger, causing us both to laugh.

My phone announcing a text message interrupts us. Looking at the screen, I smile when I see Grady's name. I turn my phone so she can see.

"Go." She waves me off. "I'm exhausted and have to be back at work at seven."

"I thought you were off tomorrow?"

"I was, but I'm picking up Lucy's shift."

"Well, goodnight." I stand and give her a hug.

"Night, Col. Don't let fear keep you from happiness."

"I won't," I assure her. Standing from the couch, I head to my room. It's not until I'm inside, the door closed that I look at his message.

Grady: Goodnight, beautiful.

He hasn't missed a morning, or an evening, since that first night I saw him in the bar. Nothing has changed; he's stayed consistent. Well, one thing is changing. I've only ever responded one other time, until tonight.

Me: Goodnight, Grady.

Before I have a chance to set my phone down, it rings. His name flashes on the screen. I debate on answering, but we're past that, and honestly, I don't want to ignore him anymore. Being angry is exhausting.

"Hey," I answer, keeping my voice low.

"You replied."

"Yeah."

"This is better," he says. "Hearing your voice before I fall asleep. So much better."

My heart flutters in my chest. "You in bed?"

"Yeah, just thinking about tonight. Thank you for dinner and for talking."

"It was time," I confess. "I don't want to be angry anymore." I might as well put it all out there.

"I'm so sorry, Collins. I swear to you I'm here for the long haul."

"We can go slow, right? Maybe work on being friends before we move on to anything else?" I didn't plan on asking that, but the words fall from my lips before I realize it.

"You set the pace, baby. I'm right beside you no matter what."

I nod even though I know he can't see me. "Goodnight, Grady."

"Goodnight, beautiful."

I can hear him breathing so I know he hasn't hung up yet. I hesitate but pull the phone from my ear and end the call. I'm not sure I'm ready for any of this. What I am sure of is that I miss him. He's always been a part of my life, the boy next door, my brother's best friend. Then he just disappeared. I don't know what the future holds for us as a couple, but I'd really like to get back to a place where we can be in the same room and not have tension between us.

One day at a time.

Chapter 21

GRADY

I T'S SUNDAY NIGHT, AND I haven't seen Collins since I had dinner at her place on Thursday. That's too damn long in my opinion. She's my neighbor, and I have yet to get one tiny glimpse of her. She got called into work on Friday, spent all day Saturday with Emily shopping and doing whatever it is they need to do for the wedding. I've missed her, more now than the last three years if that's possible. Now she's back in my life, I crave her even more.

Even though I have not seen her, I've still texted her every morning and every night. Last night, I called her, and she answered. We didn't talk long, a couple of minutes. She was yawning like crazy, and I knew my girl was exhausted. So I wished her goodnight and hung up the phone with her sweet voice in my ears as I drifted off to sleep.

Tomorrow, my life gets more complicated. It's my first day of residency. I'm ready for it. I've studied my ass off the last three years for this. I hope that Jared is looking down on me and smiling. I never want another family to go through what we went through. I know I can't save the world, but one child. One little brother or sister? That alone will make all the hours of studying and the years of college, my time away from Collins worth it.

It's early afternoon, and I'm going out of my mind missing her. I've cleaned, done laundry, and been to the store and stocked up for the week. Now, I just need to set my eyes on her, and all will be good. Grabbing my phone from the arm of the hand-me-down couch I took from my parents' basement, I send her a message.

Me: Hey, what are you getting into today?

Collins: Nothing much. Just finished laundry.

Me: Want to come over and watch a movie or something?

Collins: I don't know, Grady.

Me: Please. I'll be on my best behavior, I promise. I really want to see you.

It seems like years when in reality it's maybe a minute before she replies.

Collins: I'll be over in ten.

Me: See you soon.

I look around my apartment and its meager furnishings. It's nothing much, but it's mine. I can hold my girl on the couch, and not worry about roommates or my parents walking in on us. Once I start getting regular paychecks, I'll add a few more things. Right now, it works and it's close to her, which is the best perk of the place in my opinion.

I'm standing by the door when she knocks, and I pull it open.

"Hey." She laughs. "That was fast."

"I was waiting by the door."

"Really?"

I grab her hand and pull her into the apartment. As soon as the door is shut, I pull her into a hug. "Yes, really. I've missed you," I say, burying my face in her neck. To my surprise, she hugs me back, not as tight, but the embrace is there all the same.

"Come sit." I pull away from her and capture her hand in mine, leading her to the couch.

"Is this the one from your parents' basement?"

"Yep, home sweet home," I say with a laugh. "It's on loan. I'm just using it as a filler until I get my own. Floral is not really my thing."

She throws her head back and laughs. My eyes follow the column of her neck. Her hair is pulled up in a ponytail, exposing all that long, slender skin to me. I want to trace it with my tongue just like I did all those years ago. I can remember every moment as if it were last night.

"Yeah, I have to agree."

Grabbing the remote from the arm of the couch, I hand it to her. "You pick. I've already got Netflix pulled up."

"I get to pick? Really? I remember a time when you and Caleb never let me pick."

"Yeah." I run my index finger down her cheek. "Those days are gone, Collins."

"Really?" Her cheeks are pink. I'm not sure if it's from my touch or not, but I'm going to pretend that's the reason.

"Yes, really. I don't care what we watch. All that matters to me is that you're here. With me, and we're not fighting."

"I mean… I can pick a fight if that would make you feel better?" She laughs.

I lean in close, so close I can feel her hot breath against my lips. "No, baby. I don't want to fight with you. I want you to pick a movie. Then I want to sit here and enjoy your company. If I'm lucky, maybe hold your hand, and if luck is really on my side, hold you in my arms."

Her breathing is accelerated. "Let's uh, let's start with a movie."

"Anything you want, beautiful." I settle back on the couch and get comfortable. She scrolls through the movies and settles on *Twilight*. I bite back a smile. I know she's trying to get me to whine about it, but it's not going to happen. We could watch paint dry, and I'd still gladly sit here next to her.

"This good?" she asks, all innocent.

"Sure. You want some popcorn or anything before we start?"

"No, thanks. Maybe later."

She settles into her cushion, which is too far away from me, but I'll take it. The movie starts, and I try to pay attention, but I'm lost in thought. I assumed it would take me longer to get to this point. To us being civil, hanging out just the two of us. I turn to look at her, her eyes are riveted to the screen, so I take my time.

"You know there are four of these." She smiles over at me.

"Yeah?"

"Uh-huh, I might make you suffer through all of them if you don't pay attention." She points to the screen, and just like that, I'm busted.

"There would be zero suffering if you were here with me," I say honestly.

"Grady," she starts, but my phone rings, interrupting her. "Go ahead," she says, almost relieved.

"It's Caleb," I tell her. She nods. "Hey, man," I greet him.

"Hey, Emily and I are in the area. She wants to bring you your housewarming gift. You home?"

I want to tell him no, but I don't. "Yeah, I'm home."

"Great. We'll be there in about fifteen minutes. I need to stop for gas."

"See you then." I end the call, and Collins stands. Reaching out, I capture her hand with mine. "Hey, stay."

"Grady, I know I only heard one side, but I'm pretty sure my brother is on his way over here."

I nod. "He is. Emily bought me a housewarming gift. They want to drop it off."

"I need to go."

"Stay." My eyes bore into hers. "I don't care who knows how I feel about you, Collins."

"You ran because of him, because you were afraid to lose your best friend."

"I did. I know that there's a chance that could happen still today, but I'm not running from it. I want you. All of you. He's going to just have to get used to it. If not, it's going to make holidays and our wedding pretty damn awkward."

Shock crosses her face. "Wedding? Grady, we just started talking and not being short with each other."

"I know."

"Don't you think wedding is a little premature?"

"Nope. I told you, I'm not giving up on us. I want it all, Collins. I don't care who knows it. You're the only one who matters."

"I need to go." She pulls her hand from mine and walks to the door. I'm right behind her. When she turns to face me, her eyes are filled with pain. "You don't just get to walk back into my life and declare how things are going to go, Grady. You left me, remember."

I nod. I don't bother with words; I know I've pushed her too far. I want to beg her to stay, but it's too soon. Her actions have proven that, but dammit, I refuse not to be open and honest with her. That's what happened three years ago. I hid behind my fear, and I lost her. I'm going to fight to win her back. To prove I'm not the same guy.

"I'll call you later," I tell her.

"Sure." With that, she opens the door and walks out of my apartment.

Stepping out into the hall, I watch as she disappears behind her door. Once back into my place, I shut the door and rest my forehead against it. I hate that my time with her ended. Next time, my phone can go to voice mail. I don't care who's calling. My time with her is few and far between.

Not five minutes later, there's a knock at my door. I don't want to answer it. I want to rewind the last ten minutes and not answer my fucking phone. With a huff, I pull open the door.

"That was fast," Emily says, just as Collins did before her. The only difference is that I was waiting by the door for Collins, anxious to see her. Caleb and Emily, not so much. Any other time, I would be happy to see them, but they scared my girl away, ended my time with her.

"So, how have you been?" I ask, ignoring Emily's statement. I open the door wide and let them pass through.

"We brought you this." Emily hands me a small gift bag.

"Thank you, but you didn't have to."

"It's not much." She shrugs. "We wanted to. Open it," she urges.

"I knew you were moving into Collins's building, but I didn't know you were her neighbor," Caleb comments.

I stop pulling tissue paper out of the bag to look at him. "What part of 'I'm Collins's new neighbor' do you not get?" I ask him, laughing.

"Fuck off." He laughs as well. "I didn't think you meant literally."

"Maybe I should have said it like a teenage girl would have. Like, oh my God, I literally live next door to Collins." I throw my voice to sound more feminine.

"Ha ha, jackass. Open your present." Caleb grins.

Diving back into the gift bag, I pull out dish towels for the kitchen and some kitchen utensils. "Thanks, guys," I say, holding the items up.

"You're welcome. Not much, but we know you're starting out. We've been there," Emily says.

We catch up for a half hour or so before they head home. I want to call Collins and beg her to come back over, but I already know what her answer will be. So, instead, I make a ham sandwich, grab a bag of chips, and sit down to watch TV. My night passes in a blur of mindless television before I give up and head to bed. Grabbing my phone, I text her.

> **Me:** Goodnight, beautiful.
>
> **Collins:** Goodnight.

I want to call her to hear her voice. Instead, I place my phone on the nightstand and close my eyes. When it vibrates, I reach for it, not expecting to see her name on the screen.

> **Collins:** Good luck tomorrow, Dr. Carmichael.
>
> **Me:** Thank you. Maybe I'll see you there?
>
> **Collins:** Maybe so. Goodnight.
>
> **Me:** Night.

Setting my phone back on the nightstand, I close my eyes. I'm not nervous about tomorrow. I worked my ass off in medical school to be the best damn doctor I can be. No, what makes me nervous is the fear that I'll never win her over. That when I walked away three years ago, I lost the best fucking thing that's ever happened to me.

Chapter 22

Collins

ALL DAY, I'VE LOOKED FOR him. In the halls, in the cafeteria. Every room, around every corner and nothing. I'm not even sure which floor he's working on. I should have asked him last night, but I doubt he knew until he got here. I assume he's got some type of orientation. Just because he's a resident doesn't mean he gets out of all the hoopla that goes with new employment. At least, I assume not.

As is the life of a nurse, it's well after seven, closer to eight by the time I clock out. My shift is six in the morning until six in the evening, but in health care, there really is no schedule. If you're looking for a nine-to-five, you won't find it on the front lines of the hospital. At least, not in the emergency room where I work.

Walking to my car, I spot his 4Runner. He arrived after me this morning. I don't know what time he gets off, but this is already a long first day. Throwing my bag in the passenger seat, I pull out of the lot and head toward home.

"Hey, how was your day?" I ask Tabby when I walk through the door.

"Same old. How about yours?"

"It was good. Long, but you know how it goes." She nods.

"Mom called and invited us over for dinner. She's just throwing some chicken breasts on the grill."

Having just kicked off my shoes, I drop my purse and keys by the couch and plop down beside her. Turning to look at her, I groan. "I'm so tired."

She chuckles. "You sure?"

"Yeah, I want to take a long hot shower and head to bed."

"It does help that I'm off tomorrow."

"Girl, I can't keep up with your schedule," I tell her.

"I know, but it's great. Sure, I have to work every fourth weekend, but having days off during the week is nice to be able to get things done."

"I agree with that. Except Monday through Wednesday kill me. I need Thursday to recuperate."

"Right," she says with a laugh. "You sleep in until eight. Eight, Collins. That's not sleeping in."

"For me it is. Four thirty comes early."

"We live twenty minutes from your work. Yet, you get up over an hour before you have to leave. Crazy girl."

"Hey." I throw a pillow at her. "I can't help it. I can't just roll out of bed and go like you. I need to be alert before I get behind the wheel."

"That's what coffee is for," she quips.

"Ugh, I don't know how you drink that stuff."

"It's an acquired taste." She stands from the couch. "I'm heading out. I'll see you later."

"Bye. Tell them hello for me, and tell your mom thanks for the invite."

"Will do." She slips her feet into her flip-flops, gathers her purse, and heads out the door.

I sit here on the couch, knowing I need to get up and shower or I'll fall asleep. With a groan, I climb to my feet. After grabbing some clothes from my room, I head to the shower. I stand under the hot spray until the water starts to run cold. I know it's going to be awhile before Tabby is home, so I don't have to worry about being a bad roommate and using all of the hot water.

Making my way to the kitchen, I decide on a bowl of macaroni and cheese that was left after dinner last night. Popping it in the microwave, I stand and wait for it to beep. Adding some pepper, I grab a bottle of water and head for the couch. My phone sits on the coffee table where I left it. Even now, I want to check it to see if he sent a message. It's barely been a minute since he's been back in my life, and I'm already at the point where I look forward to hearing from him. As an act of rebellion against my heart, I leave the phone on its spot on the table and eat my heated-up bowl of mac and cheese.

With dinner done, I take my bowl to the kitchen and decide to go to bed. Retrieving my phone to plug it in, I'm making sure the door is locked when there is a light knock. Looking through the peephole, I see Grady. He looks exhausted. I take a breath before opening the door.

"Hey, beautiful." He gives me a tired smile.

"Hi." I realize we're just standing here looking at each other. "How was your first day?" I step back so he can come in.

"Long." He smiles. "I just... wanted to see you for a minute."

"Have you eaten?" I try to ignore the fact that my first instinct is to make sure he's taken care of. Regardless of the pain he put me through, he's still a great guy.

"Yeah, I just picked something up from the drive-thru on my way home."

"You wanna come in?" I ask since me stepping back wasn't a big enough hint.

He looks around me; I assume looking for Tabby. "It's just me. Tabby went to her parents' for dinner."

"Yeah." He steps through the doorway and waits for me to shut it behind him. "You didn't want to go?"

"Nah, I didn't get home until late, and I have to be up early." I take a seat on the couch, and he takes the spot right next to me.

Reaching over, he runs his thumb over my knuckles where my hand is resting on my leg. His eyes are locked on the motion. "I looked for you today," he confesses. "All day I looked." His eyes find mine. "After the anticipation, all day of possibly getting to see you, I just needed to lay my eyes on you."

I can't help but smile at him. "I did the same thing."

"You know what I kept thinking?" He doesn't wait for me to reply and just keeps talking. "If I wasn't such a fool that night, I would more than likely be coming home to you. Instead of you living here with Tabby, you would be next door with me."

My heart kicks up its rhythm at his confession. "It's in the past, no use in dwelling over it."

"Is it, Collins? Is it in the past? Because from where I stand, it's not. Not until you're in my arms where you're supposed to be. I can't forget a minute of that night. Not the way it felt to be with you or the pain I caused us both when I ran from everything you made me feel." He lifts my hand to his lips and kisses my wrist.

"I just don't understand why now? After all these years, why now, Grady? I can't stop wondering what changed your mind. Is it because you're here now and you think that if someone finds out you'll look bad? I just don't get it," I say, exasperated.

"I'm here now, not because I have to be, but because I choose to be. I could have gone anywhere for my residency, but I knew without a doubt in my mind coming home to you was my only option. Three years felt like a lifetime without you. I know it was one night, but it changed me. I worked my ass off in school. I was already enrolled there, and changing programs would have been a nightmare. I knew I had to stick it out, but before I even made it back to school, I knew I was coming back for you."

"You understand why that's hard for me to believe, right? You ignored me, Grady. I sent messages, left voice mails, begging you to call me back, to send a fucking carrier pigeon, something. Your silence was what I received."

He nods. "I know. I handled it all wrong. I was so afraid that when I heard your voice, I would walk away from it all. From medical school, from my dream of becoming a doctor. I know my own strengths and weaknesses, Collins. You were a weakness. One that I knew would change the course of my life one way or the other." He pauses, collecting his thoughts, and I don't say a word, processing what he's saying. He cradles my cheek in the palm of his hand. "I'll do whatever it takes to show you that you're what I want. What my heart wants."

"Grady...." My voice trails off because I have no idea what to say to him. He keeps going, tearing down the wall I built around my heart brick by brick.

"The entire time I was in medical school all I could think about was working harder, so I could guarantee my choice of residency. I wanted to come home to you. I want to be the man that you can be proud to have stand by your side. I want to be able to provide for you and the family I hope that we one day have. Only you can cure this ache in my chest. You're my remedy, baby."

I feel the first tear fall, but don't get a chance to wipe it away. Grady runs his thumb across my cheek. "Don't cry. I can't stand to see your tears." Leaning in, he presses a soft kiss to my cheek.

I realize that I have to make a choice. I need to decide if I can forgive him and if I do, I also need to let the past go. I'll never forget, but I can't hold it over his head either. Who am I kidding? I want him. I've always wanted him. "I want that," I confess. "I want everything you just said."

His lips press against mine, soft yet firm. It's just a quick kiss, but it affects me all the same. "You won't regret it," he whispers against my lips. "I'll prove to you every damn day that I'm worth the risk. I'll call Caleb and tell him. This is on me," he rambles on.

"Grady," I say, getting his attention, pulling away from him. "Can we just… take this slow? We don't need to tell him or anyone for that matter." There is so much between us we don't need the added pressure of my brother and maybe even our families against us. "I want the chance to actually be with you, for more than a night." I can feel a blush coating my cheeks at just the thought of being with him again. "Before they get their say."

"That's just it, Collins." His eyes bore into mine. "They don't get a say in this. No one does but you and me. I want you. I want this chance with you, and I couldn't give a fuck less who doesn't agree with it."

"He's your best friend, and our parents…."

"And you're my girl," he says softly. "Nothing is going to change that. I want this. I'm prepared for him to be mad or hell, even hate me. Would it suck? Yes, it would. Would it suck as bad as not having you? No." He's shaking his head. "Not even a little bit. As far as our parents, they love us and want us to be happy. Honestly, Collins, I don't care if they're upset. That makes me sound like a dick, but, baby, you're all I want. It's you and me, and if they aren't on board, then so be it."

"Just some time, Grady. Just to see if this is what you really want. It's been three years, and what if we piss them off, and then this isn't what you thought it would be?"

"What? The best thing that ever happened to me? I'm certain." He leans in and gives me another chaste kiss. "However, if this is what you want, that's what we'll do. Whatever you want, but I want it known that I don't want to hide you or hide us."

"Just some time," I say again. "Just so you're certain."

"I'm certain, Collins. I'll prove it to you." He shifts on the couch and pulls me into his lap, wrapping his arms around me in a hug. "Damn," he sighs. "It's been too long since I've held you."

I give in and return his hug. "Yeah," I say softly.

"I assume it's too much to ask you to come home with me so I can hold you all night?" he asks, hope in his voice.

"I don't think we're there yet."

"I know." He kisses my neck. "We'll get there." He yawns.

"You should go get some sleep. You go back tomorrow?"

"Yeah, every day this week, off Saturday work Sunday."

"Geesh."

"That's life of a resident. I'll be putting in crazy hours, but my time that I'm not there is yours."

"We'll figure it out." I stand and hold my hand out for him. "You need sleep." I lead him to the door. He surprises me when he gently pushes me against it, and his lips mold with mine. His tongue slides, explores my mouth, and I pull him closer, my hands clenching around his shirt. I let him set the pace.

"I'll see you soon." He kisses my forehead, and I step away, letting him open the door. "Lock up," he says, and I nod. After shutting the door and clicking the lock into place, I watch him through the peephole until I can no longer see him. With a sigh, I grab my phone from the table, shut off the lights, and head to bed. I'm just about to sleep when my phone alerts me to a message.

Grady: Goodnight, my beautiful Collins.

Me: Goodnight, Grady.

Setting my phone back on the nightstand, I fall asleep with the taste of him on my lips and the feel of his arms wrapped around me.

Chapter 23

GRADY

DAY TWO OF RESIDENCY, AND I'm stoked. I fell asleep last night as soon as my head hit the pillow, I was exhausted but in a good way. When we lost my little brother, Jared, I knew this is what I wanted to do with my life. Being here, that means I've made it. If my little brother would have had a physician who listened when my mom and dad were telling them Jared's symptoms, he might still be here. My parents assured me that the doctors did all they could, but I don't see it that way. Sure, I was young. Regardless, it led me here. I hope my baby brother is up there watching.

Grabbing my white lab coat with Dr. Grady Carmichael embroidered on one side and Riley Hospital for Children on the other, I report to the residents' lounge. While I am assigned to a rotation, there could be days that I'm sent to other areas of the hospital, depending on need. Walking into the lounge, there is an older gentleman there, one that I didn't meet yesterday. He turns when he hears me enter the room and walks toward me, hand outstretched.

"Dr. Carmichael, good morning, I'm Dr. Larson," he greets me.

"Nice to meet you, Dr. Larson."

"I'm the head of the emergency department. I'm down two attendings today due to unforeseen circumstances. You'll be on my rotation today."

"Sounds like a plan," I tell him. It just means that I get to experience another area of the hospital. I want to see it all, know my way around. I'm pretty sure I want to end up in private practice, but who knows, that might change while I'm here. That's the glory of residency. You get to train in all areas and find the one that works the best for you.

I follow Dr. Larson as he exits the lounge. "So, which med school?" he asks as we enter the elevator.

"Duke."

"Good school. What made you choose Riley?" he asks.

Collins. "It's a great hospital and one of the top residency programs in this area. I was born and raised here. My parents still live here. It felt like the right choice." All of that is true, but really, she was here, so there was no question as to where I would go. I busted my ass all through med school to ensure it.

"Here we are," he says, stepping off the elevator. I follow along behind him to the nurses' station. "This is Dr. Carmichael. He'll be helping out today."

I scan the faces before me and stop when I get to hers. Collins. I grin at her, not able to prevent it. She smiles back. "Nice to meet you," I say, forcing my eyes away from hers to scan back over the rest of the nursing staff. A few of them give me looks, you know the ones that say, "take me." It's amazing to me what women do, how they act once they find out you're a doctor. It's like they drop their panties and open their legs just waiting for you to take them up on their offer. They want to "catch" a doctor, live the good life. It's sad that they don't have more respect for themselves than that.

Dr. Larson turns to face me. "I want you doing the non-emergency triage today. Sore throats, sprains, breaks, colds, things of that nature. I'll take the heavier stuff. If you've got nothing else going on, you're welcome to stand in with me. Although," he looks around the room, "I don't see that happening today." He looks back at the nurses. "I need one of you with Dr. Carmichael today. He'll need an assistant at all times since he's never worked in our ER before." I watch as they all offer or raise their hands to work with me. All of them except the one I really want. "Collins," Dr. Larson calls her out. "He's all yours." With that, he turns and walks away.

A few of the nurses grumble, but the group disperses, leaving me with Collins. "Morning, beautiful," I say softly, just loud enough for her to hear.

"Dr. Carmichael." She grins.

"Is that how it's going to be?" I ask her, amused.

"I'm not sure I know what you're referring to," she says coyly. "You have a patient in bed one." She grabs the tablet from the counter and heads down the hall. I follow along behind her, wishing her scrubs were just a little more revealing. "Hello, Lucy, I'm Collins. I hear you have an earache," she asks the little girl lying in the bed.

"It hurts real bad," she says, trying to hold back her tears.

"We're going to make it all better. Mom," Collins says, "how long has Lucy been feeling bad?"

"She woke up early this morning screaming in pain. Her pediatrician just retired so we came here. She's not real fond of doctors. Ours didn't have the, uh, best bedside manner, but he was an excellent physician."

"You did the right thing," Collins assures her. "Lucy, I want you to meet someone. This"—she points over her shoulder at me—"is my friend Dr. Carmichael. He's going to listen to your heart and lungs, then check out your ears. Can you be a brave girl for me and let him do that?" She gives a reluctant nod. Collins steps back, and I take her place next to the bed.

"Hi, Lucy," I say, holding out my hand for her to shake. She gives me a toothy grin and shakes my hand. "You see this." I take off my stethoscope and show it to her. "This right here is going to help me make you better. When I place this end over your chest and back, I can hear your heart and your lungs."

"Really?" she asks, amazed.

"Really. You know what else?"

"What?"

I pull the otoscope from its place on the wall. "This funny-looking thing lets me see inside of your ear." I hold it out for her to see. "Can you do me a favor? Can you be really strong for me while I listen and take a look? I want to make you all better."

"Okay," she says softly.

"First, let's listen to your heart." Placing the otoscope back on the wall, I stick my stethoscope in my ears, and place the chest piece against her chest. Lucy is still and quiet while I listen. "Wow," I say, pulling away. "Your heart is so strong."

She giggles.

"Now, can you lean forward for me? I need to listen to your lungs, make sure they're nice and clear." She leans forward, and I place the chest piece on her back. "Lucy, can you take a nice deep breath for me and then let it out?"

"Like this," Collins demonstrates, and then together, they take a deep breath and slowly exhale. We repeat the process a few more times until I've completed that part of my exam.

"Lucy, give me five." Collins holds up her hand and Lucy smacks it with her own. She's loosening up.

"You are such a good patient," I praise. "Now, it's time to for me to look into your ears."

"Can you see my brain?" she asks.

I smile, biting my lip to keep from laughing. "No, but I can see all the parts of your ear, which is what hurts, right?" She nods. "Can you tell me which one hurts worse?" She points to her right ear. "Well, let me take a look at the left one first." I walk around the bed, and her mom steps back, letting me get close enough to look into her left ear. "All right, Lucy," I say, pulling back. "This one is red and looks irritated." I walk back around the bed and take a look at the right ear. "We have a winner," I tell her. "Your right ear is infected." I place the otoscope back on the wall. "Thank you for being such a good patient."

"You're welcome. Can you make it better?" she asks sweetly.

"Definitely," I assure her. "Mom." I look up at her mom. "That right ear looks pretty rough. I'm going to start her on a round of antibiotics. Any medication allergies?"

"None that we're aware of."

"Great. I'm going to give you a prescription for eardrops as well.

They'll help with the pain. Nurse Ward," I address Collins. "Can you go ahead and give her some drops here to help with the pain? I see she had Tylenol two hours ago, so she can't have more just yet."

"Thank you, Dr. Carmichael," Lucy's mom says.

"You're welcome. We have your pharmacy on file, so I'll send these over, and we'll get you ladies out of here."

"Thank you," Lucy says loudly as I walk out of the room.

"Give me just a few minutes," Collins says, and then she's standing next to me. "You need some help with the prescription software."

"Yes." We make our way to the nurses' station, and I watch her as she sends the prescriptions to the pharmacy electronically.

"Dr. Carmichael, if you need anything today, let me know," a busty blonde nurse says to me.

"Thanks, but Dr. Larson assigned Collins to me. We should be good."

"Well, the offer stands," she says huskily, and it's obvious to all of us what she's offering.

"I think I can handle it," Collins tells her.

Blondie shrugs, winks at me, then walks off down the hall.

Chapter 24

Collins

BREATHE IN. BREATHE OUT. BREATHE in. Breathe out. I'm not one to be involved in drama. In fact, I steer clear of it. However, since Grady has been back in my life, I feel like I'm in the middle of a sitcom. I know that part of that is my fault. I'm the one who insists we keep whatever we had and whatever we have now a secret. However, as I stand here beside him, my arms at my sides, hands balled into tight fists, I know the drama is all on me. Well, me and Darcy. I've never had an issue with her. She's a good nurse, she pulls her weight, and up until a few seconds ago, I considered her to be in the 'coworkers I like' column.

That's all changed.

"Hey," Grady says, pushing his shoulder into mine. "Did you hear anything I just said?"

"No," I admit.

"Thank you for your help." He holds up the tablet. I open my mouth to tell him that it was nothing when another nurse, Carla, comes over and sticks her hand out to Grady.

"Hi, I'm Carla. It's nice to meet you." She bats her eyelashes at him. "I checked the schedule and see that you have a day off this weekend. I thought we could go for a drink. I could show you around the area."

My mouth drops open in shock.

"Actually, I'm from here, and my girlfriend and I already have plans."

"Is it serious?" she asks him.

"Is what serious?" He acts as if he doesn't know what she's asking him.

My fists are so tight I can feel my nails biting into my skin.

"Your girlfriend. I won't tell if you won't," she purrs.

Yes, she fucking purrs at him. Her voice is low, and I'm sure she's thinking that it sounds sexy, but I've got news for her, it doesn't. Grady must feel the tension rolling off me. He steps to the side, causing our shoulders to rub.

"Yes, Carla. My relationship with my girlfriend is serious. I love her, and there is no way I would ever cheat on her. I'm sorry, your efforts are wasted on me."

Carla mumbles what sounds like "lucky bitch" under her breath, grabs a folder from the desk, then turns and walks away.

"Follow me." Grady grabs the tablet from the counter and marches down the hall. I rush to follow him as his long strides carry him away from me. At the end of the hall, he stops in front of the door that reads Supply Closet. Testing the handle, he opens the door and motions for me to go inside. I do as he asks and hear the door shut behind us, and the click of the lock.

"What are—'" I don't get to ask him what we're doing in here because he pulls me into him and crushes his mouth to mine. This kiss is not slow and calculated. It's full of heat and need. He kisses me like I'm the air he needs to breathe. When he finally pulls away, he rests his forehead against mine. We're both breathing heavily, trying to recover from the kiss.

"It's you, Collins. All I need is you. Don't let them get to you. They see my title and that's all they want. They want to latch onto a doctor, but that's not happening. At least, not with me. I've attached myself to you." He gives my hip a gentle squeeze.

"I wanted to hit her, Grady. Both of them. I've never felt the urge to harm another human being in my life, but I wanted to punch them."

He chuckles. "Easy, tiger."

"It's not funny. What is happening to me?"

"You felt threatened, but I'm telling you that you have nothing to worry about. It's you who lives in here." He places my hand over his heart. "Just you."

It's all too much. I didn't expect to feel the way I did when they were blatantly hitting on him. It's all new territory for me. Not wanting to disappear into my thoughts about Grady and where we are in this relationship, I change the subject. "You were good with her, with Lucy."

"Thank you. Kids are easy. That's one of the main reasons I went into pediatrics."

"He would be proud of you, you know that, right?"

He sucks in a breath and slowly exhales. "I'd like to think so." He pulls me into his chest and hugs me tightly. "It wasn't just him you know, that got me here. Sure, I started out wanting to be a doctor, wanting to help other families like ours. But you were my motivation in medical school. I worked hard to get top grades, so I had my choice of residency programs. I wanted to come home to you, Collins. I was determined to do so."

Lifting my head from his shoulder, I look at him. "I missed you."

His eyes soften. "I missed you, too, baby. So, much."

"We better get back to work before someone notices we're gone."

"Can we just stay here all day?"

"We could, but that's not why you spent all those years in college. You're here to help, to make a difference."

"What about you?"

I shrug. "Losing Jared affected all of us. We each chose our path with his memory guiding us."

"Collins, I—" I hold my hand up to stop him.

"We really need to get back out there." I kiss him quickly, just a peck on the lips and walk around him and out of the supply closet. I don't know what he was going to say, but I do know that this is not the time or the place to get into any deep conversations. We have a job to do. These kids, their families are depending on us.

The rest of the day we work side by side. I easily anticipate his needs, and we're a well-oiled machine. So much so that Dr. Larson congratulates us on a job well done.

"So, I'll see you at home later?" Grady asks me.

"Yeah, we can make that happen," I tell him.

"I have some charting left to do, but I won't be far behind you. Drive safe."

"You, too."

"Always, baby." He reaches out like he's going to wrap his arms around me, then his hands drop to his sides as he thinks better of it, and I swallow hard.

"See you soon," I say, leaving him standing at the deserted nurses' station to gather my things and head home.

Chapter 25

GRADY

IT'S FRIDAY NIGHT AND JUST after seven, and I'm finally on my way home. It's been one hell of a week, but I knew that going in. Nothing about residency or even being a doctor is easy, that's not why I chose this career. When my little brother died, I knew then that I wanted to help other families so they wouldn't have to go through what we did.

I'm dead on my feet, and all I want to do is go home and snuggle with Collins. I've put in some really long days, and I've only seen her for about a half hour or so each night, outside of the hospital. I've not been able to convince her to stay the night, but I'm not worried. We'll get there. Hell, I never imagined she would let me back into her life this easy, so she can take all the time she needs. She's mine, and that's all that matters. The rest will just fall into place.

Pulling into our complex, I don't bother going to my place before knocking on her door. When it swings open, her roommate, Tabby, greets me.

"Hey, Grady." She smiles. "Come on in."

"Hey. Is Collins here?"

"She's in her room." She smiles brightly. "You can go on back. First door on the left."

"Thanks." I move past her into the apartment and down the hall toward Collins's room. When I reach her door, my mouth drops open. My girl is in nothing but a pale pink lace bra and panties. Her hair is wrapped up in a towel, and she's standing in front of her closet, hands on her hips. I'm sure she's trying to figure out what to wear, but from where I'm standing, she's good now. We don't need to leave this room. Quietly, I step into her room and close the door behind me. She whips her head around to face me.

"Grady!" A blush coats her cheeks. "What are you doing in here?" she asks as I stride toward her.

"I'm here for you," I say softly as my lips press to hers. My hands find her hips, and I pull her into me. She kisses me back, just like she has every night this week.

"In my room?" She laughs, pulling away from our kiss.

"Tabby said you were in your room and that I could come on back."

"I bet she did." She shakes her head. "I'll have to remember that. Payback is a bitch."

"How was your day?" I ask, wrapping my arms around her waist. With one hand holding her close, I use the other to trace her spine softly.

"Good. I went to the store and ran some errands. Yours?"

"Better now," I say, kissing her again. "We can stay in tonight. In fact, just throw on a robe and we can head over to my place."

"You trying to get out of taking me out?"

"Never."

"Uh-huh. Let me get dressed."

"I need to go shower, but damn, I can't leave you here like this."

"Sure, you can." She pushes at my chest, but I refuse to budge.

Moving my hands back to her hips, I step back, keeping a hold of her. Slowly, I let my eyes rake over every gorgeous inch of her. "You take my breath away," I say, pulling her back into my chest and kissing her temple.

"I need a half an hour. I'll come over as soon as I'm ready."

"Just text me. I'll come to the door to get you."

"You don't have to," she assures me.

"Baby, technically this is our first date, I'm not fucking it up. You text me when you're ready, and I'll be here." With one more quick kiss to her lips, I reluctantly release her and turn and walk out of her room.

At my place, I rush through a shower and forgo shaving; instead, I use that time to run down the street and grab her some flowers. When I pull back into the parking lot of our complex, I get her text.

Collins: I'm ready.

Her message makes me feel as though I'm sixteen again and going on my first date. This might as well be. Nothing before her counts. Hell, I can't even remember much of it. Collins is all I see. I don't bother to text her back. Instead, I grab the bouquet of flowers and head inside. I knock twice and step back, holding the flowers in front of me as if they're a shield. When the door opens, my eyes widen at the sight of her. She's wearing jeans that look as though they've been painted on. Her sleeveless blue flowing top brings out the vibrant blue in her eyes, and her feet are in some kind of strappy heels that look hot as fuck.

Realizing I'm just staring at her and have yet to say anything, I lean in and kiss the corner of her mouth. "You make my heart race," I say softly. Pulling back, I hand her the flowers.

"I can take those." Tabby's arm snakes around Collins and grabs the flowers. "You kids have fun. I won't wait up," she says with a chipper voice. She hands Collins her purse and phone and pushes her out the door.

"Tabby!" Collins says loudly, laughing.

"Love you," Tabby's muffled reply comes through the door.

"You ready?" I ask, offering her my arm.

"Yeah. Where are we going again?"

I know she's worried about being seen; we talked about it earlier this week when I asked her to have dinner with me. "Don't worry, I have it all under control." I asked around, and there is a small mom and pop diner the next town over that a few of the nurses raved about—one in particular. I think she thought I was going to ask her to go. It's not until I thanked her and told her it sounded like somewhere my girlfriend would love that her face fell. I should feel guilty, but I don't. I never gave her reason to think I wanted to ask her out. That was all on her. Not to mention, she doesn't hold a candle to my Collins.

Once we're on the road, I reach over and hold her hand in mine. "You look beautiful."

"Thank you. I can't believe we're doing this. That we're together, like this." She raises our joined hands.

"Get used to it."

"You're awful confident, Dr. Carmichael." Her voice is light and flirty.

"I am Nurse Ward," I fire back. "I know what I want." I pull her hand to my lips and kiss her knuckles.

"I still worry."

"I know you do, baby. But time will show you this is right. Nothing that feels as good as this, as being with you could be wrong."

"Not that it's wrong, just that you'll change your mind. I crushed on you for years and then one night, everything I wished for came true, and then I woke up and you were gone."

My gut twists at her words. "I'm sorry."

"I know. You don't have to keep saying it. I've forgiven you. I just… still have this nagging worry in the back of my mind."

"That takes time, Collins. Take all of it that you need. I'll be here." She settles back into the seat, and we ride the rest of the way in comfortable silence. The radio plays softly in the background, and if this is all we do tonight, it's already the best date of my life, just because it's her.

"How did you find this place?" she asks thirty minutes later when I pull into the diner.

"I asked around at work." I turn off my SUV and turn to face her.

"Thank you, Grady." She smiles over at me.

"Just for the record, I don't want to hide you, hide us. I respect the fact that you want to wait, but I want to just throw that out there."

"I know. Just a little while."

"Let's get you fed." I climb out of the SUV and rush to open her door. She's already climbing out when I get to her door. Surprising me, she reaches out, taking my hand in hers. That's how we walk into the small mom and pop diner. Seeing the "Please seat yourself" sign, Collins leads us to the back of the restaurant. She slides into the booth and to my surprise, gives my hand a gentle tug. Taking the hint, I slide in next to her. Unable to resist, I move in and kiss her cheek.

"Welcome to Mabel's." A young waitress greets us with menus and silverware. "Today's special is meatloaf," she says, smiling. "I'll give y'all a minute to look over the menu. What can I get you to drink?" She rattles off our options.

"I'll have a sweet tea," Collins orders.

"Make that two."

"Did they tell you what was good?" she asks.

"Everything," I tell her. "Apparently, it's all home cooking, and you can't go wrong with any menu item."

When the waitress comes back, we both decide on the meatloaf, and then she's gone. "Tell me about medical school," Collins says.

"It was… lonely. My two roommates, Jeff and Andy, they were just as focused on school as I was. They were both there on a scholarship and couldn't afford to party it up. The three of us pretty much studied our asses off for three years."

"No wild parties?" she asks. There is teasing in her tone, but I can tell she's hesitant to hear the answer.

"No. We went to one or two, but it was always to show our faces and then head back home. I guess we were all just too focused on other things. More important things." My hand under the table reaches over and gives her leg a gentle squeeze.

"So, you just studied all the time?"

"Yeah, it's medical school." I laugh.

"Stop." She chuckles softly. "You've always been smart."

"Yeah, but it was important, you know? I mean, people's lives are going to be in my hands. I felt like I needed to give it my all. Besides, none of that interested me. I was missing you and…." I shrug.

"I missed you, too. Desperately," she adds. "Crazy, right? One night together, and I felt as though I'd lost a part of myself."

"Not so crazy. We grew up together."

"Yeah, but it was Caleb who you spent the majority of your time with."

I nod. "I know, but I felt it, too, Collins. I felt it, and it scared the hell out of me."

The waitress drops off our food, promising to be right back with refills. We both dive in, starving. Talking ceases while we eat.

"Ugh." Collins pushes her plate away. "I'm stuffed. This place is amazing."

"It is. Did you leave room for dessert?"

"No." She laughs. "I might explode."

"All right then." I wave to the waitress and signal for the check. After I settle the check, I place my hand on the small of her back and lead her back out to my SUV. "I thought we could go to the park or maybe drive around."

"It's late, and I know you're exhausted."

"I'm not ready for my time with you to end."

"How about a movie?"

"My place?" I offer.

"Yeah, we can do that." Her smile is vibrant, and I know without looking in the mirror, mine matches hers. Opening her door, I wait for her to buckle her belt before leaning in and kissing her soft lips. Pulling away, I shut the door and jog around to my side.

"How about we stop and pick up some ice cream and some popcorn?"

"I have some at my place. I'll change..." She looks down at her clothes. "...and bring it over to yours."

"You sure?"

"Yeah." She leans her head back against the seat, turns toward me, and smiles. "Thanks for tonight."

"It's not over," I remind her.

"I know. I just didn't want to forget to tell you."

Leaning over the console for one more kiss, I quickly move back to my side, buckle in and head home. With my girl. My Collins.

Finally.

Chapter 26

Collins

I SENT GRADY ON TO his place so I could change. Tonight has been perfect—low-key, great food, good company. I'm trying not to get too excited, but it's hard when he says the things that he does. He's never lied to me, and I don't feel like he is now. It's just an adjustment, to go from him slipping away in the night and being ignored for three years, to him pursuing me. It's a big change. Don't get me wrong, I'm not complaining. I love spending time with him. I'm glad he agreed to give this some time. We need it to connect. We owe it to ourselves to make sure this is what we think it could be before we add the stress of others not accepting it.

I've forgiven him, and I hope with all that I am that we can make this work. I want nothing more. I don't know what the future holds for us, but for the first time since the night he slipped away, I'm excited to find out.

"What are you doing home this early?" Tabby asks from the couch.

"Changing."

"Why?"

"We're going to watch a movie over at his place. What are you doing home on a Friday night?"

"I work tomorrow."

"Again? You worked last weekend."

"Yeah, we're short staffed. Besides, the money helps."

"No hot date?" I ask her.

"Not tonight, sadly." She laughs.

"Right. Well, I need to go change. You want to join us?" I offer. I know Grady might be disappointed, but he won't be mad. That's not the kind of guy he is.

"Nope." She pops the *P*. "I'm calling it a night soon. It's been a long-ass week."

"Yeah, Grady put in a ton of hours. He's exhausted. That's why we decided to just watch a movie. He'll probably fall asleep five minutes in."

"Yeah, right. There is no way he's going to sleep with you there."

"We'll see. We should take bets."

"Sure. I bet you bathroom duty next week, since it's my week, that you don't even come home tonight."

"We're not there yet," I tell her.

"I didn't say you'd have sex with him. I said you wouldn't be home."

"Fine. If I win, you do my bathroom duty the week after."

"Deal." She stands and holds out her hand for me to shake. "You kids have fun. I'll see you tomorrow when I get home. I'm going to bed."

"Night, Tab."

She waves over her shoulder as she disappears behind her bedroom door.

Rushing to my room, I change into a pair of black yoga shorts and a tank top. Sliding my feet into some flip-flops, I head to the kitchen. I snatch two bags of microwave popcorn and the tub of strawberry ice cream from the freezer. I know strawberry is his favorite; it's mine, too. After grabbing my phone and my keys to let myself back in, I lock the door behind me and walk the short distance to his door and knock.

"I thought you changed your mind," he says when he opens the door.

"No. Tabby was home, so we chatted for a few minutes." I don't tell him about our ridiculous bet that I already know I'm going to win. "Here." I hand him the two unpopped packages of popcorn and the ice cream.

"Strawberry." He smiles.

"Yep."

"Something we've always had in common." He leans in for a kiss, and of course, I meet his lips with mine. "Make yourself comfortable. I have the movies pulled up. Pick whatever you want."

I watch him as he walks into the kitchen. Slipping out of my flip-flops, I place them beside the door and settle on the couch. I scroll through the movies and can't really find anything that catches my eye. I'm still scrolling when Grady brings in a big bowl of popcorn and two bottles of water.

"Find something?" he asks, taking the seat right next to me on the couch.

"Not really," I say, yawning.

"I have a few things on the DVR. You can check there, too."

Clicking over to the DVR, I see *Forged in Fire.* "My dad and Caleb love this show."

"Yeah? My dad told me about it, too." He chuckles. "I don't have much time for TV, but the one episode I did watch was pretty interesting."

"Can we watch this?"

"Anything you want. I'm just glad to have you here."

It's impossible to not let myself fall when he says things like that. I choose the oldest episode and hit Play. Without a thought, I snuggle into his side. His arm wraps around my shoulders as he holds me close. Closing my eyes, I just take in the moment. The feeling of being in his arms again. I let the idea that this could be more, that we could be more settle. It's always been Grady for me. No one else even compares. I've tried to push him out of my heart, but the feat turned out to be impossible.

We're almost at the end of the first episode when I notice that Grady's breathing has evened out. Tilting my head, just barely, I see he's fallen asleep. I should get up and go home, but I'm not ready to leave him yet. Regardless of the fact that he's sound asleep, he still holds me tightly in his arms. Just one more episode, then I'll go to my place.

I startle awake, feeling as though I'm floating through the air.

"Shh, it's me. I've got you," Grady whispers softly.

"What are you doing?" The room is dark.

"Taking you to bed."

"I should go home."

"You should stay," he says, not stopping.

I assume he's taking me to his room. "Grady, we said slow," I remind him as my mind tries to catch up with what's happening.

"Just to sleep," he says, setting me on the bed. His hands cup my face. The room is dark so I can't see his face, but I can feel the want pouring out of him when he speaks. "I just want to hold you, Collins. Hold you like I should have that night. All night long, waking up with you in my arms. We can take this as slowly as you want, baby. I know how our story unfolds, but tonight, just... I want to hold you."

I lie back on the bed and groan at the softness. "Then she wins," I mumble.

I feel the bed dip beside me, then the warmth of his hand resting on my belly. "Who wins, baby? There is no one but me and you."

"Tabby." I huff out her name as if she's the devil herself. Did she know how soft his bed was? Is that why she was so smug? No, that couldn't be the reason. Damn my best friend.

"Tabby?" he asks, amused.

"Yeah, she bet me and this... me being here in your bed." I open my eyes, and I can just barely make out his features. He's close. I place my hand on his cheek, his five o'clock shadow tickling the palm of my hand. "Me being here means she wins."

"Not that I'm complaining, I'm thinking I like the fact that you lost this bet, but what exactly did you bet on?"

"She said she would see me tomorrow, that I would stay. I said no, that we're not there yet. Then you bring me into your room and lay me on this big fluffy cloud, and she wins," I sigh dramatically. Suddenly more awake as he aligns his body with mine, his hand still rests on my belly.

"What does she win?" he asks with a chuckle.

"Bathroom duty. I'm on for two weeks."

"I'll do it."

"What?"

"I said I'll do it. I'll clean the fucking bathroom every day until you move in with me."

"Move in with you? Cocky much?" I laugh, now fully awake.

"Yes. Until then, I'll keep your bathroom spotless if that keeps you in my bed at night."

"Just one night. This thing is crazy comfortable."

"I know." I hear the laughter in his voice. "Now, slide under the covers."

Doing as he says, I wiggle until I'm underneath the blankets. He slides under, too, and snuggles up next to me. My back's held tight against his front. "Goodnight, baby," he whispers huskily, kissing my neck.

"Goodnight." Closing my eyes, I let the warmth of him surrounding me lull me to sleep.

Chapter 27

GRADY

BLINKING MY EYES OPEN, I smile when I see she's still here, still wrapped up tightly in my arms. A glance at the window tells me that it's still early morning as the sun has barely started to rise. Sometime in the night, my hand that was resting on Collins's belly worked its way under her shirt. Not just her shirt, but half of my hand is under the scrap of material she calls shorts while the other half remains on her lower belly. Her skin is so fucking soft and warm. My cock that is nestled next to her is hard as steel.

What a way to wake up.

Gently, I stroke her skin with my thumb. I don't want to wake her up; she was exhausted last night, but damn, I can't resist the silky-smooth feel. This is how it should have happened that night. I should have stayed there in the camper, with her held tight against my chest. I've imagined this moment for years, but nothing I ever imagined could have prepared me for this, *this* feeling of my heart swelling as it beats rapidly against my chest. In no way could I have realized that by simply waking up with her in my arms, she would become the center of my world. I knew I wanted her, that's never changed. If I'm honest, I wanted her long before the night we crossed the line. There was not a single doubt in my mind that

I wanted to be with her, but this... this is something so profound, a magnitude I could never have imagined.

I'm irrevocably in love with her.

She moves just a little, causing my pinky to brush over a small patch of curls. Without thinking, I do it again, this time moving my hand lower. Unable to resist, I brush my thumb over her clit, causing her to moan. I freeze when I realize what I'm doing. She's told me more times than I can count that she wants to go slow and here I am taking advantage of her.

"Don't stop," her sleep-laced voice whispers.

"Collins." My voice is rigid, pleading.

"Grady." A lazy smile tilts her lips. "Don't stop." She wiggles to roll onto her back, giving me full and absolute access to her.

Another slow swipe of my thumb over her clit follows. "Good morning, beautiful," I whisper in her ear.

"It's about to be." She lifts her hand to run her fingers through my hair.

Resting my head on her chest, I take my time, slowly running my fingers through her folds. With each swipe, her wetness coats my fingers. Her shirt has ridden up, exposing her creamy skin. I place my lips just below her belly button in a tender kiss. So many times I've imagined her in my bed, and I want to cherish her now that she's here, take my time, kiss every delectable fucking inch of her.

I want to feel all of her.

But I need to go slow.

I can't push her for more. She's not ready, and the last thing I want to do is push her away when all I've done since I've been home is tug her toward me. This moment right here, it's a gift, one I will cherish. Her fingers stroke through my hair as I guide one digit inside of her. She moans, her hands stilling, as does my hand.

"You okay?"

"Yeah," she breathes. Her hands begin their exploration of my hair.

Slowly, I move my finger in and out of her. She's wet, so wet, and when she asks for more, I oblige and slide in another digit.

"This is worth bathroom duty," she pants, and I can't help but chuckle.

Lifting my head, I look at her. "Yeah?"

Her eyes are glassy with need and desire when she answers, "Definitely."

"You know, if you were here in my bed every night, I could wake you up like this every day," I say as I pump my hand a little faster.

"Mmm."

I move down the bed and place my lips on her skin once again, just below her belly button. My tongue tastes her while my lips cherish her, all while keeping my rhythm, moving my fingers in and out of her. She's writhing beneath me, which only fuels me on. I can smell her desire, and suddenly, nothing else matters but tasting her. Moving yet again, I slide off the bed. She groans when my hand slips free, and I smile. Gently tugging on her legs, moving her to the edge of the bed, I look up at her about to ask for permission, never wanting to take something she's not offering. But the look in her eyes, the way her chest is rising and falling rapidly with each breath, tells me what I need to know.

She wants me.

She wants this.

"I've missed you, Collins," I say before dropping to my knees. Placing one leg over each of my shoulders, I'm now eye-to-eye with her pretty, pink pussy. I can't believe I walked away from her.

Never again.

She's mine.

I'll fight for her.

Fight for us.

My fingers slide back into her wet heat, and my mouth covers her clit. My mind clears of everything, the past, the future, work; there is nothing but her and the taste of her on my tongue. I lose myself in her, her taste, the feel of her warmth wrapped around me. Her legs clamp around my neck as her walls squeeze my fingers. She's close. I don't let up, making love to her clit with my mouth, my fingers buried deep inside of her.

"G-Grady." My name is not a scream but a plea from her lips as she falls over the edge.

I don't stop until I feel her legs loosen and her body relax into the bed. Reluctantly pulling away, I wipe my mouth with the back of my hand and carefully remove her legs from my shoulders. After climbing back on the bed, I lie down beside her, both of our legs hanging off the edge. "Morning, beautiful."

She chuckles. "Morning."

"How did you sleep?"

"Like a rock, you?" she asks with a lazy smile.

"Sleeping with you in my dreams the last three years is no comparison to waking up with you in my arms." Her eyes sparkle at my admission and a slight blush coats her cheeks. "What do you want to do today?" It's my only day off this week, as I have to be back at the hospital tomorrow morning at ten, and I want to spend it with her.

"I'm actually supposed to go over to Caleb's. I promised Emily I'd come over and let her run the final wedding plans past me. I wasn't sure, I mean, today is your only day off. I thought maybe you had plans."

"Hey." I cup her cheek, forcing her to look at me. "You." I lean in and kiss her nose. "You are always in my plans. No matter if it's one day off or a week. I want to spend it with you."

"I know we said we were together, but I guess I just didn't want to assume."

"Assume. When it comes to me and you, assume. Always assume that I want to see you. You can bet on the fact that I want to spend all my time with you. You can be certain that you are the most important person in my life. Also, for the record, I don't want to hide us, Collins. I want the world to know how I feel about you. Nothing else matters."

"So, call Caleb. I'm not ready to tell him, but if you all are hanging out, at least we will be together, kind of," she says, scrunching up her nose.

"I won't be able to kiss you or touch you. I'm not so sure I have that kind of restraint."

She laughs. "I have faith in you. Besides, the alternative is not getting to see me until later. We'll at least be together."

Before I can reply, my phone rings. Grabbing it from the nightstand, I laugh when I see Caleb's name. I show her the screen before answering. "Hey, man."

"What are you doing today?" he asks.

"It's my only day off this week, not sure yet." What I want to say is that I'm keeping your sister hostage in my bed, so tell your fiancée she's not coming.

"Feel like coming over and helping me put a desk together? Em bought a new desk for the guest room. She and Collins are going over wedding plans today, again." He chuckles. "So, yeah, manly things need to be done, and I need to be out of the way."

"Yeah, I can do that. What time is all this going down?"

"Collins is supposed to be here around noon, so that works."

"Sounds good, man. I'll be there." We talk a few more minutes before hanging up, and I toss my phone on the bed. "Looks like we'll be at your brother's place today."

She smiles. "Good. I was kind of bummed I might not get to see you."

"We have a few hours before we have to be there."

"I'm going to run next door and get a shower."

"Or," I say, leaning in and kissing her. "You could shower here," I murmur against her lips.

"I could," she agrees, pecking my lips. "However, I don't have any clothes or any of my stuff like shampoo and bodywash. I can't go to my brother's smelling like you."

"Fuck, that's hot."

She laughs. "Yeah, I don't think you'd feel that way when Caleb's on your ass about it."

"It's going to happen, Collins. One day he's going to find out about us, and we're going to have to face it."

"I know, but not yet. Just give this some time, okay?"

"Okay," I begrudgingly agree. I want us out there to our families, to my best friend. I'm ready to start our lives together to move toward the future I want us to have. We can't do that if we're hiding, but I understand. I'll give her some time.

"Thank you for—" Her face heats.

"Never thank me for that, for bringing you pleasure. It's not a chore, not a job. It's all my pleasure, too." I lean in and kiss her lips. "Can you stay a little longer?"

"I should really go, start some laundry."

"You can go grab clothes and whatever else you need and come back here and shower and get ready. In fact, bring whatever you want to keep here."

"We're not moving in together."

"Yet." I grin.

She just shakes her head. "I should go. I'll see you later, at Caleb's."

"Can I drive you? I mean, we're neighbors after all. We could tell them we met in the hall and I offered to drive you."

"Grady, I don't know."

"Come on, Collins. It's simple and a nice gesture."

"Fine. I need to go so I can get ready."

"Come here." Sliding my hand behind her neck, I pull her into a kiss, one that she's sure to remember. It's a kiss that tells her exactly how I feel about her.

"Text me when you're ready to go."

She nods, standing and pulling her sleep shorts back on. I rush to her side and place my hand on the small of her back, walking her to the door. When she opens the door, I make sure mine is unlocked so I can get back in and follow along with her, just mere feet away.

"I could have made the walk of shame on my own." She smiles up at me.

"No. There is no shame here, baby. Nothing but respect, passion, and love." The last word is whispered. "So much fucking love, there could never be any shame." I kiss her temple.

She nods. "See you in a few hours."

I watch as she disappears behind the door before turning and heading back to my place. Once inside, I flop down on the ugly-ass floral couch and replay the night and morning. There is nothing I would change about my time with her. Well, maybe her having to leave, but we'll get there. I can feel it.

Chapter 28

Collins

ONCE INSIDE MY APARTMENT, I dance around like a crazy person. Last night was more than I could have hoped for, just being with him and then this morning… Let's just say that it was worth months of bathroom duty.

Heading to the kitchen, I grab a granola bar to satisfy my hunger before rushing to the shower. I have plenty of time, but honestly, I can't wait to go back to him. To spend more time with him, just us. Today is going to be hard. I just hope we can get through it without spilling the beans. I'm not ready for Caleb or anyone else, well, other than Tabby, to know just yet. I want to make sure he's really in this. Yes, I've forgiven him, and he's given me no reason to think that he's not being honest. In fact, he's gone out of his way to make sure I know he is. I just want to keep him all to myself. Since our night together was only ever between us, I feel like I need to keep this, keep *him* close to my chest, so to speak.

By the time I'm finished with my shower and ready, it's only a few minutes after ten. Grabbing my phone, I pace across the living room debating on what I should do. I really want to spend more time with him, and since we're both riding together, we could go grab a late breakfast or brunch or whatever in the hell you call it. Food. We could get some food.

I debate whether or not I should call him. My phone vibrates in my hand, pulling me out of my mental debate. I can't hide my grin when I see his name on my screen.

Grady: I miss you already.

Decision made, I grab my purse and keys and lock up the apartment. I walk down the hall and knock on his door. I shift from one foot to the other while I wait for him to answer. I don't know why I'm nervous; we're in this together. When he opens the door, a slow grin tilts his lips.

"Hey." He reaches for me. His hand lands on my waist as he tugs me close. "This is a nice surprise." Bending, he kisses the corner of my mouth.

"Yeah, I might have missed you, too. A little." I hold up my thumb and index finger and show him just a little space in between the two.

"Yeah, I'll take it." Both arms wrap around me in a hug. All too soon, he's pulling away, and with his hand on the small of my back, he leads me into his apartment. As soon as the door is shut, I'm pushed up against it, and his mouth fuses with mine. He kisses me like it's been years since he's seen me, not hours. When he angles away, his forehead rests against mine.

"Don't you want to know why I'm here?" I ask him.

"Nope."

"What if I'm here to tell you that this is too much and we're over?"

He pulls back, cupping my face in his hands. "I'd tell you that I'm going to fight for you, for us. I'm not going to let anything come between us. I've been down that road, Collins. It's not one I care to travel ever again."

I swallow hard. "I-I just wanted to know if you were interested in grabbing some food before we went to Caleb's."

"What am I going to do with you?" he asks, kissing me chastely on the lips. "Yes, to food. We have to go somewhere local. We won't have time to go far."

"Yeah, maybe we can, I don't know… hit a drive-thru or something."

"Or we could go wherever you want and not worry about who sees us."

"One day."

"One day soon, Collins. You're not a dirty little secret."

"I know. Just… come on, Grady, it's been what, a minute since we agreed to see if whatever this is between us is going to withstand our past?"

"It's been longer than a minute, and it will. I'll make damn sure it does." He kisses me again, a quick peck on the lips. "Let me grab my phone and keys, and we can go."

Fifteen minutes later, we're sitting outside a small deli not far from my brother's place. "They're going to know we rode together, so stopping to grab something to eat is normal, right?"

Grady chuckles. "Come on, you." He reaches for the handle and climbs out of his SUV. He meets me on the sidewalk and reaches for my hand. I pull away as if I've been burned and a frown mars his gorgeous face that was just seconds ago covered in happiness. "I don't like it," he grumbles.

"I think I'll get the turkey," I say, walking toward the deli door. I don't answer him because what can I say? *I've forgiven you, but I'm still scared this is a dream, so no one can know about us?* Today is going to be a hell of a lot harder than I first thought.

At the counter, I order my turkey while Grady orders roast beef. I find a small booth in the back corner and slide into my seat. Grady slides in across from me. "Sorry," he says, handing me my sandwich. "I just hate this, baby. Maybe we should tell him today?"

"N-no," I say, and even I can hear the panic in my voice. If that's not a good indicator, the way my heart is thundering would be a dead giveaway.

"Collins," he sighs.

"Please."

He gives me a soft smile. "You're lucky I love you."

I freeze, my sandwich in midair, halfway to my mouth. My mouth moves, but no words come out. I place my sandwich back on my wrapper and still nothing. Did I hear him right?

Without missing a beat, Grady reaches over the table and places his large hand over mine. "Not exactly the way I wanted to tell you, but I refuse to take it back. I love you, Collins." He's looking into my eyes, and I want to crawl across the table and attach myself to him for life, but I don't. I can't. I need to process this. He loves me? "Eat, baby." He smiles. "We're going to be late."

Just like that, the heart-stopping conversation is behind us. I pick up my sandwich and take a bite, but don't taste anything. I can't get his words out of my head. The worst part is that I didn't say it back. I didn't say it, but I do love him. I love him with everything in me, and I have for years now. I'm just shocked, I guess. I spent our time apart being angry with him, and now he's back and everything I thought he felt for me is wrong. Now he's telling me he loves me and… it's overwhelming.

"What's your schedule like next week?" he asks, changing the subject.

Taking a sip of water, I gather my wits then answer him, "Same old, Monday through Wednesday. Yours?"

"Tomorrow, I'm off Tuesday then work the rest of the week. Off Saturday work Sunday."

"Crazy schedule."

"Yeah, but it's nice, you know? After busting my ass in medical school all these years, I finally get to see patients. Makes all the hard work, all the distance from you worthwhile."

"Yeah, you needed to be there."

"I did, but hindsight is twenty-twenty. I could have brought you with me. The house we rented, you could have lived there with me."

"I would have," I admit. I would have gladly changed schools to be with him. Sure, Tabby and I had a plan, but plans change, and my best friend would have understood.

"I couldn't have asked you to do that. Not after one night. Not to mention, I was a chicken shit. I should have, but I didn't." He takes the last bite of his sandwich. I should be eating mine, but instead, I can't tear my eyes away from his chiseled jaw and the five o'clock shadow he seems to always be sporting.

He loves me.

"I'm ready," I say, wrapping up my half-eaten lunch in the wrapper and placing it on our tray. Grady adds his trash and slides out of the booth, taking our tray to the trash. I follow him to the door he holds open for me. I want to remind him we can't act this way; we have to just be two friends going in the same place, but I can't find my words.

He loves me.

He pulls onto the street, and I find my voice. "Can you turn right here?" He doesn't question me, just turns right like I asked. "Left," I instruct. I continue to give him directions until we come to a deserted parking lot. It's just before noon, and we have to be at my brother's soon, but I need to do one thing first. "Park over there." I point to the back of the building. Once the SUV is parked, I take off my seat belt and turn to face him.

"What's wrong?"

"Nothing. Nothing at all is wrong." I climb over the console and straddle his lap. My hands cradle his face. "Grady Carmichael, I love you, too," I whisper. "I've loved you for so long, that when you said it, I thought maybe I was hearing things. I know it sounds crazy," I ramble on, "I just... had to process it, but I love you, too."

His green eyes are shining brightly. One large hand slides behind my neck as he pulls me into him. His lips hover over mine. "You are the love of my life," he says before his lips mold with mine. This kiss is soft and slow, and I can feel everything he's trying to say. Leaning out of the kiss, he keeps me held close. "You can trust this, Collins. Trust my love for you."

"Baby steps." I smile. This sounds crazy, it feels crazy that we're in this place, both admitting our love for each other. I want to keep this, keep him to myself just for a little longer. I want to enjoy this time with no complications, no drama. All of which will be front and center in our lives as soon as my brother finds out about us.

"Yeah, we can do that." With a chaste kiss, I climb off his lap and back into my seat. "They're going to see right through me," he says once I'm buckled in.

"Who?"

"Caleb and Emily. They're going to be able to tell how I feel about you. It's not something I can just hide away."

"Come on, it will be like a game, just between us."

"I'm going to lose." He laughs.

"We've got this. I just want some time with you before the drama takes root. He's not going to be happy, and I want this time with you."

"Okay, baby." He kisses the corner of my mouth before he settles back in his seat and drives us to my brother's.

Chapter 29

GRADY

W E PULL UP TO CALEB'S, and I have to wipe my sweaty palms on my shorts. Collins wants to keep us a secret and I respect that for now, but honestly, I'm not sure I can do it. She's like a magnet, and I'm unable to resist her pull. I know that I have to, but fuck, it's going to be a challenge.

When I hear the door shut, I realize Collins is already on her way to the door. Grabbing my phone and keys, I hop out and jog to catch up with her. I want to wrap my arm around her, place my hand on the small of her back, pull her to the side, and kiss the hell out of her. Fuck, all of the above, but I can't.

"Hey," Caleb says, answering the door. He looks over at me, then back to his sister.

"We rode together," Collins says, reading the question in his eyes. "Grady was leaving his apartment the same time as me and offered for us to drive together."

Caleb sticks his hand out for me to shake, and I take it. "Thanks, man."

I feel like the world's biggest asshole for lying to him, but I want my girl to feel comfortable, and she's right; we are too new. The last thing we need is to be fighting. I'm just going to have to grin and bear it. At least, it's just the four of us.

"Hey, guys," Emily greets us as we enter the living room. "Collins, I have everything set up in the kitchen."

"Great. So are you all set?" Collins asks her.

"I think so." Her grin is huge.

I glance over at Caleb, and he's looking at her like she's everything that is good in his world. I know that feeling. It's the same one I get when I look or even think about Collins. I'm trying damn hard to not give her that same look while we're here. "Where's this desk?" I ask, pulling his attention away from his fiancée.

"Spare bedroom. You need me, Em?" Caleb asks.

"Nope. We're all set." She turns to Collins. "I have a ton of books and things you can save for when you get married."

"Hold up." Collins laughs. "You have to have a fiancé to get married. Hell, even a boyfriend. I have neither."

I notice she keeps her eyes locked on Emily when she says that. Not able to resist, I pull my phone out of my pocket and fire off a text.

> **Me:** You have a boyfriend, and the other can be arranged. Love you.

Sliding my phone back in my pocket, I slap Caleb on the shoulder. "Let's go do manly things," I say, causing him to laugh. I follow him down the hall to the spare bedroom, and we get to work on the new desk.

We have the pieces laid out on the floor. Caleb is reading the directions when my phone vibrates in my pocket.

> **Collins:** Do I?

> **Collins:** I love you, too.

> **Me:** What do you mean... do I?

Her reply is immediate.

> **Collins:** Have a boyfriend?

Me:	Collins.
Me:	What would you call what we're doing?
Collins:	Dating.
Me:	YOU HAVE A BOYFRIEND
Collins:	I'm pretty sure I'd know if I did.
Collins:	I can't recall being asked.
Me:	I can ask you now. In fact. I'll be right there.
Collins:	No!
Me:	Say it.
Collins:	We have enough lies going on right now.
Me:	We will talk about this later.
Collins:	What if I have plans?

She's toying with me on purpose. I want nothing more than to leave this room, march into the kitchen, and kiss the hell out of her.

Me:	My girl's got jokes.
Collins:	Love you!
Me:	Love you, too.
Me:	This isn't over.
Collins:	I have no doubt. Get back to work.

I'm grinning like a fool when I slide my phone back into my pocket. We are definitely going to talk more about this tonight.

"Who's got you grinning like you just won the lottery?" Caleb asks.

"My girlfriend." I realize my mistake as soon as the words leave my lips. Shit. I knew this was a bad idea.

"Girlfriend? Since when?"

"It's recent."

"Someone I know?"

"Not ready to talk about it. You know, don't want to jinx it and all that."

"You must really like her. I've never heard you say you have a girlfriend before."

Here goes nothing. I turn to look at him. I wait until he's holding my stare. "I'm really into her. She's everything that's good, and no way do I want to do anything to fuck it up."

His eyes widen as he nods his understanding. "Fair enough. Hey, why don't you bring her to the annual Fourth of July party the 'rents throw?"

Our parents, being best friends and neighbors, always throw a combined Fourth of July bash. It started years ago. Hell, it's been going on as long as I can remember. Our houses sit next to each other on one acre lots. A huge tent is set up between the two properties. The Wards have an in-ground pool, while we have a small pond. Swimming, fishing, volleyball nets are put up. We both have hot tubs, Dad and Roger man the grill, while Mom and Monica take care of the sides. It's a blast, and I realize I've missed it the last three years.

"She has plans with her family," I lie. Well, not really. Collins does have plans with her family, mine, too. He just doesn't realize her family is him. What a fucked-up mess this is.

"Sure, she does." He laughs. "Why are you hiding her? Being so secretive?"

"I'm not," I say, way too defensively. "It's new, like I said. Well, not so new, we've uh, just reconnected." Son of a bitch, I need to keep my mouth shut.

"Who is she? From around here? You doing the long-distance thing?" he presses.

"What's with the third degree? I thought we had a desk to put together?"

"I need another wrench, and a beer. Come on." He stands, and I follow him to the kitchen. I should have stayed there and got my shit in order, a good internal pep talk to shut my big-ass mouth, but Collins is in the kitchen so yeah, I'm following him.

"How's it going, ladies?" Caleb asks, kissing first his fiancée and then his little sister, my girlfriend, on top of their heads.

"Great. I think we've been through it all. For all my planning, it's really not that elaborate." Emily laughs.

"As long as you're happy." This time he leans over her and kisses her on the lips, upside down.

It's wrong because he's my best friend, but I'm jealous as hell right now. I want to pull Collins into me, kiss her openly. Fuck, if I'm honest, I'm ready for it all. The white picket fence, the dog, the bills, the kids, the minivan, whatever she sees for us, I'm ready for it.

"Oh, guess what?" Caleb hands me a beer, smirking. "This guy," he points to me, "has a secret girlfriend."

I watch Collins closely, and her eyes widen, but otherwise, she keeps her cool. "Come on, man. I told you we're just reconnecting." I then turn to Collins. "You good to drive home?" I hold up the beer, showing her, and she nods.

"Awe, I love it," Emily coos. "What's her name?"

"Yeah, Grady, what's her name?" Caleb taunts. "Oh, that's right, she's a secret." He turns his attention to Collins. "I tried to get him to bring her to the Fourth bash, but apparently, she has plans with her family."

When Collins's eyes find mine, I shrug and she grins. "Yeah, Grady, you should bring her."

I can hear the humor in her voice. "You think so? I mean, she wants to keep things on the down low for a while, just until we see where this is going." I pause, letting my audience of three soak in my words. It's time to go in for the kill. "Honestly, I'd bring her. I'm in love with her, and I don't care who knows it. I'm trying to respect her wishes."

Collins chokes on the drink of water she was taking. Emily reaches over and pats her on the back.

"You're in love with her?" Caleb asks, surprised.

I tip the bottle to my lips. "Yep," I say, popping the *p* before taking a long drink.

"No shit?" Caleb comes over and gives me one of those bro hugs, you know one of the lean in, back slap, handshake things that us guys do.

"No shit."

"Have you told her?" Emily asks with hearts in her eyes. She's all about the love connection with their upcoming nuptials.

"She knows." I take another sip of my beer, my eyes finding Collins over the bottle.

"Come on, man, I need a name." Caleb tries again to find out more information.

"Nope. I love her enough to respect her wishes."

"Tell me this," Caleb starts. "Do we know her?"

"Yes." No hesitation. I feel bad enough that I'm lying to him, the least amount of lies we put out there the better.

"Damn, I need to start paying better attention." He laughs.

"Are you done with the inquisition? We have a desk to finish." I walk to the trash can and toss my now empty bottle of beer.

"Yeah, let's do this."

"I thought we could go out for dinner after this, you guys game?" Emily asks.

I look over at Collins. "It's your call."

"Sure." She smiles brightly.

I try not to show my disappointment. I love my best friend and his future wife, but damn if I'm not ready to go home and spend some time with my girlfriend. Not to mention, we need to have a little chat about her title in my life.

"Great, now get to work, chop, chop. We're hungry." Emily waves us off.

Caleb kisses her quickly, just a peck, and turns back to the bedroom. It takes extreme control to not do the same with Collins. Instead, I avoid eye contact and follow him down the hall. The sooner the desk is together, and dinner is over, the sooner I get her back in my arms.

"Let's do this," I say, grabbing a side panel and getting to work.

Chapter 30

Collins

"FINALLY," EMILY SAYS DRAMATICALLY. THE smile on her face tells me she's just being silly. "We were ready to starve to death," she tells the guys as they enter the kitchen an hour later.

"Hush, woman." Caleb leans in and taps his cheek. She obliges him, giving him a loud smacking kiss. "You ladies are ready I take it?"

We both stand. I'm starving considering I didn't eat much of my lunch with Grady. Not with the *"I love you"* bomb he dropped on me.

"I'll drive," Emily says.

With a nod, we follow her out to her Ford Fusion. Caleb slips into the passenger seat, while Emily slides behind the wheel. Grady and I take our seats in the back, and his legs are so long that he's invading a little of my legroom. Caleb messes with the radio, chattering to Emily about a band that's coming to town this winter.

When I feel his pinky link with mine, I fight the urge to react. Instead, I sit still. I don't look over at him. I don't smile, keeping my reaction neutral, when inside I'm anything but. Luckily, our legs are hiding our hands.

It's our little secret.

Part of me wants to just tell my brother and our families, to get it over with. Let the cards fall where they may. The other part of me likes having him all to myself. Although, that little "I have a girlfriend" confession earlier was a close call. We'll need to talk about it later.

"I was thinking pizza," Emily says, glancing up in the rearview mirror.

"Babe, you're going to turn into a pizza," Caleb teases her.

"Hey! I happen to love it, and you love me, so deal."

"Can I just say, I love that you are not obsessed with weight and the dress," he tells her.

"You've seen me at my worst. It's supposed to be one of the happiest days of our lives. Why ruin it with worry about five pounds? I want to enjoy my life with you."

"And that is why I love you so much." Caleb leans over the console and kisses her neck.

Grady slightly nudges my knee with his. I'm not sure if he's trying to get me to look at him or not, but it's not happening. It's daylight, and the risk of this pinky holding thing we're doing is bad enough. I know I can't look at him right now, being this close, and not being able to show how I feel for him. So, instead, I keep my focus straight ahead.

We pull into Mama's, which is a small family-owned pizza joint that has been around as long as I can remember. I take my time getting out of the car. Grady falls in step beside me, but I still won't look at him. When we reach the door, his palm settles on the small of my back as he guides me inside. Caleb and Emily are in front of us, so they are none the wiser.

"Do you know how bad I want to kiss my girlfriend right now?" he says, his lips close to my ear.

I ignore him, but my body does not as goose bumps break out across my skin. Fighting the pull he has on me, I slide into the booth that Emily has picked out for us. "It's been forever since I've been here," I say, grabbing a menu. Grady slides in beside me. He keeps his hands under the table, one hand landing on my knee, giving it a gentle squeeze. I fail miserably at not paying attention to him as I turn toward him and smile.

"What are you having?" Emily asks, wearing a knowing grin.

Damn it! Busted. I turn back to the menu in my hand and study it. "I don't know yet. Are we all sharing or what?" I ask, not taking my eyes off my menu.

"We getting a Calzone, wings, and breadsticks?" Caleb asks Emily.

"We are so predictable." She laughs.

"Split a Hawaiian and breadsticks?" Grady asks me.

I pretend to not be surprised that he knows my favorite pizza. He must have been paying attention all those years. "Sure. I actually need to use the restroom. Can you let me out?"

He nods, releases his hold on my knee, and slides out of the booth. "What do you want to drink? Sweet tea?"

"Yes, please. I'll be right back." As if my ass is on fire, I scurry away to the restroom. I just need a minute to breathe. I suck at lying, and all of us hanging out is bound to be trouble.

"Care to tell me why you're hiding in here?" Emily asks. She's standing just inside the bathroom door, arms crossed over her chest, a grin on her lips. I have no idea how long she's been standing there.

Turning on the water, I begin to wash my hands. "I'm not hiding."

"Uh-huh. I've been standing here watching you, and you didn't even hear me come in."

"Just tired, I guess. It's been a long week."

"You can tell me, Collins."

If only. "Really, I'm good." My phone vibrates in my back pocket. Quickly, I dry my hands and retrieve it.

Grady: You okay?

Me: Fine. Be back in a second.

Grady: We can just tell them.

Me: No. It's fine, really. Just needed a minute.

Grady: Okay.

"I saw the way you looked at him. Does he know?" Emily says, pulling me away from my phone.

"What? Does who know? How I looked at who?" I play dumb.

"Grady. Does he know you're into him?"

Oh, he knows all right. "I'm not. I mean, he's easy on the eyes, but there's nothing there." I feel like a total bitch for lying, but I can't come clean, not like this, in the bathroom with my future sister-in-law. We need a little more time. At least, that's what I keep telling myself.

"That he is. I say go for it."

"What? You do realize he's Caleb's best friend, right?"

"So? He's a great guy."

"He is," I admit.

"So?" she prompts.

"Can we just go back to the table and eat? Table this for another day?" I wave around the bathroom. "Different location maybe?"

She throws her head back and laughs. "Yeah, we can do that. But for what it's worth, I say go for it. You only live once." She turns and walks out the door, and I follow along behind her.

The guys spot us immediately and stand to let us slide back into our seats. Grady slides a small plate in front of me and places a breadstick on it. He proceeds to add some sauce before going back to eating his food. I've seen my dad and even Caleb do this more times than I can count, but with their wife or girlfriend, now fiancée. Chancing a glance at my brother, he doesn't seem to notice, and he and Em talk about I don't know what. I relax into my seat and dive into my breadstick.

"So, Grady, how's residency?" Emily asks.

"Good. Exhausting and exciting all at the same time. It's nice to finally be able to put all those years of college to use."

"Do you guys work on the same floor?" Caleb asks.

"I'm a floater, so I'm always bouncing around the hospital," I explain.

"Yeah, we've not crossed paths yet, but I will be working in all areas of the hospital over the next three years as well, so we're bound to work together at some point."

"I don't know how you do it, either of you. Needles and blood and all that." Caleb shivers as if the thought alone is just too horrifying to think about.

"Meh, you get used to it," Grady and I say at the exact same time. He turns to look at me, a smile lighting up his handsome face. I want to lean in and kiss him. The urge is strong, but I hold out.

"Jinx," he says, his voice low and way too husky for what the situation would call for. Then again, we're not normal.

"How about you?" I divert the conversation to my brother. "You ready for this big-time lawyer job you've accepted? It's still hard for me to believe that my goofball big brother is an attorney."

"Yeah, well it's hard for me to believe sometimes, too." Caleb laughs. "And my best friend is a fucking doctor. Who would have thought?"

I don't answer him... but me... I knew Grady would do it. He's always talked about being a doctor and saving families from going through what they did when they lost his younger brother. Then again, I hung on every word he ever said. If I'm honest, part of the reason I want to keep this between us is from fear that we're both searching for something that should be left in the past. I've always loved him, but is that real adult love? Is it my childhood crush that I've harbored for years playing out? Do we have staying power? And Grady, is it that he feels guilty now that he's home? Is he doing this to save face with my brother and our families? It doesn't feel that way, but am I ignoring it because he's the only man I've ever wanted? I need to work all this shit out in my head before we add more drama to the mix.

He leans in and whispers in my ear, "You okay?" pulling me out of my thoughts.

Looking across the booth, I see Caleb is gone and Emily is on the phone not paying any attention to us. "Yeah, just thinking."

"Don't," he says. "Don't think about this, about us when I can't hold you."

That makes me smile. "Where's Caleb?"

"Here," my brother says, causing me to jump. "Paid the bill, you ready?"

Grady argues with him about the bill, but not me. If my lawyer brother wants to buy me dinner, who am I to refuse? Emily ends her call, all smiles. I assume from the bits and pieces that I heard it was one of her sisters about the wedding. We pile back into Emily's car and head home. When we get back to their apartment, I claim to be exhausted and ask Grady if he's ready to go. He pulls his keys from his pocket and hands them to me.

"You had one beer," I tell him.

"Not taking that chance wi—not taking the chance, Collins."

I nod, taking the keys. "Thank you for dinner." I give my brother a hug. "Em, the wedding is going to be beautiful. I'm so excited for the two of you."

"Be safe," Caleb says, waving as we climb into Grady's SUV. I adjust the seat from his long-ass legs, the mirrors, and pull out of the lot. As soon as the apartment complex is in the distance, Grady reaches over and places his hand on my thigh.

"You ready to have that talk?" he asks.

At the stop sign, I glance over at him. His head is resting back against the headrest, and he's watching me, a soft expression I can't quite read on his handsome face. "Eager?" I chuckle.

"I am. I'm eager to hear you tell me that you're my girlfriend. I mean, I told your family, my best friend, surely that makes it official."

"What was that by the way?"

"I'm trying to limit the lies we tell, or I tell. Besides, when he finds out it's you, he'll remember this. He'll remember that I told him that I love you. Hell if I know if that will make it better, but it can't hurt, right?"

I don't reply right away. I pull into the parking lot of our complex and turn off the engine. "I guess so," I finally say.

"What's going on in that beautiful head of yours?" He reaches over and tucks a stray strand of hair behind my ear.

"You just laid it all out on the table, and what happens when you change your mind? What happens then, Grady?"

Reaching over, he grabs the keys out of the ignition and climbs out of the SUV. My heart starts to race, and I prepare myself for the worst. I should have kept my big mouth shut so I could have enjoyed this time with him a little longer. I watch him as he stalks around the front of the car and pulls open my door. He offers me his hand and helps me climb out. My feet hit the ground and I step toward him, allowing him to close the door. As soon as the door is closed, he bends and places his hands on the back of my thighs, lifting me in the air. Instinctively, I wrap my legs around his waist. He steps forward until my back hits his SUV. When his lips take mine, controlling, demanding, I don't hesitate to open for him.

He grinds into me, and there is no preventing the moan that slips from deep in my throat. His tongue explores every inch of my mouth, and I love it. All of it.

I love him.

When we both need air, he pulls away and rests his forehead against mine. "I won't be changing my mind, Collins. This is real." He grinds his hardness against my center one more time as if I need proof. "What I feel for you is real. No amount of time away from you was able to stop what happened that night. You captured me, all of me. My body, my heart, and my mind. It's all yours. In fact, I wish he would drive by right now so he could see us. I want it out there that you are my girlfriend, that I love you more than anything else in this world, and that we are building a life together. Tell me that's what you want?"

"Yes."

"Yes, what?"

"Yes, I want that. All of it. I've wanted that, *you* for so long. Even after you left without a word, I wanted you. I tried to pretend that I didn't, but it was only ever you."

A car drives by and blows the horn, causing him to laugh. "Let's get you inside." Slowly, he slides me down his body, so that I'm sure to feel once more the effect that I have on him. He leads me upstairs and straight to his place. We don't stop until we're in his bedroom, lying on the big fluffy cloud of a bed facing each other, arms and legs intertwined. "Tell me you're my girlfriend. I know it's insignificant to what you are to me, to how I feel about you. You are so much fucking more than that to me, Collins, but I know we need to start slow and I need to hear you say it."

"I'm yours."

"Not good enough, baby." He slips his hand under my shirt, his hand working its way to my breast, over my bra. "Tell me."

"I'm your girlfriend."

His thumb grazes my nipple through my lace bra. "Yes, you are. Tell me you know you're so much more than that. That when I tell you this is real, you believe it. I know I left you, but I promise you with everything that I am that is never going to happen again. Not ever."

"I hear you, and the look in your eyes tells me I can believe you. My heart believes you."

"Yeah?" he asks softly. His thumb continues to trace over my nipple. "What do we need to do to get your head there, too?"

"Time."

"Okay. You keep going back to that, and I promised to give you some time, but, baby, don't fight me, okay. Let this happen. Let this current that ignites between us help get your head and your heart on the same page."

"Okay." The word is a whisper against his lips as he leans in for a kiss. His hands caress my body, and his kisses fuel my desire, making me crazy with wanting him. He never takes it further, and no matter how badly I wish that he would, I don't either. I settle for making out like teenagers.

I have no idea how much time has passed. The sun has since fully set, and the apartment is dark and quiet, nothing but the sounds of our kisses and beating hearts to fill the room. "Stay," he whispers. "I need to hold you again."

"I really should go."

"You should stay here wrapped in my arms all night. Where you belong," he counters.

How do you argue with that? "Okay." That's all he needs to hear before his lips are back on mine. We kiss for hours, explore each other's bodies without really doing anything more than heavy petting. When we fall asleep, as he promised, he holds me tightly against him. No matter where this goes, this night will forever be one I will never forget.

Chapter 31

GRADY

TODAY IS WEDNESDAY, THE FOURTH of July, and I'm off. I had hoped that I would be asked to pick up, but it didn't happen. Don't get me wrong, I'd love to spend time with Collins and our families, but it's going to be hard. No, scratch that, it's going to all but kill me to pretend she's not the reason my world turns around. It's been almost two weeks since the night I convinced her to be my girlfriend, and things have just gotten better from there. Most nights, I get home after she does, and my girl always has dinner ready for me. I don't expect it, but damn if it's not nice to come home to her and a homecooked meal. Not to mention that she spends more nights in my bed than not. In fact, there have been a total of three nights since that night that she's been at her place instead of mine. I remember all three of them vividly as I slept like shit.

I never would have dreamed that having her next to me, in my arms, would lead to the best sleep I've ever had in my entire life. It is. Without a doubt. We've talked a lot. We're getting closer, and each day I feel as though she's letting go of the past. Not that I expect her to do that. Not completely anyway. It will always be there as a part of our history, but moving forward, we're not the same people. I'm not the same scared guy starting medical school. I'm the man who busted his ass for three years to be good enough for her. I'm the man who lived those three years without her. After just one night, I knew there would be no one else. I knew without a shadow of a doubt that she was it for me.

She is.

She's all I see.

She's all I ever want.

Today is going to suck. She'll be there, with our friends and family, and I can't hold her, touch her, kiss her. Fuck me, it's going to be torture. I check my phone one more time, just making sure that I didn't get called into work. Wishful thinking on my part. Grabbing my keys, I know I can't put off leaving any longer. I head out the door.

Collins and Tabby left over an hour ago. I wanted us to ride together, but she refused. I get it, but it would have been nice to have some time with her before we got there, to sneak in a kiss or two. Did I mention that last night she stayed at her place? Something about girls' night with her and Tabby. I didn't fight it, but I admit I did pout a little. Fuck if I care who knows. I want her with me all the damn time. I don't care if that makes me a pussy.

Pulling up to my parents' place, the drive is full, so I park in the yard beside the garage. Taking a deep breath, I then slowly exhale. This day is bound to test my patience. Climbing out of my SUV, I head around back. I find Mom and Dad on the back deck, Dad with a beer in his hand and Mom with her signature cranberry and vodka. However, I know that it's strictly cranberry at this point in the day. She never indulges until the food has been eaten and put away. My mother is always putting others before herself.

"'Bout time you got here," Dad says as I join him and Mom on the deck. He pulls me into a hug, but it's short-lived before Mom is tugging on my arm and pulling me into her embrace as well.

"We've not seen much of you these last few weeks," she scolds.

"I know, I'm sorry. Residency is keeping me busy. Long days, six days a week." I feel guilty that I've not been to see them, but I'm telling the truth about the long days. I just leave out that after each and every one of those long ass days, there is nothing I want more than to curl up with Collins on the couch and decompress. Okay, and kiss... lots of kissing.

As I pull back from Mom's embrace, I hear, "Oh, Grady, it's so good to see you."

Turning, I see Roger and Monica Ward, also known as my girlfriend and best friend's parents standing behind me. "How have you been?" I ask, leaning down to give Monica a hug.

"Oh, we're fine." She waves me off. "So good to have you home."

Monica always has been like a second mother to me. One day she will be. That's if I can convince Collins to spend the rest of her life with me. I know that's what I want. I've told her as much. I'm just not sure she's there yet.

"Grady," Roger says, shaking my hand. "Damn proud of you, son. Both of you boys have done us proud." He says it as if I'm his son.

That's how close our families are. Hence, the hesitation from Collins to tell them about us. I'd like to believe they love us both enough that if we're happy, they're happy, at least when it comes to our parents. I honestly have no idea how Caleb is going to react. When we were younger, I was the one helping him keep our friends from Collins. It started out as a duty, a code of honor if you will, to my best friend. Then, as time went on, it was for purely selfish reasons. I didn't want anyone to have her but me.

"Thank you."

"Caleb and the guys are over at our place," Monica informs me.

"I'm headed that way." I drop a kiss on Mom's, then Monica's, cheek and head next door. Jogging down the steps, I have to make myself slow down as I make my way to the Ward's backyard.

"It's about time you got here!" Bryce yells out.

Raising my hand in the air, I flip him off, causing everyone to laugh. When I reach the patio table, I take the only seat left, which is between Alec and Bryce. Collins is next to Bryce, Tabby next to Collins. Emily is sitting on Caleb's lap. "What's going on?" I ask the group. I don't make eye contact with my girl, not yet. That would be too obvious, right? Tabby is the only one here that knows about us.

"We're trying to get these two to go for a swim with us," Alec says, pointing to Collins and then Tabby.

Fuck me. With all of the scenarios that have run through my mind about today, none of them included watching her parade around in a bikini, hell even a one piece. Damn it. "Yeah?" I manage to croak out.

"We're wearing them down." Bryce laughs, putting his arm around Collins's shoulders and pulling her into him.

I ball my fists at my sides. I'm ready to stand to tell him to get his paws off my girl when she removes his arm and scoots away from him. She catches my eye from across the table and gives me a slight head nod, letting me know she's okay. Of course, she's okay, but I still don't like his hands on her.

"Easy, tiger." Tabby leans into me and whispers.

"Right," I scoff.

"She only has eyes for you," she says even lower to be sure no one can hear us.

"What are you two whispering about over there?" Collins asks.

My head pops up and what I find makes me extremely happy. She's glaring at us, and jealousy is written all over her. I know I shouldn't be happy about that. I should hope that she keeps herself in check because of who we're with, but I couldn't give a fuck less. I'm ready to stand up and kiss the hell out of her. Brother be damned.

"Actually," Collins says, standing from her chair, "I'm ready to cool off. Let me go change."

"I'll come with you." Tabby is up and out of her seat followed by Emily.

"Me, too," Emily says.

My eyes follow the three of them until they disappear into the house. I'm not worried about Caleb because I know his eyes are following his fiancée, too.

"Dude!" Caleb says, pulling all of our attention. "That's my little sister."

I'm ready to defend myself to tell him that I need her to breathe when I realize he's not looking at me. He's looking at Bryce.

"She's hot, Ward." He shrugs unapologetically.

"She's off limits to you."

"Come on, man. She's old enough to make her own decisions."

"She is, but not with you. You think I want her to be another notch on your bedpost. She's not a plaything, Bryce."

"Everyone enjoys sex," Bryce counters.

"Just leave it alone, Bryce," Alec says. "Is it really worth fighting with him over, not to mention this guy." He points at me. "They've both been protective of her all her life."

"Why is that?" Bryce asks, wearing a smirk.

He thinks he knows, and he might, but I'll never admit it to him, not when he's baiting me. Collins would never forgive me. "She's his little sister. I'm his best friend."

"What am I?"

"You have to respect his wishes to keep best friend status." I'm being a dick, but I can't seem to find it in me to care. He put his hands on her.

"Enough!" Collins yells from beside us. We were all too focused on our intense conversation to realize that they were already back outside. "I'll date or have sex with whoever I want. You," she points to Caleb, "and you," she points to me, "have zero say so in the matter." She turns to face Bryce. "As for you, it's not happening. Not today, not tomorrow, not ever, so you're wasting your time." With that, she walks off toward the pool, Emily and Tabby trailing behind her.

I want to be mad that she says I have no say so. I know that I do, because I'm her fucking boyfriend, but she can't tell them that. She has to keep up appearances. Right? Fuck! I wish I could pull her away and talk to her. Hold her close and kiss those soft lips of hers just so I know that we're okay. That although she's angry, she's still mine. I fucking hate this secrecy bullshit.

The guys and I stay on the deck, shooting the shit. Eventually, the tension eases away, and we're once again just four friends catching up. I keep my eyes on her as much as I can. When it's time to eat, I make it a point to sit in a seat that would put her in my direct line of sight. That way when I look at her, it's because she's there, not because I can't keep my eyes off her.

The girls head back to the pool while the four of us guys play corn hole. That's how we spend the majority of the afternoon until Alec and Bryce have to leave. They both work for our local fire department and are helping set off the fireworks display later this evening.

"Stay safe, boys," Mom tells them as they say their goodbyes.

"How about a game of chicken?" Tabby suggests. "I'll be the judge."

"Why do we need a judge?" Caleb asks. "Whoever falls off first, loses."

"I have to make sure the two of you don't cheat." She points her finger at him, and we all laugh.

"Me?" He slaps his hand to his chest in mock horror.

"Yes, you. Now get in the pool."

Caleb salutes her and wades into the water. Pulling my T-shirt over my head, I toss it into a chair and follow behind him. "Ladies, mount up." Caleb grins, diving underwater and swimming toward Emily. She shrieks when he reaches her and pulls her under with him.

"Hey, baby." I'm standing behind her, so close I can feel the heat from her body.

She turns to face me, a smile on her lips. "You ready for this, Carmichael?"

"Let's see." My index finger traces her belly. From the way we're standing, no one can see that I'm touching her. "Am I ready to have those sexy legs wrapped around my head? That's a hell fucking yes."

She throws her head back and laughs. I want to lick the column of her throat. Instead, I settle for the feel of her smooth skin beneath my fingertips. "Tell me you're mine." I step a little closer, too close for where we are, but I need her to feel what being this close to her does to me. When my hard length presses against her belly, exactly where my hand was tracing just seconds before, she sucks in a breath.

"Nothing's changed."

"Then I do have a say so in who you have sex with?"

She sighs. "You know you do. I didn't know what else to say."

"You did good, baby. Put us in our place, but I'm just making sure my place is still with you."

"Until you decide otherwise, yes."

"So, forever then?"

Her eyes light up as they bore into mine. "You really want that?"

"You, Collins, I really want you. Forever doesn't seem long enough."

"You two done planning your attack? We're not getting any younger," Caleb calls.

Immediately, we step away from each other. Collins turns to face them. I'm glad she's standing in front of me to block the view of how she affects me. Sure, I'm underwater and the chances of them noticing are unlikely, but it's a risk she wouldn't want to take. Of that I'm certain.

"Oh, we're ready," she taunts.

"Mount up." He sniggers before dipping underwater and emerging with Emily on his shoulders. I do the same. When I stand back to my full height, Collins reaches down and pushes my wet hair out of my eyes. Tabby counts us off, and the girls shriek with enjoyment as they battle it out, trying to knock the other off. Caleb and I are laughing our asses off, trying to stay upright.

"Come on, ladies!" Tabby shouts. Collins and Emily are laughing hysterically and the next thing I know, they're both falling backward into the pool. "You cheated," Tabby scolds.

My girl sputters up from the water, a smile lighting up her face. "We were too evenly matched. It never would have ended," she says.

Tabby just shakes her head. "I've failed you." She pretends to be offended.

"Oh, hush." Collins waves her off, still smiling.

"We're going to go change," Caleb tells us. From the look on his face and the way he can't keep his hands off her, I'd say they are going for more than that. "It's about time to head out for the fireworks."

"I guess we should change, too," Collins says to me.

"Yeah. These shorts are hybrid, they dry fast, and my shirt is dry."

"Well, I need to go change for sure."

"You riding with me?"

"Sure, Tabby and I will ride with you."

"Um, count me out. I'm meeting Holden. He just got off work about thirty minutes ago."

"Is he meeting you to watch the fireworks?" I ask her.

"Nope." She's grinning like a fool.

"Go." Collins laughs. "Call me if you need me."

"Later," Tabby calls over her shoulder.

"Wait, didn't you ride with Tabby?"

"I did."

"So, how are you getting home?"

She peers up at me. "I was hoping this guy I'm seeing would drive me."

"Oh, so you're seeing someone?"

"Uh-huh. He's a great guy. Smart as hell, sexy, too."

"Does he know you're mine?"

"I don't know. Do you know that you're mine?"

"Yes. A thousand times yes." We're still standing in the middle of the pool. "I want to kiss you so fucking bad right now." My hand gives her hip a gentle squeeze.

Even though the sun has gone down, I can still make out the sparkle in her blue eyes. "Come here." She motions me closer. "Bend down." I do as she asks, and she places her lips next to my ear. "I love you." Before I can even respond, she's turning and swimming away from me. I want to chase after her, grab her around the waist, and throw her over my shoulder. Instead, I watch her go. Not taking my eyes off her until she disappears into the house. This night isn't turning out so bad after all.

Chapter 32

Collins

GRADY ENDED UP DRIVING US to the fireworks. Our parents and most of the party goers stayed behind, but we've always gone to see the show. You're never too old for fireworks. It was hard to not reach for his hand while he was driving, but it could be worse, right? I mean, at least we're getting to spend time together.

"Is it just me or does the show get smaller each year?" Caleb asks from the back seat.

"I think we're just getting older. The magic of the moment is not what it once used to be."

"When I was a kid, I loved it," Emily chimes in. "It's not that I don't enjoy it now, but I think Collins is right. When you're younger, it's almost magical. Standing with your boyfriend under the shower, snuggling close." She laughs when Caleb growls.

"Enough about that," he grumbles.

"Face it, big brother, we're getting older."

"Speaking of, have you talked to your girl tonight, Grady?" Caleb asks.

"Yep." That's all he gives him.

"You should have her stop by later."

"She's busy with family."

"Let's call her, so we can all say hello," Caleb suggests.

Grady doesn't lose his cool. "You did hear me when I told you I was in love with her, right?" he asks, glancing in the rearview mirror. "Why in the hell would I let her talk to you before I know she's all mine?" he counters.

"He's got you there," Emily jokes.

"Collins, have you met her?" my brother asks. "I mean, you live next door to the guy you've had to have run into her?"

"Not yet. But we don't run into each other that often. Our shifts are out of sync. Hell, I hardly see Tabby."

"But you all obviously ride share," he points out.

"Yeah, but we were headed to the same place at the same time. Grady was leaving his apartment at the same time I left mine. The stars must have been aligned or something."

"What's with the third degree?" Emily asks. "He'll let us meet her when he's ready."

"What about you, Collins?" Caleb turns the heat on me.

"There's a guy," I tell him, following Grady's lead and not wanting to add even more lies to the mix.

"Who?"

"Just a guy I've been out with a couple of times."

"I want to meet him. Make sure he's good enough for you."

"Hey!" Emily scolds him. "Turn it down a notch, will you? She's an adult, and so is Grady, why are you suddenly so interested in their love lives?"

"She's my little sister and he's my best friend. It's my job to be in the know."

Emily laughs. "Yeah, it's really not. You need to stay out of it. We will meet the people in their lives when they're ready for us to meet them."

"Really? What if it was one of your sisters?"

"Samantha is dating someone," she tells him. "Some guy she met at a coffee shop."

"Why didn't you tell me?" he asks her.

"I didn't realize I was supposed to."

"They're going to be my sisters. I need to check this guy out," he tells her.

"Caleb, I love you, but you're too damn nosey."

"Agreed," Grady and I say at the same time. The four of us burst into laughter.

When we get back to the house, the party is still in full swing, not that I expected anything different. Caleb and Emily get stopped by my aunt asking about wedding plans. I keep walking. Grady's parents have a small pond at the back of their lot, and that's where I'm headed. Just to get away from it all for a few minutes. To get away from him and the pull he has toward me. The night is clear, and there seems to be a million stars in the sky. The further I get from the house, the more they become prominent in the night sky. Looking ahead with just the light of the moon, I see it, the scene of the crime also known as the camper. The one where my relationship with Grady took a turn. If you had asked me three months ago, I would have said for the worse, but now I'm starting to realize that we just weren't ready. We were both so young and were enrolled in colleges states away. I'd like to believe that things are working out as they should.

We're together now.

It's still hard for me to believe, but every time he kisses me, sends me a text telling me he loves me, my heart melts and in my mind, I know he's not just saving face. He's putting in way too much effort to just be worried about the fallout from my brother. In fact, I believe him when he says he doesn't care how it turns out as long as we're together. I know he would be crushed to lose Caleb. I also know losing me is not a risk he's willing to take to keep that from happening.

It's in this moment I realize I've let it go. I forgave him weeks ago, but the pain, it's still there in the shadows, but the love he showers me with everyday mutes the effects it once had on me.

"Hey, beautiful." He wraps his strong arms around me. "What are you doing out here all by yourself?"

"Did you follow me?"

"You know I did." His lips press against my neck, and I tilt my head, giving him better access. We have to take advantage of these stolen moments while we can.

"Did anyone see you?"

"No, but I don't care if they did."

We're both quiet for a few minutes. The sound of the party filters its way to us through the night air. "That brings back memories, huh?" I point to the camper.

"Yeah," he agrees softly.

"Can we go inside?"

"It might be locked, but we can check." He pulls away and laces his fingers through mine, and together we approach the door of the camper. With a slight tug, it comes open. Grady looks at me over his shoulder and grins. "After you." He steps back, allowing me to enter the camper in front of him.

As soon as I step through the door, the memories of that night assault me. The feeling of being wanted, not just being wanted, but it was Grady who wanted me. How it felt to be skin to skin with him, the way he was so gentle when he slid inside of me for the first time. All of it, every single second of that night was a fairy tale. All except the end when I woke up to find him gone.

"Don't think about it," he says, wrapping his arms around me from behind. "Don't let that night dictate our future."

"It does though. That's where we started. No matter what happened between then and now, it's always going to be a part of who we are." We're both quiet for a few minutes when I say, "Maybe once it all blows over, it will be a funny story to tell our kids one day." He stills behind me, and I'm worried I've said the wrong thing.

He releases me and moves to step in front of me. With gentle hands, he cradles my face. "What does that mean, baby? I'm trying really fucking hard to not let my mind make up its own meaning."

"What do you want it to mean?"

"That you're mine. That you believe me when I tell you that I'll love you forever. That you're ready to stop hiding us, that I can hold you and kiss you any time I want."

"Then you would be right—" I don't get to finish what I'm going to say before his lips crash into mine. I open for him, getting my first taste of the day. Nothing compares to kissing Grady.

"But," I say with a peck to his lips and pulling away, "I want to wait until after the wedding. I don't want to ruin their big day for any reason. So, as soon as the wedding is over, and the honeymoon, we'll tell them. I know that's a few more weeks, but I can't stand the thought of ruining that moment for them."

"How long until the wedding?" he asks, trailing kisses down my neck.

"Uh, three. Three weeks until the wedding."

"How long is the honeymoon?" More kisses.

"A w-week. A week in Mexico."

"So, a month. One month and I get to tell the world that you're mine?"

"If that's what you want."

"Baby, you know that's what I want." He nips at my ear. "You know what else I want?"

"What?"

"You. Now. I want you here."

"What if they come looking for us?" I ask, even though I'm already sold on the idea.

"Don't care. Let them find us."

"Grady," I sigh.

"Shh, let me make love to you. This time, I'll be there when you wake up. Maybe not here in the camper, but at home in my bed. I'll be there with you wrapped so tightly in my arms you'll have to fight to break free."

"Not here. I want to, trust me I do. I just… I want to be in your bed. I want to be able to roll over and fall asleep in your arms. We can't do that here, and the risk of getting caught is too much."

"Fine," he says, sliding his hand under my shirt and pinching my nipple. "Then we leave now."

"That's kind of obvious, don't you think?"

"Nope. I have to work tomorrow, and your ride left you. You're tired and calling it a night." My shirt is lifted, and the cup of my bra is pulled down, and his lips latch onto me. He tugs with his teeth and soothes the ache with his tongue.

My hands find their way to his hair and I hold him to me. "We can't do this, not here," I say, even though my grip on him says otherwise.

"You sure about that?" He moves to the other breast and lavishes it with attention.

"Y-yes, I'm sure."

"Then we're leaving." Pulling away, he tucks my breasts back into my bra and rearranges my tank top. "I love you," he says, kissing my lips.

"I love you, too."

"Here's the plan. You head back, claim to have a headache. I'll join you later to say goodbye since I have to work in the morning. I'll offer you a ride home. It makes sense us being neighbors and all."

"Okay."

One more chaste kiss, and he guides me out of the camper. "Be careful walking back."

"It's not that far," I counter.

"Just humor me." Another kiss and I leave.

When I reach the houses, I hear my dad and Grady's laughter, so I follow the sound. I find them on the back deck of Grady's house.

"There she is," my mom says. "Caleb and Emily were looking for you. They headed home."

"Yeah, I was upstairs in my old room. I have a headache. I'm going to call a cab to take me home."

"Why do you need to call a cab? I've not seen you drink tonight," Mom inquires.

"I rode here with Tabby. She left early for a date. I was just going to have Caleb drop me off at home."

"Grady," his dad calls over my shoulder. "Can you take Collins home? She's not feeling well," his dad asks, not having the first clue that he's playing right into the scenario we were trying to create.

"Sure. I was just coming to say goodbye anyway. I have to be at work tomorrow."

"Where have you been?" his mom asks.

"Work called. A patient I was treating yesterday… they had questions about the history."

"Well, Caleb said to call him. He and Emily left about ten minutes ago," his mom tells him.

"I'll call him after work tomorrow," he responds. "You ready to go? Need help carrying anything?" He already knows that I was here last night helping Mom before Tabby and I had our girls' night. He's too good at this.

"I'm good." I hug my parents, then his, and follow him to his SUV that's parked next to their garage. Without a word, I climb into the passenger seat and rest my head back against the seat, closing my eyes. I don't know who's watching. Not just that, but the desire that's coursing through my veins is within lethal limits. I'm trying to prevent myself from pouncing on him as soon as we pull out of the drive.

When his hand rests on my thigh, I open my eyes and turn to look at him. "You okay?"

"Yeah, just wasn't sure if anyone was watching."

"Dad made it too easy." He gives me a wink and a grin, and I pinch myself on the leg to make sure I'm not dreaming. The pain is there, so this must be real.

Chapter 33

GRADY

"DO YOU NEED ANYTHING FROM your place?" I ask Collins as we head into the building.

"Yeah, I need to get some clothes to change into. I should probably take a shower as well."

"We'll stop and grab some clothes. Then we can shower at my place." I'm expecting her to tell me she can just come over after, but she surprises me when she agrees. I wait for her to unlock her apartment door and follow her back the hall to her room. She tosses a tote bag on the bed and throws in some clothes before disappearing into the bathroom. I grab another set of bra and panties, T-shirt, and lounge pants and toss them in the bag. A set for just because. Besides, I like the idea of her things being there mixed in with mine.

"What are these?" she asks, holding up the clothes I added.

"Just extras to leave at my place." I'm again prepared for her to tell me that it's too soon, but she just shrugs, tosses them in the bag, and to my surprise, adds a few more items such as socks and some pajama pants. She's not going to need them, but it's more of her at my place, so I don't bother mentioning that little tidbit of information.

"You ready?"

"Yes."

Standing from the bed, I throw the bag over my shoulder, reach for her hand, and lead her out of her place, making sure the door locks behind us, and into mine. "Go ahead and unpack. There are a couple of drawers in the dresser and room in the closet for your stuff. Same goes for the bathroom."

"What are you going to do?"

"Caleb just texted me." I hold up my phone to show her. "I'm going to call him back before he comes over here."

"What does he want?"

"He wants to know where I ran off to and if I happened to see you since he couldn't find you, and your parents are not answering their phones."

"I'll be quiet." She stands on tiptoes and kisses the corner of my mouth before disappearing down the hall toward our room. Yes, I said our room. Everything that is mine is hers. No question.

I dial his number, never taking my eyes off her until she disappears down the hall. "Hey, man," I say when he picks up.

"Hey, did you see Collins? We tried to find her before we left. Mom and Dad are not answering, and I'm kind of worried over here."

"I saw her. She was talking to our parents as I was leaving. She was calling a cab to come get her because she had a headache. Dad asked me to bring her home. I was coming home anyway since I have to work tomorrow."

"So, she's home?"

"Yeah, just dropped her off. Made sure she was in before I came to my place." The lie tastes sour on my lips, but it's what she wants. At least, I know that we have an end in sight. As soon as they're back from the honeymoon, this will all be out in the open, consequences be damned.

"Where were you? I tried to find you."

He doesn't sound suspicious, which is a good thing. Just curious like my nosey lawyer friend tends to be. He always needs the details, always has. That's part of what makes him a good attorney. "I stepped into the house. I got a call from work about a patient's history." Another lie, but I just keep reminding myself it's not to hurt anyone, and, in the end, it will all be worth it.

"Got ya. Well, it was good to see you, man. Sucks that you have to work tomorrow. I'll be thinking about you," he jokes.

"Yeah, yeah. Live it up while you can. Once that new job of yours starts, your free time will be gone, too."

"As long as I have my wife, I'm good with it. Catch ya later, man. I'm gonna call Collins and see if she needs anything." And with that, the line goes dead.

I walk through and turn off the lights. As I enter my room, I hear her answer her phone. I'm trying not to be pissed off that he thinks I wouldn't take care of her, but I have to remind myself that he doesn't know that she's mine. Not yet. Fuck, this secrecy thing is killing me.

"Yeah, I'm good," she tells him. "Just a headache. No, I don't need anything. Grady checked before he dropped me off." She smiles over at me and instantly my ruffled feathers are once again smooth. Walking across the room, I stand behind her and wrap my arms around her waist. Resting my chin on top of her head, I hold her while she talks to him. "I'm good, promise. I'm just going to call it a night. I'm getting ready for bed now." She's quiet while he replies. "Night."

"He's going to be pissed," I tell her.

"He is."

"I hate that you're going to be in the middle of that and on the receiving end of his anger, but damn if I can let you go. Not now, not ever."

"We're in this together, right? We just explain we wanted to take it slow, and once it happened, we didn't want to ruin their wedding, which is all true."

"Ready for a shower?" I ask, changing the subject. I never should have brought it up in the first place. I don't want her to think about any of that right now. Her answer is to hold her hand out for me and lead us into the bathroom. My lips are on her as soon as her feet stop moving.

Turning in my arms, she smiles up at me. Her eyes are blue flames of desire. "I never thought we'd get here."

"I hoped." She raises her hands over her head, and I strip her out of her tank top. Underneath, she's wearing a sheer white bra. I've seen it in the moonlight, but here it's even more iridescent. Reaching behind her back, I unclasp her bra, slowly pulling the straps down one shoulder at a time before letting it fall at our feet.

Her hands slide under my shirt, and I lift my arms, bending over and helping her remove my shirt. She surprises me when her arms wrap around my waist, and she hugs me tightly. Moving one hand to the back of her neck, the other traces her back. Her skin is silky softness under my fingertips.

"I love you." The words fall freely from my mouth, and no truer words have ever been spoken.

Big blue eyes peer up at me. "I love you, too." She steps out of my hold and discards her shorts and panties all at once. "You've got some catching up to do." She quirks an eyebrow, causing me to laugh.

Reaching behind her, I turn on the shower, letting the water warm before ridding myself of the rest of my clothes. Bending, I place my hands on the backs of her thighs and lift her. Her legs wrap around my waist as I step under the spray. My mouth slants over hers. She opens for me, trusting and giving me all that she is. Sliding my tongue past her lips, I explore her mouth. I take my time devouring her, giving myself time to commit this to memory. The feel of her slick wet body molded against mine, the taste of her on my tongue... I never want to forget a single detail about this moment.

I can feel it. She's all in. It's a turning point for us, and when I make love to her in our bed, everything is going to be different than before. She's going to know that when she wakes up, I'll still be there. I'm going to know that when I wake up, she's really mine. She's not just a dream, a wish of what-ifs. She's real, she's my heart, and I wouldn't have it any other way.

Leisurely, my tongue traces hers, exploring her, just enjoying having her here in my arms. "I'm glad you're here," I say what I've been thinking.

"Where else would I be?" She rests her head on my shoulder.

"Nowhere, baby. This is where you belong."

Lifting her head, she smiles shyly. "Will you make love to me?"

My cock throbs, wanting to do just that. "I am. But not here." I can see the question in her eyes. "Our first time, I was an asshole. I took you and then left. This time, it's going to be in our bed, and I'm not leaving you." I set her back on her feet.

Without a word, she reaches for her bodywash and begins to wash off the day. I take a step away from her and do the same. Together, we shower as if it's the most normal thing in the world. And it will be, once I can convince her to move in with me. This is how we need to start every single day. Why would I need caffeine when I have Collins?

Once we're rinsed off, I turn off the water and step out. Grabbing a towel, I wrap it around my waist then grab another, draping it over her shoulders. "I need one for my hair." Grabbing another, I run it over her hair.

"I can dry my hair, Grady," she says with a chuckle.

"So can I." I kiss the tip of her nose. "I like taking care of you."

"You don't have to take care of me. That's not what this is about."

"No, you're right. I don't have to. I want to. There's a big difference between the two. I feel no obligation. It's more of a need on my part. I like knowing I can do nice things for you."

"Just love me," she whispers.

"That's something you never have to ask of me." We finish drying, turn off the lights, and find our way back to my room in the darkness. I go straight to the bed, tugging back the covers, "Climb in," I say, following in behind her. "Come here." I pull her close, aligning her naked body with mine. "I have no expectations for tonight. I just want you here, in this bed with me all night long. If we could keep the clothes on the bathroom floor, that's a plus but not a requirement."

She giggles. "This is easy. Being with you like this."

"It's supposed to be."

"We're good at it."

"Yeah, you know, except for the lying to our families part."

"I feel guilty, too, but with the wedding so close, I don't want to ruin it. I would be pissed at Caleb if he did that to me. And Emily... I don't want to ruin her big day. It's just a few more weeks. We have an end in sight."

We're both quiet after that. I'm not sure what she's thinking, but I'm just enjoying holding her like this. I used to lie in bed at night and imagine what it would be like to have her in my life like this. I'd dream about it, and let me tell you, dreams and reality are two very different things.

I'm startled out of my thoughts when I feel her small hand grip my dick. "Collins?"

"You promised."

"Tell me this is what you want. I made a promise to myself that night that if I ever got you back, I would always do right by you. That includes giving you all the time you need."

"I want you to make love to me." Her delicate hand strokes me slowly from root to tip, causing me to groan. "Or we could just do this," she says with another stroke.

"As good as that feels, that's not going to work for me. It's been too damn long, baby."

"You've really not been with anyone since that night?"

"No. Not even a kiss. Had a few who tried, but they weren't you. I wish I could explain it to you, but I don't really have the words. That night, being inside of you, it changed me. I knew no one would measure up so why bother. Besides, I was working my ass off to get my choice of residency, so I could come home to you. That was always my end game."

"I've never wanted anyone but you," she whispers as she continues to stroke me.

I place my hand over hers, stopping her movement. Her words along with her soft hands have me ready to come unglued. Rolling on top of her, she opens for me, so my thighs are nestled between hers. Resting my weight on my elbows, I run my fingers through her hair, moving it out of her eyes. The dim light of the moon makes her creamy skin look even more flawless. I lower my mouth to hers and kiss her softly, taking my time, savoring her.

"Grady," she breathes against my lips. "I need you."

"I need you, too." I circle my hips to show her just how much.

"Please," she begs.

"I need to grab a condom." I bought a new box when I moved in, never wanting to be unprepared should this moment present itself.

"I've only ever been with you."

"What are you saying, Collins?"

"I'm on the pill, and it's only ever been you."

"There's been no one since you, baby."

"Make love to me, Grady," she whispers in my ear.

Pulling back, I align myself at her entrance. "You sure about this?"

"Never been more sure about anything."

Her legs clamp around my waist and with the pressure of her hold, I slide home. Home, a place I've only been once before but never forgot what it felt like. My pulse races, and my heart pounds. I want to move, but if I do, I'll lose it. I'll spill over inside of her, and this is over before it ever really began.

"Move," she breathes.

"I can't," I say through gritted teeth. "You're so fucking tight, and warm, and if I move, I'm going to come."

"We have all night, right? I mean, that's what you said," she backtracks.

"We have all night, Collins. We have the rest of our lives, and I plan to be here…" I pull out and slowly push back in. "…more times than either of us will be able to count." Again, I pull out then push back in, this time a little faster, a little harder than before, and soon we have a steady rhythm. Flipping us over, I look up at her. Her hair hangs over her shoulders, hands resting on my abs, legs straddling my thighs. She's fucking perfect. "You take control. You set the pace," I tell her.

"I've never… I mean, I-I don't know what to do."

I want to beat on my chest like a caveman. It's only ever been me inside of her. I'm the only one who gets to see her this way, feel her warmth, capture her moans with my lips. It's all just for me. There is nothing in life that tops this feeling. "Do what feels good." I place my hands on her hips and begin to slowly rock her back and forth. It doesn't take her long to catch on and find her rhythm.

"T-that's good," she says, closing her eyes and tilting her head back. Her hair cascades down her back and brushes across my thighs. My cock jerks inside of her, causing her to moan deep in the back of her throat.

Keeping one hand on her hip, I bite down on my bottom lip, trying to control my orgasm. Her perfect tits are bouncing with each rock of her hips. Her walls are pulsing around and keeping a tight hold on my cock. It's sensation overload, and I'm about to blow. Needing to get her there, I place my thumb over her clit and rotate in small circles.

"W-what are you doing?" Her tempo doesn't falter.

"I'm getting you there." My voice is thick and husky with need. I'm ready to lose it. I don't know how much longer I can hang on. She swivels her hips as she cups her breasts in her hands. I watch as she pinches her already puckered nipples with her thumb and forefinger, giving them a gentle tug. I work her clit faster. I'm about to go without her, and I can't have that. "I'm close, baby."

"I-I'm…. Ahhh!" she shouts as her walls clench around my cock, and I lose all control, spilling inside of her. Pulse after pulse course through me, sending jolts up my spine. My memories of our one and only time together didn't do justice to the real thing. I remember the details of that night, and how she felt like coming home, but with time that feeling faded.

Until now.

I remember her warmth.

I remember what it feels like to hover over her, her big blue eyes staring up at me.

Trust.

I remember what it was like to have her trust that night, and tonight is no different. She never would have let me inside of her otherwise. There will never be anyone for me but her.

Sitting up, I wrap my arms around her and hold her tightly. My cock jerks inside of her, and she moans. Burying my face in her neck, I breathe her in.

"Grady," she says softly. Pulling back, I look into her eyes. "I-I love you," she says, her voice cracking with emotion.

"I love you, too." My already racing heart skips at her whispered confession. "Hey, what's with the tears?" I can see her eyes shimmering in the moonlight.

"I never thought we'd be here. I wanted to hate you, but I just couldn't, so I was resolved to loving you from a distance, and now this. These are happy tears."

"I don't like tears on you. Period," I say, kissing one cheek and then the other. Wrapping my arms around her, I tell her with my body what she means to me. My grip is firm, letting her know that she's where I need her to be. In my arms. Always.

I hold her until she says, "I should go clean up." Before I can stop her, she's lifting up on her knees and swinging her legs over. Her bare feet pad across the floor and out the bedroom door and into the bathroom. The light flicks on and I know I should go to her, but something tells me she needs some time. Instead, I grab my towel from our earlier shower and clean up before climbing back in bed. Just when I think I need to go look for her, I hear the bathroom door open, and she's back in my room, climbing under the covers.

"Come here, you." I hold my arms open, and she snuggles up next to me. "You okay?" She doesn't answer right away, and worry starts to take hold inside of me. This can't be it for us.

"I am. I can't remember a time when I've been this happy and content with where my life is going. I know we have Caleb to worry about, but… I feel like with you by my side, everything will work out."

Placing a kiss on top of her head, I tighten my grip. I can't seem to ever have her close enough. "We make a great team, you and me." She kisses my bare chest. "We're going to have more nights like this, Collins. More snuggling and making love. Sure, once we have kids it's going to change, but there are so many more nights with you in my arms that we have to look forward to."

"There is zero hesitation in your voice," she points out.

"Why would there be? It's you, the love of my life that I see in my future. Nothing has ever looked better."

"Who would have thought, Grady Carmichael, a closet romantic."

I chuckle. "Only for you, baby. Only for you."

"I'm going to hold you to that," she says over a yawn.

"Night, beautiful."

"Night."

We drift off to sleep, happy, sated, and exactly how we should have three years ago. This time, there will be a different outcome. This time it's forever.

Chapter 34

Collins

THERE IS SOMETHING TO BE said about being woke up with kisses. Kisses to the shoulder. Kisses to the neck. All kinds of kisses. There is even more to be said about the giver of those kisses.

Grady.

"I know you're tired, baby, and I promise you can go right back to sleep, but I need you to wake up for me. I can't leave for work until I know for certain that you know I stayed with you. Open those baby blues for me, Collins."

Forcing my eyes open, I roll over and snuggle into him. "Morning," I say groggily.

He chuckles. "Morning, beautiful." He touches his lips to my forehead. "I need to go or I'm going to be late. I left a key on the counter for you. Stay as long as you want, or hell, move in. I'll be home around six to help with the heavy lifting."

"Funny man. Why do I need a key?" I ask over a yawn.

"Because I want you here, and with my shit hours, I never know when I'm going to be home for certain, so if you need to be in here to get anything you left or to leave more"—he winks—"I want you to be able to get inside."

"Okay."

"That's it, okay? You're not going to argue with me and tell me how it's too soon?"

"Nope."

"Really? And to what do I owe this change of heart?"

"I'm tired of fighting it. I want what I want, and there's no changing that."

"And what do you want?" he asks, sliding his hand up my bare leg.

"You." It's a simple answer to a complex question. One word sums it all up. I just want him, anyway that I can have him.

"I love you, and if I could get out of work today, I would, but unfortunately, that's not happening."

"Go, be awesome, save lives, and all that. Text me when you are on your way home, and I love you, too."

He kisses me hard on the lips before jumping off the bed and grabbing his phone from the nightstand. "Have a good day, dear," he calls over his shoulder.

I listen for the door to close then snuggle back into his fluffy cloud of a bed and catch a few more hours of sleep.

When I wake a few hours later, the sun is shining brightly through the window. Reaching for my phone, I see it's a little after ten. It's been ages since I've slept this late. I also see missed text messages from Grady.

Grady: I hated leaving you.

Grady: You must still be sleeping. Good. I like knowing you're still in my bed.

I smile before I respond.

Me: Just woke up. Hope you're having a good day.

Grady: It's not too terrible. Would be better if I was there with you.

Grady:	Stay in bed. Be there when I get home.
Me:	I can't stay in your bed all day.
Grady:	A man can dream.
Me:	Get back to work, Dr. Carmichael.
Grady:	Love you.
Me:	You, too.

Setting my phone on the nightstand, I climb out of bed and head to the shower. I take my time because really, I have nowhere to be today. My laundry is caught up, and the apartment is clean. Looking around Grady's place, I decide to tidy it up a little for him. He's been working six days a week and spending all his spare time with me. In the past few weeks, I've spent more time here than I have my own place. It's the least I can do.

I start in the bedroom and notice the pile of laundry. I go ahead and throw a load in the washer while I'm at it. I'm here so I might as well. Once I dust, I change the sheets, of which I was shocked he had an extra set in the hall closet. It has his mom written all over it. I then run the vacuum around and make my way to the bathroom. Before I realize it, I've cleaned the entire apartment and did three loads of laundry. It's still only two in the afternoon, and I'm starving. Going to the kitchen and opening the fridge, there is nothing. Poor guy hasn't even had time to go to the store. Grabbing my purse and keys, which now includes the one he left for me, I lock up and head to my place.

Taking a quick inventory, as well as the list that Tabby has on the fridge, I decide to go shopping. Two hours later, I'm pulling into our complex with a trunk full of groceries for both places. It takes me forever to get them all unloaded and put away. I'm just putting the milk into the refrigerator at Grady's when my phone rings. I smile when I see his picture pop up.

"Hey, you. How's your day?"

"Long, I'm going to be here a little later than I thought. The resident who is replacing me is running late."

"That makes for a long day. What time is he supposed to be there?"

"Around eight. I guess his car broke down, or he had a flat tire or something. I didn't really ask questions. Just told them I would stay, not that I have much of a choice being a first-year resident, and called you."

"Well, keep me updated. I'd planned on making us dinner tonight."

He groans. "I'm starving."

"Did you not eat lunch?"

"Not yet. It's been too busy."

Looking at the clock on the microwave, I see it's almost five. "Anything I can do?"

"Just be there when I get home. You're the best part of each day."

"I can do that. Call me if anything changes."

"Will do, babe. I gotta go. Love you." And just like that, the line goes dead.

I had planned on making a chicken pot pie for dinner, nothing outlandish. Just some pot pie style soup and Bisquick, easy peasy. Maybe I should make it and take him dinner? Then people will see that I'm there and ask questions, and I'm sure all kinds of red flags will fly when they find out I was there for him. Sexy Dr. Carmichael that all the nurses are swooning over. It's a gamble, but I hate the thought that he hasn't eaten all day. Needing another opinion, I text Tabby.

Me: Hey, you got a minute.

Tabby: Yep, what's up.

Me: Grady just called. He's stuck at work and hasn't eaten all day.

Me: I kinda want to take him some food.

Tabby: Okay?

Me: It will look bad, right? Like we're a thing?

Tabby: You are a thing.

Me: I know that and you know that but no one else does.

Tabby: Just blow it off as you grew up together. He's your big bro's BFF.

I think about that, and it could work. I could go with the friend of the family angle. Hell, I've already used it a few times when people talk about him.

Tabby: And you're neighbors.

Tabby: And coworkers. Just do it.

Me: I'm gonna do it. I'll leave some for you in the fridge as well.

Tabby: Go get 'em!

Tabby: What are we having?

Me: Chicken Pot Pie

Tabby: Yum! Thanks. Let me know how it goes.

Leaving his place and heading back to mine, I start dinner. This version of chicken pot pie is seriously the easiest thing to make ever. Once I slide it in the oven, I set out a container, and pull my lunch bag from off the top of the fridge. I add napkins, a fork, and for dessert, a Little Debbie Oatmeal Cream Pie, because who doesn't love an oatmeal cream pie? While dinner is baking, I go to Tabby's room and see if she has any laundry. I help her out from time to time since I have so many days off in a week. Working three twelve-hour days is a bitch, but being off the remainder of the week, not so much. I throw in a load of her scrubs and write her a note on the fridge, reminding her to put them in the dryer when she gets home. If she gets off work on time, which is a rarity. I might pass her as I'm leaving.

With Grady's lunch packed, the leftovers covered on the stove for Tabby, I scarf down a small portion and head out the door. The drive to the hospital feels weird this time of day. It takes me no time to get there as traffic is heavy in the opposite direction. I know that Grady is working on the fourth floor, which is the intensive care unit, so I hit number four on the elevator. Taking a deep breath, I slowly exhale. I've got this.

As soon as I'm off the elevator, I see Mary, the head night nurse. "Collins, what are you doing here? You come to work?" She looks over my street clothes and answers her own question. "Guess not." She laughs.

"Hey, Mary. I'm here to bring dinner to Dr. Carmichael; his mom knew he was working late." The lie falls out of my mouth before I can stop it. They just keep adding up.

"Oh, how sweet. I didn't realize you knew him?"

"Yeah, we grew up together. He and my brother are best friends."

"Well, I can tell you he's easy on the eyes that one. The nurses all love him."

"He's a good guy, you know, beyond his handsome good looks."

"You think I'm handsome?" I jump at the sound of his voice.

Turning, I smile up at him. "You know you are. Your uh, mom said you were working late and thought you might be hungry. I offered to drop it off for her."

"She did, did she?" He smirks.

"Luckily, I have a few minutes. Come sit with me while I eat?"

"Sure." I turn back to Mary. "Bye, Mary."

I follow Grady to the break room, neither one of us saying a word. When we get there, there's a nurse, I think her name is Sasha, who is eating alone.

"Oh, Dr. Carmichael, we can eat together. I hate eating alone." She stands to join him when I step to the side so she can see me.

"Hi." I wave awkwardly. She gives me a dirty look like I just kicked her puppy.

"Sure, you can join us," Grady tells her.

I want to protest, but I remind myself that this was my decision. If I left it up to Grady, the entire hospital would already know that we're together. Just a few more weeks. We can do this for a few more weeks.

"So, she thought you would be hungry. There's chicken pot pie, and a Little Debbie for dessert," I tell him, my face heating.

"How do you two know each other?" Sasha blurts. "Did you make him dinner?"

"No, we grew up together." I'm quick to correct her, and I see the way his face falls. "He and my older brother are best friends."

"I see." She smiles, assuming she's back in the game. She's not. Not even close.

"Thank you for bringing this."

"I don't mind. So, how has your day been?" I try to make small talk that won't give us away. I want to lean into him, give him a hug, maybe a kiss, but then there's Sasha.

"It's been crazy today. Then when Martin called and said he was going to be late, I had to miss dinner."

"Well, now you can refuel."

"Thank you, Collins, really. This was sweet of you." He digs in, taking a huge bite. "This is delicious."

"You act like you've never had your mom's cooking before," Sasha smarts off. She's miffed she's not getting his attention I'm sure.

"I haven't eaten all day," he tells her before turning to look at me. "Thank you." His voice is softer. "You didn't have to bring this."

"I wanted to," I tell him honestly.

Someone I've never met before pops their head in the room. "Sasha, we need you. Wasn't your break over like ten minutes ago?" she asks.

"Yeah, I-uh sorry. Lost track of time." Grady keeps on shoveling in food, which makes me glad I decided to come. Sasha gathers her things and slips out of the room, embarrassed I'm sure.

"She wants you," I tell him.

He nods. "I know, but she's not getting me."

I'm shocked by his answer. "You know?"

"Yeah, she's hit on me a few times, asked me to lunch, but I always turn her down."

"Why didn't you tell me?"

"Nothing to tell, Collins. She's nothing to me, and never will be." Reaching over, he runs his finger along my jaw. "You're all I see."

"Eat your dinner," I say, pulling back.

"Are you mad?" He stares at me with his mouth hanging open.

"No, but it pisses me off."

"Well, there's nothing I can do about that. You insisted we keep us a secret. I can tell her I have a girlfriend all day long, but girls like her, they don't care. They see that I'm a doctor and want to latch on. Think it will be an easy ride through life."

"You still getting off around eight?"

"If Martin shows up. Thank you for this, really." He places the lid back on the container and tears into the pie. "I need to get back to work. It's been nonstop all day."

"I don't want to keep you. I just wanted you to eat."

"Thank you, baby." He leans in and presses his lips to mine. "Will you be there when I get home?"

"Yes." There really is no other place I'd rather be. We work together to pack up the empty dish, and with one more quick kiss, I'm following him out of the break room. When I pass the nurses' station, Sasha is there and glares at me. I smile widely, wave, and keep on walking. I want to scream and yell that he's mine, but I trust him, so there's no need. He's been all in since the day he got back to town. This time, things are different. I can feel it.

Chapter 35

GRADY

EIGHT O'CLOCK TURNED INTO TEN, and by the time I had finished charting and passed on my patients, it was almost eleven thirty. That's why I'm just now walking through the door a few minutes before midnight. I'd texted Collins and kept her updated. She said she was going home, but I begged her to stay. Nothing is better than coming home to her. She didn't commit either way, just told me to be safe. I don't bother with the lights until I reach the bathroom. I turn that light on and start the shower, then walk back out of the room and to my bedroom door. Peering inside, I see her curled up sleeping peacefully. My shoulders relax and the tension from the day rolls away.

Just because she's here.

Making my way back to the bathroom, I strip down and step under the hot spray. In medical school, they tell you stories about residency. Long hours, asshole attendings, and when your peers don't pull their weight that leaves you to do it all on your own. It's not that I didn't believe the stories, I did. It's altogether different when you experience it firsthand. I've been lucky in my short stint so far. The attendings have been nice, and the staff as well. There are a few nurses who keep hitting on me, some more obvious than others. I don't give them any hope. I tell them I'm taken. They don't even pique my interest, not when I know I get to come home to her.

Collins.

I still can't believe she's let me back into her life after walking away like I did. I knew she was different. I'll never take her for granted. That's why when Sasha hit on me again tonight, I took it to my attending. Luckily, that happened to be Laura Smithfield. When I told her that Sasha was coming on too strong, touches here and there, badgering me about getting a drink, she didn't once question me. I made sure to tell her that I was in a committed relationship, one that if I had anything to do with it would go the distance. She assured me she would handle it. I didn't see Sasha again. My guess is her shift ended, but I hope she backs off. I could tell that she made Collins uncomfortable, and since they both work there, and in just a few short weeks everyone will know she's mine, this needs to be handled.

Toweling off, I hit the light and head across the hall to my room. Quietly, not wanting to wake her, I slide into bed. Instantly, she snuggles up next to me. "Missed you," she mumbles.

I hug her tightly to my chest and kiss the top of her head. That's the last thing I remember before exhaustion takes over and I drift off to sleep.

I'm jolted awake when I feel her pull away from me. I tighten my hold and bury my face in her neck. "Where are you going?" I mumble.

"I have to pee," she replies with soft laughter.

"Come right back." I kiss her neck and reluctantly release her. She climbs out of bed and scurries across the hall to the bathroom.

The bed feels cold without her. Hell, I'm cold without her snuggled up against me. When she comes back into the room, I hold the covers up for her, and she dives under them, taking her spot, resting her head against my chest.

"It's cold in here."

"I have the air set pretty low. It's hot as hell outside."

"It's like an ice box."

"I bet I can warm you up," I tell her.

"Hmmm, you think so?" She places a tender kiss to my chest.

"I know so."

"Maybe once you've gotten some more sleep."

"Sleep? Who needs sleep when I have you in my arms?"

"You have to go to work in a couple of hours."

"Nope. I'm off today."

"I thought you had to work."

"Me, too, but Sally needed to switch, so I'm off until Sunday."

"Really? I get you for two days in a row? Whatever will we do?"

"We," I say, kissing her temple, "are not leaving this bed for forty-eight hours."

"I'm thinking that's unrealistic. A girl's gotta eat," she teases.

"Fine," I sigh as if giving into her is killing me. "I amend my statement. We're not leaving this apartment. We'll just order takeout."

"We can cook," she counters.

"If we cook, we have to go to the store."

"I went yesterday. I went for Tabby and me, and picked up some things for you, too."

Just when I think she can't be anymore amazing. "What else did you do while I was slaving away at the hospital?"

"Well, I cleaned this place, did your laundry, just stuff that needed done."

"Baby, while I appreciate all of that, more than you know, you're my girlfriend, not my maid."

"I know, but I was here and had all of my stuff caught up. I wanted to do something nice for you."

"I thought the sheets smelled good last night. I just assumed it was you."

"Wait." She raises her head to look at me. "What did you switch her?"

"What?"

"Sally, you said she needed to switch. What did you switch her?"

"Oh, I was off next Wednesday, and it's her son's birthday. I'm working Wednesday, and she's working for me today."

"They just let you do that? Switch when you want?"

"Well, we have to get the chief resident's approval, but yeah. We can do that."

"Good to know."

"Now, you go back to sleep while I make us some breakfast."

"I was thinking I would have you for breakfast," I say, flipping her over and settling my thighs between hers.

"As great as that sounds, we need real food."

"Okay," I relent. "We can have it your way after I have it mine." I move to the bottom of the bed, gently gripping her ankles, and pull her to the edge. My hands run up her legs. "These have gotta go," I tell her once I reach her booty shorts she loves to sleep in.

"You think you can help me, Doctor?" Her voice is breathy, and I love knowing that she's already turned on. That she wants this as much as I do.

"Why Nurse Ward, I'd be happy to." Sliding my fingers under the waistband of her tight-as-hell shorts, which really look like underwear with more fabric, I slide them and her thong down her legs. I toss them over my shoulder.

"Hey, I just cleaned," she scolds.

My reply is to kiss her just above her pussy, where I know she really wants me. Lifting my head, I find her leaning on her elbows watching me. My dick pulses. "I'll make it up to you," I tell her before running my tongue up her slit.

"Oh," she moans and falls back to the bed.

I don't stop. I feast on her, just like I told her I would. When she squirms, I add the pulse of my fingers inside of her. In and out, slow and steady. My tongue traces every inch of her, tasting, licking, nipping at her pussy like it's my last meal.

"Grady," she moans.

I pull back and lick my lips. "What do you need, baby?"

"You, I need you inside of me."

"I'm inside of you." I push in two fingers to prove my point.

She half laughs, half moans. "That's not exactly what I meant," she pants.

"Tell me what you meant, Collins." I graze her clit with my thumb. "You want me to stop?" I stop all movement, and she groans.

"Y-you know that's not what I want," she says; her voice is scolding.

"Tell me, baby. What do you want?"

"I want you to fuck me," she says, her voice rising.

My hand once again begins to move inside of her, faster than before. "Like this?"

"No. Damnit, Grady." Her body jolts when I press my thumb against her clit and begin to rub in small circles.

Pushing herself back up on her elbows, she peers down at me. Her eyes are hooded with desire. "I want you to remove your fingers and replace them with your cock."

"Why didn't you just say so?" I smile cheekily. Bending, I swipe my tongue over her clit one more time before removing my mouth and my fingers and standing. She wastes no time wrapping her legs around my waist and pulling me into her.

"Finally," she says, exasperated, causing me to chuckle.

"Baby, if you wanted my cock, all you had to do was tell me." I align myself at her entrance. "You ready?" Her reply is to squeeze her legs, instigating me to move forward and my cock to slide inside of her.

"Finally," she breathes.

Leaning in close, I take her lips with mine. She opens for me, her tongue ready for the battle with my own as she kisses me back. When we come up for air, her eyes are blue flames staring at me.

"I don't want you to be soft and slow, Grady. I want you to take me. I want to feel you everywhere."

My cock pulses inside of her. Hands on her thighs, I push for her to let me free and slide out of her warmth. "Turn over, on your knees," I say, my voice gruff with desire. She doesn't even hesitate as she turns over, settles on her knees with her ass in the air. "Spread your legs." She does as I ask. I grip the globes of her ass and pull and step in a little closer. Without warning, I grip my cock and slide back into her. I resume my grip on her and begin to thrust, short fast thrusts as her pussy clamps down on me. She's so fucking tight and wet, and I can't seem to stop myself as my thrusts grow faster. Harder.

"T-that. Don't s-stop." Her plea urges me on even more.

"Fuck, Collins," I pant, never stopping my stride. Thrust after thrust, I pound into her. My balls tighten and tingles race up my spine. "I need you there."

"I—Oh, fuck!" she shouts, and the way her pussy is squeezing me, the way her legs quiver, I know she's found her oasis.

One more thrust, my grip tightens as I explode inside of her. Pulse after pulse, I spill over. She collapses on the bed, her head to the side and a content smile on her face. Carefully, I pull out of her and lie next to her on the bed. She wastes no time, curling up against my chest.

"So, an entire forty-eight hours of that?"

"Anything you want," I say, not just because she just made me come harder than I have in my entire life, but because it's her. Collins. I can never say no to her.

"I want. But some recovery time would be nice."

"Yeah." I chuckle, kissing the top of her head.

"You go back to sleep. I'm going to clean up and make us some breakfast."

"I'm good. Let's take a shower, and we can cook together. I'll sleep when you do."

"Deal." Slowly, we climb out of bed and head for the shower.

Two hours later, we're snuggled up on the couch. I'm in a pair of basketball shorts, and she's in one of my T-shirts and those boy shorts she loves, sans bra, per Dr. Carmichael's request of course. Those tiny little shorts are sexy as fuck.

We're watching the Lifetime network, and I can't keep from spouting off about how the doctor did it. You know, being one yourself gives you the insight into these things. We're in the final ten minutes about to reveal the killer when there's a knock at the door.

"You expecting someone?" Collins whispers, not wanting whoever it is to hear her.

"No. Just you."

"Grady, come on, man. We saw your 4Runner outside. We know you're home. Open up," her brother's voice booms.

"Shit!" she hisses and jumps off the couch.

"Hey, calm down." I pull her close and hold her to my chest. "Let's just tell him, Collins."

"No, we have two weeks until the wedding, Grady. Two weeks," she repeats, keeping her voice low.

"Fine. Go hide in the bedroom. I'll see what he wants."

"Grady!" Another knock. This time, another male voice.

"Fuck, that sounds like Alec."

Scanning the living room, she gathers her shoes, and keys, and phone. I watch as she makes sure her phone is set to silent. "You see anything else that's mine?" she asks.

"I do." I nod.

She looks around the room again, scanning for what it might be. "What? I don't see anything," she says, turning her gaze back to mine.

"Me." I grin. "Just relax, baby. I'll get rid of them."

"Hold on!" I yell out when there's another knock.

She accepts the kiss I give her and scurries away to my room. I listen as she shuts the door quietly. I'm sure her ear is glued to the door trying to listen to what's going on. Taking another look at the place, making sure nothing that can directly identify her is lying around, I open the door.

"What the fuck took so long?" Caleb grumbles.

"I was watching a movie, and it was just getting to the good part."

"Ass." Alec laughs, followed by Bryce as the three of them make themselves at home in my apartment.

"Let's go shoot some hoops. Grab a drink after," Caleb says.

"Nope."

"Why the hell not?"

"Because I worked over sixteen hours yesterday. I'm fucking beat, and I just want to chill." I want to add here in my apartment with my girlfriend.

"When do you work again?"

"Not until Sunday, and tomorrow I plan to be holed up with my girlfriend all day before you get any ideas in your head."

"When do we get to meet this girl? I mean, as soon as she meets me, she's going to throw your ass to the curb," Bryce jokes.

"Keep dreaming, smartass. Not for a while. It's new, and we're seeing where things go."

"You said you loved her," Caleb reminds me.

I look him straight in the eye. I want him to know that I mean what I say. "I do love her. If I had my way, she'd be living here with me."

"Why isn't she?" Alec asks.

"It's complicated. Look, guys, just leave it be. I promise you that as soon as she's ready for me to tell you, we will."

"So, it's her. She's embarrassed by you?" Bryce asks.

"Fuck you," I fire back. "She's not embarrassed. It's new. We don't need you fuckers or anyone else sticking their nose in our business. She wants to be sure."

"Wants to be sure of what? That she wants to be with you? I'm sorry, man, but this sounds off to me," Caleb says.

"I hurt her, okay. It was a few years ago, and she's worried that I'm not here, that I'm not in this for the long haul."

"Are you?"

I can tell by the tone of his voice that he's serious. He's not just fucking off. If I didn't know any better, I would think he knows it's Collins that I'm talking about. "Yes. I regretted it as soon as it happened. I needed to go, and she needed to stay, but not once in the time I was away from her did I not think about her."

"That's why you left?" he says, as if it's all finally making sense to him.

"Yeah, that's why I left. I fucked up, man. I'm just trying to make it right. To show her that she's it for me."

"It for you? Like marriage and shit?" Bryce asks.

"Yeah, like marriage and shit. I've loved her from afar for years, and now that I'm back, I'm fighting to prove it to her."

"That's some heavy shit," Alec says.

I nod. "Yeah, so lay off a little, will ya? When she's ready, I'll tell you. Trust me, I want to shout it from the fucking rooftops."

"Pussy." Bryce grins.

"If loving her makes me a pussy, it's a badge I'll gladly wear."

"Damn." Alec turns to look at Bryce. "We're the last two holdouts."

"I'll be holding out for a long damn time. Having too much fun being single."

"Trust me," Caleb chimes in, "one woman is not as bad as you make it sound."

"Nope. You know every inch of her body. She lets you in anytime you want. All you have to do is love her and be faithful." I smirk.

"Yeah, you two can keep spouting that shit. I'm out."

"You're all out. I'm having a quiet, relaxing day, remember?"

"She's on her way over, isn't she?" Alec asks.

"No, but she'll be here later, and I don't plan to leave this apartment until I have to go to work on Sunday morning. And I won't be answering the locked door either," I say pointedly.

It takes me thirty more minutes to get them out the door. I double check the lock and then rush to the bedroom to find Collins. I fucking hate that she was hiding in my room. Caleb's wedding can't come fast enough. Opening my bedroom door, I find her curled up on the bed, the pillow I slept on last night clutched in her arms, sleeping peacefully. She's gorgeous. As quiet as I can, I snuggle in next to her, wrapping her in my arms. I can't think of a better way to spend the day.

Chapter 36

Collins

"WE MADE IT THROUGH IT," I tell Grady as we're climbing into bed. Tonight was Caleb and Emily's rehearsal dinner, and we made it through without giving away our secret. It was difficult to say the least. We're paired up in the wedding, so I had to walk down the aisle with him. I can feign indifference from a distance. But when he's right next to me, my hand resting in the crook of his arm, the heat of his body seeping into mine, that's a challenge.

"We did," he says, wrapping his arms around me. "Now the wedding and then next week, when they get back, we get to tell them."

"One more week of hiding."

"Thank fuck. I want the world to know you're mine."

"He's not going to be happy, Grady. I hate the thought of coming between the two of you."

"There is no choice here, Collins. Your brother and I have been through a lot together. He's been my best friend my entire life, but you... what I feel for you trumps all of that. It would suck to have him hate me, to lose his friendship, but it would kill me to lose you. I can't... no, I won't, not again. I fucked up all those years ago. I own that. I'm not making the same mistake twice."

"I hope he comes around."

"He will. When we have kids and he's missing out on being a part of our lives, a part of their lives, he'll come around. It might take him some time, but I'm confident he'll accept us in the long run."

"Kids?" It's hard for me to wrap my head around the fact that he's planning our future. A future with kids. Plural.

He laughs. "Is that the only part of that you heard?"

"No." I smack his chest playfully. "I heard you, but that part stuck out." How could it not? I've dreamed of this moment, of falling madly in love and starting a family. It was always, Grady that was there by my side. My heart swells knowing that he feels the same way.

"You do want kids, right? I mean, we've not talked about it. I just assumed."

"Do you?" I counter.

"Stop answering my questions with a question, but yes, I do. I want a little girl who looks just like her momma."

"Funny, I was thinking a little Grady might be nice."

His lips take mine in a tender kiss. "How many?" he asks when he pulls away.

"At least two, maybe three."

"Three, maybe four," he bargains.

"Let's just see how it goes."

"Yeah? You saying you want to marry me, Collins Ward?"

"Are you asking?"

"There you go again." He tickles my side, and I squirm in his hold.

"Not officially, but I will be."

"You can't get married without your best friend." It's tearing at my heart to think about the fallout that is bound to come from this. I hope Caleb can see how in love we are and accept that Grady is good to me. That we are fully committed to each other. I hope he can accept that his little sister is madly in love with his best friend.

"You're right, that's why I'm marrying her."

Lifting up on my elbows, I look at him. "What did you just say?"

"I said, I'm marrying her. I won't be getting married without my best friend because she'll be standing beside me. Sure, I have the guys, and I hope that Caleb is there standing next to me as well, but at the end of the day, it's you, Collins. You're the first person I think of when I have a good day, and the first I want to see when I have a bad one. Caleb will always be my best friend, but the top spot, that's reserved all for you."

I take a minute to compose myself as his words have me choked up. "Thank you for waiting. For giving us this time together. I feel like our past is just that, the past. I no longer feel as though you're going to up and leave me. I needed this time to have you all to myself. I know it was hard, and that it goes against what you wanted to do, but thank you for agreeing to it."

"Don't you know by now that I can't say no to you? Baby, I'd give you the world if I could."

"How about forever instead?"

"Are you asking me to marry you?"

"What if I was?"

"Yes." It's one word, a simple three letters, but they stop my heart all the same.

"One day," I say, choking out the words. What I really want to say is let's hop a flight to Vegas, or Gatlinburg, or the courthouse on Monday. Tomorrow is my brother's day. We're going to get through this wedding, send the happy couple off on their honeymoon, and then drop the bomb we've been hiding. If we make it through that, then we'll be ready to face anything.

"One day soon," he says, kissing me softly.

We kiss until we're both breathless. Grady surprises me when he kisses my temple and whispers goodnight. I love that about us. I love that our relationship has substance, that it's not all about sex. Tonight, we had intimacy without intercourse, and it was perfect. I don't know that three years ago we would have been ready for this. I'm starting to think that Grady did the right thing. His actions that night led us here, and this is where I want to be, where we both want to be. I make a mental note as I drift off to sleep to tell him thank you.

I'm up early the next morning. I have to meet Mom, Emily, her mom, and sisters at the venue to get our hair done. "Hey." I kiss Grady's bare shoulder to wake him up. He rolls over and wraps his arms around my waist where I'm sitting on the edge of the bed.

"Come back to bed," he mumbles.

"I can't. I'm meeting the girls to get our hair and nails done. I won't see you again until we get to the venue."

"What time is it?" he mumbles.

"Eight." I run my fingers through his hair. "You don't have to be there until noon. The wedding is at three."

"Why do you have to be there so early?" he asks, his voice muffled as he speaks into the pillow.

"Because us ladies, need to go get beautiful."

"Pfft, you're already beautiful. Come back to bed." He tries to pull me down with him, but with my feet planted on the floor, I have some leverage.

"You're sweet, but I need to go. This is all a part of being in the wedding. Besides, you'll be with the guys later."

"One more week." He says exactly what I'm thinking.

"One more week. In fact, I thought maybe we can have dinner with our parents next week? I'm not as concerned about them as I am Caleb. As long as we keep what happened in the past out of it."

"That's a part of who we are."

"Yeah, maybe we can leave out the fact that I gave you my virginity? Keep it PG for the parentals?"

He chuckles. "Might be a good angle."

"Indeed. I have to go. I'll see you later at the venue." I stand from my spot on the bed and his hands fall away. Bending over, I kiss his cheek. "Love you."

"Love you, too," he mumbles, and I know he's going right back to sleep.

When I arrive, everyone else is already there. Mom pulls me into a hug, and then Emily scoops me up. There is an entire team of stylists from a local salon doing our hair, nails, and makeup. There is an assortment of bagels, pastries, and fresh fruit that we graze on throughout the morning.

"I love your hair," Emily's sister, Samantha, tells me.

"Thank you. I've been contemplating getting it cut, but I always chicken out."

"No!" she exclaims. "Don't cut it. It's gorgeous."

I smile at her, but before I can reply, my mom interrupts me. "Collins, can you go check on the guys? You know all of them, so you'll know who to look for. Emily is worried they're not all here."

"It's too quiet," Emily chimes in. "We all know Bryce and Alec are not quiet," she says, making those of us who know them well burst with laughter.

"Yeah, I'll go check on them." Looking down, I'm already in my dress. "Wait, should I slip out of my dress?" I ask the room.

"You're not the bride, silly." Mom laughs. "Just go check on your brother and the boys and report back to us."

"Got it." I salute to them and slip out the door. It's not until I'm out of the room and roaming the halls do I realize I'm not sure where the guys are getting ready. After all the details and wedding planning, it's one thing that never came up. Not that it needed to. I mean, we're all here at the same venue, but this place is huge. I still don't understand why they chose such a huge place for just under one hundred guests. Oh, well, it's not my wedding, and regardless, it's going to be a beautiful ceremony.

I reach the main ballroom, and stop and look around, taking it all in. Not much has changed since last night except for the fresh flowers and their sweet floral smell. Tears of happiness prick the back of my eyes for my brother and Emily. I can only hope that when this day comes for me, that it's Grady by my side and that my brother will feel the same joy for us as I feel for them. I send up a silent prayer that everything works out.

Breaking out of the thoughts, I head to the other side of the building where I assume the guys will be. I hear a commotion at the end of the hall, and that's where I'm headed when someone snags my arms and pulls me into them. I yelp in surprise, but immediately recognize his voice and his smell.

Grady.

"Hey, baby," he says softly, kissing my bare shoulder. His hand is gripping my waist, and he's shirtless.

"W-where is your shirt?" I stutter, because let me tell you, Grady Carmichael shirtless will render you speechless. Trust me.

"I had to use the bathroom. What are you doing on this side? Not that I'm not happy to see you."

"I'm coming to make sure everyone is here. Emily had this feeling that Alec and Bryce might be late."

"Nah, we're all here. You look beautiful." He kisses me on the shoulder one more time. "I'm glad you left your hair down."

"We all did," I tell him. Emily has hers up, but her sisters and I left ours down. "You better get back. Go ahead of me. I'll wait before I come to the room."

"One more week," he says, kissing me softly. Stepping back, he drops his hand from my hip, turns and walks away.

I count to two hundred slowly before making my way down the hall and knocking on the door. Grady answers. "Hey." He smiles big, stepping back to let me in.

"Everyone decent?" I say loudly, covering my eyes with my hands.

"No way I'd let you in otherwise, baby," his deep voice whispers in my ear.

"Hey!" Caleb is standing before me in just a few long strides. "What are you doing here, little sister?" He wraps me in a hug. "You look beautiful," he says.

I catch Grady's eye over his shoulder, and he's wearing an "I told you so" grin. "Thank you. I'm just checking on things for Em, making sure everyone is here and accounted for."

"Aww, is my bride nervous?" His smile is huge.

"Nope. Cool as a cucumber. We just haven't heard anything from any of you, so she wanted to make sure everything was set, and all of you"—

I point to Grady, Bryce, and Alec—"were here and ready to go."

"Come on, Collins," Bryce says, stepping next to me and putting his arm around my shoulders. "You know the real reason you came on our side of the lot." He winks. "You wanted to see me." He pulls me a little closer, and I hear a growl. Normally, I would roll my eyes at such an obvious act of possessiveness, but the growl, it came from Grady. When it's my man, it's a turn-on. However, there is not time for that now. I have to diffuse the situation before my growly boyfriend gives us away.

Thinking it's Caleb, I look at him, but he's smiling. Grady, however, looks murderous. "Nope," I say, removing his arm from around my shoulder and stepping away. "Great, the gang's all here. I'll report back. See you in about an hour or so," I say, not knowing the exact time, but knowing that the wedding is drawing closer.

"Tell my *wife* she has nothing to worry about," Caleb says. I can't help but notice the emphasis he put on the word wife.

"Got it. You four stay out of trouble." I wave over my shoulder and rush out the door. I thought Grady was going to give us away. I had to get out of there. This day has barely even started. Thankfully, I'm walking with him in the wedding party. I'm not sure how things would have turned out if I were paired with Alec or Bryce. We were lucky the night he drew and got me. Maybe, just maybe that luck will continue when we tell my brother about us.

Chapter 37

GRADY

I DON'T TAKE MY EYES off her as she leaves the room. I'm still standing here staring at the door, trying to get myself in check. I don't know what it is, but when I see Bryce's hands on her, it drives me mad. Maybe because I know that behind all the kidding and smiles, that he really wants her. He used to talk about how hot she was when we were younger.

Before that night.

Before everything changed.

Now here I am, clenching and unclenching my fists to keep from punching him in the damn face, when in reality, he didn't do anything wrong. He doesn't know she's mine. None of them do. Slowly, I inhale a deep breath and release it. After today, it no longer matters. I'll make sure everyone knows she's mine. We've agreed to tell our parents this week. In fact, I already sent my mom a text and asked if we could have dinner next week. I hope Collins was serious because I'm ready.

I've been ready.

"Hey, can the two of you go check in with Dad and make sure nothing else needs to be done? He mentioned we might need ushers. If that's the case, I thought maybe you guys could help out before the ceremony?" Caleb asks.

I don't turn around. I don't know if he's asking me, but I need another minute. I can't look at Bryce just yet without still wanting to knock Bryce on his ass.

"Sure, Grady, you coming?" Alec asks.

"Actually, I need someone to stay here and help me with this damn tie. Besides, he's not even dressed yet."

He's right. I'm not. I'm in nothing but my gray dress pants. I can be ready in a matter of minutes, but as the groom, I'm sure he wants to make sure that everything goes off without a hitch for Emily. I hear the door and take another deep breath.

"When were you going to tell me?" Caleb asks from behind me.

Slowly, I turn to face him. "Tell you what?" I ask the question, but I already know the answer. Somehow he's figured it out. He knows me better than anyone, and my reaction to Bryce didn't go unnoticed. All I can think about is that Collins is going to be pissed. Today of all days he has to figure it out? We worked so hard to not ruin this day.

Even the best-laid plans can go astray.

He laughs humorlessly. "Fuck off, Grady. Just tell me."

"Look, man," I hold my hands up in surrender, "I'm a doctor, not a damn mind reader. Tell me what you're talking about." I continue to play dumb on the off chance that my suspicion is not correct. Maybe there's a small chance he hasn't figured it out.

"You wanna play that way? Fine. How long have you been sleeping with my sister?"

And there it is. "That's a complicated question."

"Un-complicate it."

"What gave us away?"

He's standing before me, hands on his hips, shaking his head. "The way she looks at you. Hell, the way you look at her. Your eyes follow her no matter where she is in the room. Not to mention, you were ready to tear Bryce's arms off for touching her."

"He's always fucking touching her," I grumble under my breath.

"Why does that bother you?" he prompts.

"Why doesn't it bother you?" I counter.

"Because I know my sister. I know she would never go there, not with Bryce. And lately, it seems like you've got her covered."

I can tell by the look in his eye the jig is up. I debate on holding out and pretending like I have no clue what he's talking about, but this is my best friend. I'm surprised we've made it this long without him noticing. "I'm in love with her. I have been for a long damn time. Before you yell at me, or punch me, which you have every right to do, you need to know she's not just a fling, man. I love her, like crazy, head-over-heels would-marry-her-today-if-I-thought-she-would-say-yes in love with her."

He's quiet for a few minutes then says, "I can see that. What I don't understand is why you didn't tell me?"

"I wanted to." I hesitate, not wanting to throw Collins under the bus. "*We* wanted to, but we didn't know how you would take it. We were going to tell our parents next week, and then you and Emily when you came home from your honeymoon. We didn't want to ruin your big day."

"Really?" he scoffs. "You think you being with Collins would ruin my wedding?"

"Well, I mean, she and I are both in the wedding party, and we didn't want things to be tense and uncomfortable. We just wanted it to be a good day for the two of you."

"We've been friends since we could walk," he reminds me.

"Look, Caleb. I know. I'm an asshole. I get it. I know you're pissed as you should be. Yes, you are my best friend, but, man, so is she. No, that's not right. She's more than that. There is not a minute in the day that I don't think about her. She's always the best part of every day, good or bad. I love you, brother, you know that. But if you make me choose, it's going to be her. It's always going to be her." My shoulders slump. I've put it all out there and now I just wait for the inevitable. The punch… I'm sure it's coming, the screaming soon to follow.

He surprises me when he asks. "You said a long time. How long?"

Fuck. No holding back now. "Everything changed for me three years ago." I can see him starting to put the pieces together. I've told him I left and messed things up. He's working it out in his head.

"Collins. My baby sister is the reason you ran like your ass was on fire and never looked back?"

"She is."

"What did you do to her?"

"What? Nothing, I mean, I left because she made me feel too much. I was worried about what you would think, and then there was medical school. I was states away, Caleb. She had just finished her first year of college. How could I ask her to do long distance? Fuck, man, there is no way I could have. I was only able to stay away because I knew she was mad at me."

"So why come back? What changed your mind and make you realize she was worth it?" His voice is calm, and his face is void of emotion. I can usually tell what he's thinking, but right now, I can't get a read on him. I'm not sure if it's me, or my emotions from Bryce, and now Caleb discovering us. Maybe it's the fact that my girl is going to be pissed if this ruins the wedding.

"I knew the minute I pulled my SUV out of my parents' driveway. I also knew that I wasn't ready. Not in the way you think," I'm quick to add. "I wasn't ready to leave medical school, and I couldn't ask her to come with me. I knew we both had things we needed to do before we could be together." I take a breath. "I know I hurt her, but I hurt myself, too. Coming home, it's what we both needed."

"Why's that? So, what? You asked her to wait? You get to play around, living it up while you expected her to wait?"

"No," I say adamantly. "Not at all. There was no one in my life, no women, just school and work after I went back. I knew there was no point. I would just be comparing them to her. That wasn't fair to anyone. So I kept my nose buried in a book and busted my ass at medical school. That way I could have my choice of residency. I busted my ass to come home to her. It cured both of our broken hearts. I told her she was my remedy, but now I see that I was hers as well. We were both not really living. We held onto hope that one day we could fix this, we could be together, and we're there. I won't hurt her again."

A knock sounds at the door. Neither one of us makes a move. Silence surrounds us, then another knock, this time followed by her sweet voice.

"Are you guys in there? Are you ready to go?" Collins asks. My anxiety peaks knowing that all hell could break loose at any moment. Collins made sure we waited to not ruin this day for Caleb and Emily, and my dumb ass had to fuck it all up. I wouldn't have been able to control my reaction to Bryce's hands on her if I tried. The growl slipped out. I knew then that the secret was more than likely out of the bag. I just didn't want to believe it.

Caleb stalks toward the door and pulls it open. Grabbing her arm, he pulls her into the room.

"Watch it," I warn him.

"What's going on?" Collins looks back and forth between the two of us.

"He knows."

"Oh." Her mouth drops open.

"He figured it out. Apparently, I'm not good at hiding how much I love you."

Her face softens. "It was only a matter of time."

Holding my hand out for her, she takes it and allows me to pull her into my hold. "Look, Caleb. I'm sorry you found out this way. I'm sorry we kept it from you, but I assure you we had the best of intentions. I'll apologize as much as I need to make this right. However, I won't apologize for being with her. I love you both, but differently."

"Yeah," he speaks up. "You already told me you'd choose her over me."

Collins looks up at me, her big blue eyes shimmering with tears. "It will all work out," I say softly, kissing her forehead.

When I look back at him, Caleb is watching us closely. "I have one last question. What made you think I would be mad about this?"

Collins and I look at one another shocked. Is he saying what I think he is? "I'm your best friend. She's your little sister. There are rules against these things."

"Says who?" he asks.

I look down at Collins, and she shrugs. "We just assumed that you wouldn't be happy about it. I've heard you warn off Alec and Bryce several times," she explains.

"Alec and Bryce, they're my friends, but they are also two of the biggest man-whores I've ever met. Of course, I want better for you." He pauses, staring us down, waiting for one of us to speak. We're too stunned, so he keeps going. "I could see it back then, too. The looks the two of you would give each other. The way you never cared if she tagged along. I always thought one day something might happen between the two of you. I just never thought I would be the last to know."

"You're not, technically only Tabby knows about us. I'm so sorry, Caleb." Collins pulls out of my hold and steps toward him. He opens his arms for her, and she doesn't hesitate to step into his hold. "I love him."

"I know you do. He loves you, too," he tells her.

"Are you... are you okay with this? You're not mad?"

"Of course, I'm okay with it. I've always thought of Grady as a brother to me, but not to you. He's an awesome guy. That's why he's my best friend. If he can hold that title for me, he can hold whatever title it is he holds with you."

"He's... everything."

My arms hang at my sides as I watch them embrace. I have to fight to make myself stand still and not pull her away from him. Not because of jealousy, but because my heart is beating so hard, I feel as though it might beat right out of my chest. Her words have caused a swarm of emotions to race through me. Love, happiness, contentment. She's my everything.

"You treat her right."

"Always. I promise you there is no one out there who will love her like I do."

He chuckles. "From the way you were ready to tear Bryce's head off, I believe you." With another tight squeeze, he releases Collins, and she's back in my arms where she belongs.

"So, you're okay with this? With us?" She glances up at me before looking back at Caleb.

"Yeah, I'm okay with it. I wish you would have told me, but I get it."

"Wow," she breathes. "I was expecting yelling and some fists to be thrown. I was prepared to argue our case. I was expecting you to not talk to us for a while. I mean, I hoped that you would come around, but I never expected this."

"Why would I not want my little sister with one of the best guys I know? I'm disappointed and hurt you didn't tell me, but I get it. I know both of you, and I know you were coming from a good place."

"All's good, my man," Bryce says, barging into the room.

I tighten my hold on Collins, my hand on her hip as I hold her possessively to me. Bryce notices, raising his brows in question.

"I need to get back. We need to get you married," Collins says.

"Damn right," Caleb adamantly agrees.

She looks up at me. "See you in a few." Standing on her tiptoes, she meets me halfway as I press my lips against hers.

"Sounds good, baby." Reluctantly, I release her and watch her walk out of the door.

"Hold up, what was that?" Alec asks.

"Turns out this guy," Caleb points at me, "is in love with my little sister."

"No shit?" Alec says.

"Wait! No punches were thrown?" Bryce asks.

"Nope."

"What the hell, Ward? You've always threatened me she's off limits."

"She was to you. You stick your dick in anything. She deserves better than that."

Bryce crosses his arms over his chest. "He's that person?"

"Yep! Now, are you all ready? I have a beautiful bride waiting for me."

Bryce seems to simmer, and Alec just looks lost as we follow Caleb out of the room. We shake hands and do the man-hug back-slap thing, and he leaves to go stand at the arch of flowers. We stand at the closed door, waiting for the girls and the bride.

"Damn," Alec says when Collins and the girls come walking toward us.

"I'm next," I tell them.

"You're serious?" Bryce asks.

"Never been more serious."

He clamps his hand on my shoulder, and that's that. The fight we thought was coming was not a fight at all. And I get to do this. In a few long strides, I reach her. Snaking my arm around her waist, I bend down and kiss her neck, knowing if I mess up her makeup there will be hell to pay from the bride.

"Yes!" Emily cheers. "I knew it!" She smiles big, then the smile drops from her face. "Does Caleb know?"

"Yeah," I tell her. "He knows."

"It's all good, Em," Collins assures her.

"Good. Let's get me married."

We pair off, my girl on my arm, and suddenly, I'm smiling as if this were my wedding day. I look over at Collins, who is smiling at something Emily's sister, Cindy, says.

We'll have our day.

Soon.

Very soon.

Chapter 38

Collins

THE WEDDING WENT OFF WITHOUT a hitch. I cried and smiled all the way through it. Grady held my stare throughout the ceremony, and I know it sounds crazy, but I could feel the love we have for each other in just a look.

"When do I get to dance with you?" he whispers in my ear.

We're sitting at the front of the room reserved for the wedding party. "They have to have their first dance first. Then we'll join them."

"Too long," he grumbles.

I feel his lips press against my bare shoulder. "Look." I give a subtle nod toward the table where our parents sit, and there are four sets of eyes watching us.

"Oops." He chuckles. "Guess we forgot a few people were still in the dark."

I'm just about ready to suggest that we go talk to them when Caleb and Emily are announced as they enter the ballroom. Their smiles are wide and blinding as the room erupts in cheers. They stop in the middle of the dance floor and go straight into their first dance as husband and wife.

"You ready for all of that?" his deep voice asks me.

"Are you?" I counter.

He laughs softly. "Always answering my questions with one of your own."

"I have to keep you on your toes."

"And I'll keep curling yours," he says, kissing my neck again.

"Now, if we could have the wedding party join the happy couple," the announcer's voice says over the sound system.

Grady stands and pulls my chair out for me. "Come on, baby. Let's show them how it's done."

I place my hand in his, and he leads me toward the dance floor; however, we take the long way and stop at the table our parents are seated at. "Hey," Grady greets them, pulling me into his side. "We just wanted to let you know, we're together. I'm in love with her." He looks down at me. "And I'm pretty sure she loves me, too." I nod my agreement. "We were going to tell you this week at dinner, but Caleb discovered us, and we're tired of hiding. Let's just enjoy tonight, and we will answer all of your questions later." He waves and guides us to the dance floor. Not before I notice the shocked expression on our fathers' faces and the tears in our mothers' eyes. I was never worried about their reactions. I knew our moms, if they even thought it was possible we were together, would be planning our wedding before the first date was over. It was wrong to lie to them, but I'm glad that we had that time, just for us. Our families are so connected, it was good to find who we were together before including them.

"You didn't let them say a word." I playfully smack at his chest.

"Nope. This is Caleb's night, but they were bound to ask. It's out there, and we can talk about it later. Tonight, I'm holding you, kissing you, and touching you anytime I fucking want. I'm going to enjoy the hell out of the fact that we no longer have to hide. We can talk to them tomorrow. Tonight, we fade into the background with each other. We let Caleb and Emily have the show."

"I love you, Grady Carmichael."

"I love you, too."

I rest my head against his chest as we shuffle around the dance floor. Nothing has ever felt this right. This moment with him, it's perfect. I can't wait to see what the future holds for us. I can imagine the day that the wedding is ours. When we're the couple being celebrated. When we start the journey of becoming husband and wife. It's a dream, one I hope comes true.

"Hey." My new sister-in-law taps me on my shoulder a while later. We've just finished dinner, which was delicious.

"Yeah?"

"You mind helping me in the bathroom?"

"Not at all." I stand, and Grady grabs my hand.

"What's up?"

"We're going to the restroom."

He brings my hand to his lips. "Love you."

He doesn't lower his voice. It's not a whisper, just his deep timbre telling anyone within hearing distance how he feels about me. Leaning over, I kiss him on his cheek and follow Emily to the restrooms.

"Spill," she says once we're there.

"Hey." I act offended. She knows well enough to know that I'm not. "I thought you had to use the restroom."

"I do, but I don't need help. I need details."

"This is your day, Em."

"Exactly, this is my day, and I want details." She grins, disappearing behind the stall door.

"You sure you don't need help?"

"I got this. Start talking."

So, I do. I tell her what happened earlier and how cool Caleb was about it all. "I'm still kind of shocked," I admit.

"You shouldn't be. Grady is a great guy, and your brother knows that. You should have told us. Told me at least."

"I couldn't ask you to keep that from him."

"You're right." She flushes. "It looks serious," she says, coming out of the stall and then washing her hands.

"Yeah, it is. I mean, we love each other."

"One day, I want it all." She catches my eye in the mirror. "There's more to this story, and I can't wait to hear it."

"When you get back from your honeymoon, we'll have a girls' night, and I'll spill all. Deal?"

"Deal." We shake on it, both of us laughing at our antics.

When we get back to the table, Grady pulls me into his lap and nuzzles my neck. The announcer tells the bride and groom it's time to cut the cake and then takes us through bride and father, groom and mother dances and so on. Once all of the scheduled dances are over, Grady leads me to the dance floor and that's how we spend the rest of the night. We cut loose with our friends and family during the fast songs, and he holds me close and tells me how much he loves me during the slow ones.

"Hey," Caleb says, breaking us out of our trance. "We're getting ready to head out."

I pull away from Grady and hug my big brother tightly. "I'm so happy for you."

"You, too, little sister."

"I'm sorry," I tell him.

"Don't be. He loves you."

"I love him, too."

"That's all I care about."

"Congratulations, man," Grady says.

Caleb releases me and hugs his best friend. "Take care of her." I hear Caleb tell him.

I hug Emily, and she again makes me promise to tell her the story, not leaving out a single detail, and I happily agree, glad I can finally talk about him. About us.

Standing behind me, Grady wraps his arms around my waist as we watch them leave.

"You kids ready to talk yet?" my dad asks.

Turning, I look at him. He doesn't look angry, which is a good thing. "How about lunch tomorrow?" No matter how old I get, I still feel like a sixteen-year-old girl standing before her daddy before her first date.

"Our place," Grady's mom chimes in. "Noon."

"We'll be there," Grady assures her.

Surprisingly, that pacifies the four of them. We accept hugs from our mothers before our fathers pull them out to the dance floor.

"That was easier than I thought it would be," I tell Grady, watching our parents dancing.

"They can see it, Collins."

"What? They can see what?"

"How much we love each other. No parent is going to argue with that." Again, my heart melts. I love seeing this softer side of him. The one he gives to me. The one that's not afraid to not just tell me but show me how much he loves me.

"So, you're saying our daughter comes home with her brother's best friend you're going to be okay with it?"

He turns me in his arms and crushes his lips to mine. "Not that I'm complaining but what was that for?" I ask when he pulls away.

"You said our daughter. I think that's the first time you've ever talked about us and a future, that kind of future."

"You sure?"

He throws his head back and laughs. "I'm sure, baby. There are a lot of factors that come into play, but if he's a good guy, then yeah, I'll be happy for both of them. As long as she's at least thirty." He kisses my temple. "Make that forty," he says, and I have to bite my lips to keep the laugh from bursting free.

"Come on, crazy man. Dance with me."

"Gladly."

We spend the rest of the night laughing and dancing. Enjoying the fact that we no longer have to hide. It's freeing and exhilarating all at once. I never want to lose this feeling.

Chapter 39

GRADY

IT WAS AFTER TWO THIS morning before we got back to my place and in bed. Collins was asleep as soon as her head hit the pillow. I wasn't far behind her. I set my alarm to make sure we didn't miss lunch with our parents, pulled her into me, and fell fast asleep. Now here I am at a little after ten, and wide awake. The alarm is set to go off in fifteen minutes, so I turn it off, letting her have that time to sleep. It also gives me time to watch her.

Yesterday was more than I could have hoped for. I was sure Caleb would be pissed. He wasn't. That's great, it is, but it also means the main reason I ran, it was for nothing. We still would have had to be in a long-distance relationship with medical school and her nursing school. We'll never know if we could have made it work, and at this point, it doesn't matter. We made it back to each other, and we're no longer hiding how much we love each other. That's what matters. Never again will I let fear control me. I let the possibility of the unknown keep me from her for way too long. "Never again," I whisper, tightening my hold on her. Never again will I let fear keep me from what could be amazing.

Reaching for my cell, I pull up my mother's contact and send her a text message.

Me:	I'm ready.
Mom:	Good morning to you, too.
Mom:	Ready for what? Lunch? I haven't even started.
Me:	No. I'm ready. Do you still have Grandma's ring?
Mom:	Oh.
Mom:	Of course, I do. I told you I would hold onto it until you were ready.
Me:	I'm ready.

I wait for her reply. I smile when I think about her dancing around the kitchen.

Mom:	Okay. I'll have it out and ready for you.
Me:	Thank you, Mom.
Me:	I love you.
Mom:	I love you, too, Grady.

"Who are you texting?" Collins sleep-laced voice asks.

"My dad. He asked if I could come over and help him move a few things in the garage before lunch."

"I need to go to my place and shower anyway."

"How about I come back and pick you up so we can be there together?"

"Grady, it's our parents. I'm not afraid of them. Besides, they didn't seem to be upset, just wanted answers. I'll be there as soon as I'm ready."

"Okay, baby." I kiss her and climb out of bed. She follows, wearing my T-shirt and those boy shorts. She takes a pair of shorts out of her dresser drawer and slides them on.

"The perks of living next door." She grins when she finds me watching her.

"Just think of the perks if you actually lived here."

"Special privileges?" she asks, smiling.

"Loads," I reply, kissing her.

"Maybe we should talk about that."

Placing my hands on her shoulders, I wait until she looks at me. "You serious?"

She shrugs. "Yeah, I mean, if that's still what you want. We don't have to. I'd have to talk to Tabby, and—"

I kiss her. I kiss her until we are both breathless and needing air. Breaking the kiss, excitement bubbles over at the thought of our future together. "Yes. I want that so much. Today, when we get back?" I ask, hopeful.

"Slow down there, bud," she says, tapping my chest. "I have to talk to Tabby. I won't leave her hanging."

"Pay your portion. I've got things covered here," I tell her.

"Later." She kisses my chin. "I'll see you in a little while."

Realizing I have a limited amount of time, I rush to the shower. She has no idea that she's just made my plans for today that much sweeter.

Fifteen minutes later, I'm in my SUV and headed toward my parents' place. However, instead of pulling into my parents' driveway, I pull into hers. Grabbing my keys and my phone, I climb out and approach the front door.

"Grady, where's Collins? Is everything okay?" her mom asks when she answers the door and sees it's only me.

"She's getting ready for lunch. I wanted to know if I could talk to you and Mr. Ward?"

"Come on now, we've always been Roger and Monica. Nothing has changed. Come on in." She steps back, allowing me to enter.

I wait for her to close the door and follow her to the living room where Roger is sitting in his recliner. "Roger," Monica says. "Grady wants to talk to us."

"Have a seat, son."

He called me son. That's a good sign, right? "I love her," I blurt. "More than anything, I love her. I want nothing more than to spend the rest of my life doing just that." Roger nods and Monica places her hand over her mouth, tears in her eyes.

"She feels the same. I can tell from the way she looks at you."

This time it's me who nods. Wiping my sweaty hands on my jeans, I go for it. "I'd like to ask your permission to marry her." The room falls silent as I stare her father in the eye, waiting for his reply.

"If you are who she chooses, you have our blessing." He looks to his wife, and she nods, a tear falling down her cheek.

"She does."

"You sound pretty certain." Roger chuckles.

"I've never been more certain."

"When do you plan to do it?" Monica asks.

"Today. I have my grandmother's ring. Mom's been holding it for me, and I asked her to have it out and ready."

"Sounds like our lunch is turning into a celebration of sorts," Roger replies.

"Every day I have with her is a celebration."

"Just curious," he says, tapping his chin. "What would you have done if I had said no?"

I don't hesitate. "I would have asked her anyway. I respect you, Roger." I look at Monica. "I respect both of you, but I can't live without her."

"Good answer," he says, standing and offering me his hand to shake. "I like knowing that you put her first before all."

"Always."

After a hug from Monica, I head to my parents' house knowing that Collins should be getting here soon. I pull out of the Wards' drive and into ours. Mom is at the front door to greet me. She hands me the ring with tears in her eyes.

"When did this happen?" Dad asks, coming up behind her and putting his arm around her shoulders.

"It's been a long time coming. We reconnected when I got home and well…." I hold up the ring box and grin.

"She's the one, huh?"

"Yes."

"You need to—"

I cut him off holding up my hands. "I just talked to Roger and Monica. I have their blessing."

"Caleb?" Mom asks.

"He so much as gave it to me last night. I didn't tell him I was proposing, but he accepts that we're together. He's good with it."

"When are you asking her?" Mom asks, stars in her eyes.

"Today."

"What?" She covers her mouth with her hand much like Monica just did moments ago.

"I don't want to wait. We hid this for so long, making sure it was solid, and we are. I want to start the next phase. I want her to be my wife."

"Well, all right then." Dad laughs.

"Knock, knock." We hear Monica at the patio door. That could only mean Collins is here.

I grin at my parents. Taking the ring out of the box, I shove it into my pocket, toss the box in the drawer of the hall table, and head in that direction to meet my girl.

"So," Mom says once we are all seated on the back deck. "Start from the beginning."

I open my mouth to reply, but Collins beats me to it. I'm glad in a way as they all know how I feel. This is her chance to let her side be told. She doesn't realize I got here early and told them how I feel. Told them where I hope our future is headed.

"We've always felt something." She looks at me, and I nod. "But just recently, since Grady has been home, we've… become closer."

"That's obvious," her dad says. "Why hide it?"

"We wanted to be sure we were solid. There was more than just us to think about. Caleb and Grady have been friends since they were in diapers. Then once we knew," she looks at me and smiles softly, "when we were sure it was real and solid, we were a few weeks out from the

Remedy | 231

wedding. We didn't want to do anything to cause upset and potentially ruin the wedding."

"So, what happened?" Dad asks.

"Well," Collins says with a laugh, "Caleb figured it out. Seems we were not as good at hiding it as we thought."

That causes our parents to chuckle. "So, you two are together? You're dating?" her mom asks.

"Yeah, we're dating."

"About that," I say, bringing her hand that's been held tightly in mine to my lips for a soft kiss. I stand from my chair, pushing it back from the table, and pull hers out. She turns in her seat to face me, which puts her in the perfect position. "I love you," I say, dropping to both knees. Her mouth drops open in shock as what I'm about to do registers. Reaching for her hands, I hold them in mine. "I know there is never going to be anyone but you in here." I place our hands over my heart. "I want what they have." I motion to our parents, who are watching with rapt attention. "I want to build a life with you. I want the babies and the carpools. I want the memories, the laughter, the tears. All of it. I want all of it with you." Taking a deep breath, I release her hands and dig the ring out of my pocket. With a steady hand, I hold it up for her. "Collins, you're no longer my weakness but my biggest strength. Will you do me the incredible honor of being my wife?"

"Is that… is that your grandmother's ring?"

I smile and nod, emotion clogging my throat. I know she's always loved this ring. Growing up, anytime she would see my grandmother, she would fawn all over it.

Silent tears flow over her cheeks. "Yes," she finally whispers.

I can't speak. The knot in my throat is too large, too restricting. The tears in my own eyes blur my vision. Standing, I take her hand in mine and slide the ring on her finger.

"It's a perfect fit."

Her watery smile slays me. "We're a perfect fit, baby."

"I love you."

"I love you, too."

Our parents cheer and offer hugs and handshakes of congratulations. I never thought this day would happen. That night all those years ago, I fell madly in love with her. One night was all it took for me to know that she was my forever. As luck would have it, she feels the same way about me. I made it to college and then to medical school, graduated, and now in my residency, I've accomplished my goals, but this one, marrying Collins, will forever be my greatest accomplishment.

She's my remedy.

Epilogue

Collins

Three years later

TODAY IS A SPECIAL DAY in the Carmichael household. Today I get to watch a ceremony held by the hospital for the residents who have successfully completed their program. My husband is one of them. I was worried how my peers and upper management would take the news of Grady and I being engaged, but turns out it was fine. There are no rules against it in the handbook. Although, there were a few people who were rather upset. I can still remember the day that the nurses, namely the three who threw themselves at him, at least the ones I knew about, learned of our engagement. Sasha insisted we were punking them. After a few weeks of me wearing my ring, Grady referring to me as his fiancée with not a care in the world for who heard him, they finally got the hint and left him alone. It's been smooth sailing ever since.

We married two years ago in the same venue as Caleb and Emily. It was a fairy-tale day that I will never forget. Surrounded by our friends and family, we pledged our love for one another. We're a perfect example of how dreams really do come true, both personally and professionally.

"There she is," Emily says as she takes a seat next to me.

"Hey, where's my nephew?" Caleb and Emily's six-month-old son, Connor, coos from across the room. Turning, I see Caleb holding him while talking to our parents.

"Daddy's boy." She grins.

"You are in so much trouble. Two Calebs in the world," I say, and we both laugh.

"I wouldn't want it any other way. However, a little Emily might be nice, too."

"Are you?" I ask excitedly.

"No, but we definitely want more. What about you?"

"Yeah, we're working on it," I tell her.

"Collins, are we late? Did we miss it?" my mother-in-law asks frantically, taking her seat next to me.

"Not at all; you still have a few minutes to spare."

"Thank goodness. There was an accident on the way here. I thought we were going to miss it."

"You're good," I tell her.

We chat for a few more minutes until the announcer asks that we take our seats. Mom and Dad, followed by Caleb and baby Connor, settle in our row. The announcer, who happens to be the chief medical officer of the hospital, goes on to tell us that he is proud to have been able to mentor such a great group of doctors. One by one, he calls them by name to stand as he presents them with a certificate. When it's Grady's turn, our row cheers loudly. Even baby Connor squeals and claps his little hands.

There are ten residents in this group, so the ceremony is quick. Once dismissed, they scatter throughout the room to their families. My husband heads straight for me but is intercepted by his parents, then mine. My brother stops him, too, and I know it's on purpose. Grady steals Connor from Caleb and stalks toward me, bouncing him in his arms.

"Hey, baby," I greet him with a smile.

"Mrs. Carmichael," he says, kissing me. Connor grabs a chunk of my hair and pulls. "No, little man, that's Aunt Collins's hair. Ouch," Grady tells him.

My nephew just gives him a gummy smile. Little stinker. "It's been two years, Grady. Are you ever going to stop greeting me like that?" Even though I give him a hard time for it, I don't think I will ever tire of him greeting me that way.

"Nope. Not ever."

Playfully, I roll my eyes and smile up at him. "Never say never."

"Trust me, wife, I'll still be greeting you that way when we're old and gray."

"Can I have my son back?" Caleb says, already reaching for Connor.

"Hey." Grady twists out of his hold. "You're a baby hog."

"He's my baby," Caleb counters.

"He's my nephew," Grady fires back.

"Have one of your own. Give me my son," he grumbles good-naturedly. Connor takes the choice out of their hands as he rests his head on Grady's shoulder.

I smile at them as they banter back and forth. I know Grady would love nothing more than for us to give Connor a little cousin. Over the last six months or so, that seems to be all he talks about. He's not the only one. I'm ready for us to start our own family.

"See, he likes me better," Grady goads Caleb.

"He's tired," Emily chimes in. At the sound of his momma's voice, Connor reaches for her, and she takes him, smiling widely.

"Son," Caleb says, "we've got to work on this." He kisses the top of his head, wrapping his arms around his wife and son.

Enfolding my arms around Grady's waist, I peer up at him. "You did it. I'm so damn proud of you." I take a deep breath to hold back the tears that are threatening to fall. "Jared would be, too. I have a feeling he's smiling down on you."

He swallows hard and hugs me tighter. "Thanks, baby." He buries his face in my neck. He just holds me, breathing me in. I'm sure he's fighting off his emotions. He kisses me, just under my ear, before standing to his full height.

"So, dinner at our place," my mother-in-law, Debbie, says. She's oblivious to the moment we just shared and I'm okay with that. I don't want to upset her or make this day about sadness. I simply wanted him to know that the person who started him on this journey, although no longer here on earth, would be damn proud of him.

Grady clears his throat. "Sure, Mom, we're right behind you."

"See you there," Caleb tells us. "Good job, brother." They shake hands and follow our parents out the door.

GRADY

It's been one hell of a long road, but it's worth this moment. To have my wife, and our family there to cheer me on, nothing could top this day. I have two weeks off then I start my new job at a local private pediatric practice here in town. I did my rotation there and fell in love with the atmosphere. The physicians and staff are friendly and went out of their way to make me feel welcome. I learned a lot from them and I can't wait to start this next phase of my career.

"What are you thinking about over there?"

"Just how nothing could top today. I've busted my ass for years, leaving you, fighting to get you back. It's all brought us here, and I'm so damn proud to be right where I am."

"It has been a great day," she agrees.

"The best." Reaching over the console, I link her fingers with mine. She grows quiet and when I glance over at her, I can tell something is on her mind. "What's up, baby?"

Turning her head, she smiles. "Just trying to decide when I should give you your present."

"I thought we agreed on no present. We just put all that money out for the down payment on our house." We bought a four-bedroom about two miles from our parents and another three from Caleb and Emily. It's the perfect size for a soon to be growing family with a big backyard.

"Yeah, I know. I still… have something for you."

"What am I going to do with you?"

"Love me?"

"Always." I bring our joined hand to my lips.

"Can we stop at the park?" She points just ahead.

"Sure, it's been years since I've been here."

"Yeah, we spent a lot of time here as kids."

"It's not too far from our place. We'll have to bring our kids here," I say, pulling into the lot and turning off the ignition.

"Yeah." She smiles. "We should definitely do that." Collins reaches into the back seat and produces a small gift bag with graduation caps on it. "I know it's not technically a graduation, but I thought it fit."

"It fits. I love it."

"How do you know?" She laughs. "You haven't even opened it yet."

"Because it's from you."

"Open it, Grady."

I nod, reaching into the bag. I pull out what feels like a picture frame. Carefully, I remove the tissue paper and my eyes rake over the frame. "My daddy MD," I read the heading aloud. I read the passage, and then I realize the picture is not just any picture, it's an ultrasound image. "Collins?"

"You're going to be a daddy." She's smiling through her tears.

Immediately, I unbuckle my seat belt and climb out of the SUV. I'm at her door, just as she removes hers, and I pull her into my arms. Stepping away from the door, I spin her around. When we stop spinning, her legs are dangling in the air, and tears have coated our cheeks. "We're having a baby?"

"We are."

Dropping to my knees, I kiss her still flat belly. I don't bother to try and hide the quiver in my voice when I whisper, "I love you little one." I rest my forehead against where our child is growing inside of her. I've never met this little peanut, just found out of his or her existence today, yet the love I have for our baby is astounding. Standing back up, I kiss her long and hard. "I love you, baby momma," I say, breaking the kiss. She throws her head back with laughter. No matter how many times I think things can't be better, that there is no way that I could be happier in the life I share with her, she proves me wrong. I'm looking forward to a lifetime of surprises, love, and laughter with her and our little peanut, and any future peanuts we are lucky enough to have.

"I love you, too, Dr. Carmichael."

Contact
KAYLEE RYAN

I cannot thank you enough for taking the time to read Remedy. I appreciate each and every one of you. I'd love to hear from you.

Facebook - http://bit.ly/2C5DgdF

Reader Group - http://bit.ly/2o0yWDx

Goodreads - http://bit.ly/2HodJvx

BookBub - http://bit.ly/2KulVvH

Website - www.kayleeryan.com/

Other works by
KAYLEE RYAN

With You Series

Anywhere With You

More With You

Everything With You

Stand Alone Titles

Tempting Tatum

Unwrapping Tatum

Levitate

Just Say When

Unexpected Reality

I Just Want You

Reminding Avery

Hey, Whiskey

When Sparks Collide

Pull You Through

Beyond the Bases

Other works by
KAYLEE RYAN

Soul Serenade Series

Emphatic

Assured

Definite

Insistent

Southern Heart Series

Southern Pleasure

Southern Desire

Southern Attraction

Southern Devotion

Acknowledgments

To my readers:

Thank you! Your never ending support is humbling. Thank you for reading.

To my family:

I'm blessed beyond measure with the support that you provide. I could not do this without you.

Sara Eirew:

Thank you for another cover worthy image. You brought Grady and Collins to life.

Tami Integrity Formatting:

Thank you for making my words beautiful. You're amazing and I cannot thank you enough for all that you do.

Sommer Stein:

Your talent never ceases to amaze me. Thank you for yet another stunning cover. You've brought this book to life and for that I thank you.

My beta team:

Jamie, Stacy, Lauren, and Franci I would be lost without you. You read my words as much as I do, and I can't tell you what your input and all the time you give means to me. Thank you from the bottom of my heart for taking this wild ride with me.

Give Me Books:

   With every release, your team works diligently to get my book in the hands of bloggers. I cannot tell you how thankful I am for your services.

Becca Manuel: You nailed the trailer for Remedy. Thank you so much for doing what you do.

Tempting Illustrations:

   Thank you for everything. I would be lost without you.

Bloggers:

   Thank you, doesn't seem like enough. You don't get paid to do what you do. It's from the kindness of your heart and your love of reading that fuels you. Without you, without your pages, your voice, your reviews, spreading the word it would be so much harder if not impossible to get my words in reader's hands. I can't tell you how much your never-ending support means to me. Thank you for being you, thank you for all that you do.

To my Kick Ass Crew:

   The name of the group speaks for itself. You ladies truly do KICK ASS! I'm honored to have you on this journey with me. Thank you for reading, sharing, commenting, suggesting, the teasers, the messages all of it. Thank you from the bottom of my heart for all that you do. Your support is everything!

   With Love,

   Kaylee Ryan
   AUTHOR